INSTRUCTING ISABEL

GROVER TOWN DISCIPLINE, BOOK FIVE

YASMINE HYDE

Published by Blushing Books
An Imprint of
ABCD Graphics and Design, Inc.
A Virginia Corporation
977 Seminole Trail #233
Charlottesville, VA 22901

Yasmine Hyde
Instructing Isabel

Ebook ISBN: 978-1-64563-542-0
Print ISBN: 978-1-64563-546-8
VI

ONE

"Papa, Robert mentioned that he would be coming to see you tomorrow at your town office, or maybe we could invite him to dinner." Sophia sat at the table and twirled one wheat-colored lock, a perfect, thick coil, around her finger as the fingers of her other hand grasped her fork with the smallest piece of roasted brisket balanced at the tip of the tines.

Papa continued to slice through the thick portion of his own meat as he glanced over at Sophia, who sat to his right. "Why would *Deputy* Nelson feel the need to come and see me?"

Her father had placed an emphasis on the young man's title, Isabel was sure, to remind her sister of what was proper.

Isabel took a healthy bite out of her yeast roll as she stared at her sister's animation. Sophia's eyes brightened, and her thin lips pulled into a long smile that practically reached each ear at their father's question.

"Because I do believe..." Sophia paused for effect, ever the overdramatic, then blurted out, "Robert...Deputy Nelson," she corrected, "will ask you for my hand!"

Isabel never paused in chewing. It wasn't a surprise to her

that Sophia and Robert's two-month relationship had moved to such a level. Ever since the barn dance a couple of months ago, when Robert, the twenty and six-year-old night deputy who worked for the sheriff, had asked her sister to dance, it was all that Sophia wanted to talk about. They'd followed up the dance with a buggy ride after Sunday service—on which Isabel had been forced to accompany them—and too many picnics and walks through town to count.

For her own sake, Isabel hoped they would marry so she could stop playing the chaperone to her sister's courting.

Her father, James Reynolds—his family had called him Jim when he was growing up—rested both his hands on the table on the sides of his plate filled with half eaten brisket, fresh boiled green beans with potatoes, and his second yeast roll, as he slowly chewed his last bite. His gaze wasn't rested on her sister, but her mother who sat at the end of the six-person dining room table.

Their mother, Lillian, who had the same wheat-colored hair and dark blue eyes as Sophia and who never liked confrontation, didn't glance up as she speared a green bean trying to avoid their father's gaze.

Her father finally glanced away from his wife to her younger sister. "Sophia Lynn, we have had this conversation before. I don't plan to repeat myself again. But until your older sister marries, I will not agree or pay for any wedding for you."

Sophia gasped and clutched at her throat as if she didn't know what their father's response would be.

Isabel kept herself from the rude act of rolling her eyes at her sister's theatrics. It was a ridiculous rule to her too, but she was doing her best to stay out of the conversation.

"But, Papa—"

"No." Their father rubbed at the upper part of his stomach

with the side of the fist of his right hand that still held the knife as if the conversation gave him indigestion. "It is not right for a younger daughter to marry before her older sister. Do you want the town to think something is wrong with Isabel?"

Her sister's red face and furious dark gaze landed on her across the table. "Something is wrong with her. What girl prefers learning and teaching ignorant dusty workers to takin' walks in the meadows, dancing, and all-around fun and marrying a man who adores her? My sister Isabel. Even Serenity Morgan finally found a man to love her and is married and raising babies and churches in New Mexico. While I will be stuck as a spinster." In full dramatic form, Sophia rose from her seat and threw her linen napkin down beside her plate, prepared to storm from the table.

Isabel did feel bad for her sister and the rules that her father imposed upon the house. Soon her father would just have to give in because she refused to be married now, or possibly ever. There were bigger dreams at play for her.

"Sit!" their father barked. "I would like to eat my food without a tall glass of histrionics one night."

Sophia lowered herself back to her seat, bottom lip poked out so far, it practically covered up her round chin. "Mama, can't you talk to him?"

Lillian Reynolds finally looked to her husband with pleading eyes. She set down her utensils, hands trembling, then hid her hands in her lap. "James, isn't it our job to ensure our girls are happy?"

When their father shot an eyebrow up at their mother, she stammered, "N-not that they aren't. It's just that Sophia has always talked about marrying, while..." Her mother glanced at her and sighed. "Isabel has had other things on her mind. We shouldn't hurt one daughter because the other remains stubborn."

"First, wife, it is my job to feed, clothe, and provide a roof over their heads. Their future husbands can worry about their happiness. Second, I will not pay for Isabel to go away to some teaching academy, so she might as well settle into the life before her. Once that is done, Sophia can marry anyone of her choosing."

"Papa." It was her turn to be upset. Every time her sister brought up the subject of marriage, it was she who got denied her plans. "If Sophia wants Mister Nelson, I don't see why she can't marry. Everyone in town always says how fine a teacher I am; it's my dream."

Her father stared at her now, his pale green eyes a mirror of her own, as he declared, "Dreams are for people who don't have the funds to live in the now, Isabel Carrie. With your inheritance, you could have a pick of any man. So pick!"

She didn't care about the land or money, and she refused to be held in Grover Town for the rest of her life. At least not as some man's wife. Besides, she wasn't like her sister; men in town young and old stumbled over themselves to get her to offer them a smile. Sophia was like their mother, willowy and sylphlike in manners and dress, with perfect thin, bow-shaped lips. They both had lovely hair that was a shiny golden brown and made their curls look like someone had turned wheat into silk. For her, she was buxom, breasts too full and hips too wide and her lips round and red like she'd spent the day sucking on too many cherry sweet sticks. Her thick dark hair just added to her bulk, so she never wore it down and always kept it pulled back and bundled tightly with a fistful of pins to keep the heavy locks secure. No, men were not galloping down the road asking for her hand. However, she knew better than to attempt to argue with her father when he was in such a mood.

When he used her first and middle name, he couldn't be budged. "I've lost my appetite. May I be excused, Papa?"

He grunted at not hearing her agreement to his terms but nodded.

Sophia let out small sniffles as if her world had come to an end because she couldn't marry Robert.

Their mother started eating again, more of a distraction Isabel was sure then actual need for sustenance.

Quietly, Isabel placed her napkin beside her plate then rose and left the table. She was fuming mad, but it would do her no good to show those emotions to their father; it would only incite his own anger. Their father's views were simple and archaic, to Isabel's thoughts. A young lady should want to marry and have children, maybe have an appropriate small business, knitting, dress making, or painting pretty pictures. Her father didn't see the need for a woman, who didn't need money to help her family, to even work.

In her room in the big L-shaped house, she flopped on her bed. Her stomach was already growling from the lack of food. Unlike her sister, who ate like a bird to maintain a delicate size, Isabel found pleasure in eating just as she did teaching. She hoped Mrs. Turner, their cook, would wrap up her plate for later. After the household had retired, she could sneak into the kitchen and finish her food. It was cold out now; three inches of snow was on the ground. Her room was warm like the rest of the house. There was a small potbelly that sat in the corner, with a long flue that continued up and out the roof.

As she lay there staring at the wide, black stack, she tried to figure out what she could do to get out of the town. Her father had refused since she was seventeen to send her east to her mother's sister. Her aunt, Josie, had married a young politician whose stagecoach had broken down outside of Grover Town over twenty years ago. She'd journeyed to Philadelphia, Pennsylvania with her new husband after he'd completed schooling in Manhattan. Once, when she was nine and Sophia seven, her father had taken them to Pennsylvania for a visit. Her father had garnered a few business opportunities that carried him from a simple farmer in Grover Town to one of the biggest landowners.

After a few months, her mother had thought the city too hectic and she preferred the small-town life, and since her father had no more need of it after he hired a solicitor to take care of his interests, they had moved back. Sophia had been too young to remember it as anything but a long trip. However, Isabel remembered the wonder of living in a growing city. She'd hungered to return, and when she learned in the schoolhouse that Miss Beadle, the schoolmarm, had lived on the east coast while she went through her training, it had set in Isabel's mind. It had been her way out of the small town.

Over the years, she'd realized she loved instruction, and it became her career goal. Unfortunately, her papa didn't see it that way. He'd forbade her at every turn. The only thing he allowed her to do was use the schoolhouse once a week after supper to instruct some of the ignorant workers who'd come to Grover Town. Only, with one of the sheriff's deputies present and the house maid accompanying her.

Understanding that her father was not going to fund her training, she would have to think of other options. Soon. Now that her sister had someone wanting to speak to their father about her hand, the pressure would be relentless for him to see her settled first. His views at the table moments ago were not a surprise to her; she had just believed that she could wear him down and eventually, he'd relent and let her go. It was clear to her now that was never going to happen.

With an idea in her mind, she rolled to a seated position

then went to her desk. It was covered with books and education articles that she'd borrowed from Miss Beadle. Pulling open the slim drawer under the desk, she removed paper, pen, and ink. Ensuring her flute pen was filled, she began to write.

MY DEAREST AUNT JOSIE,
I hope that this letter finds you and Uncle Albert well...

———

YOU MUST COME HOME. *Both your brother and his wife have passed due to sickness that is running through the reservation. Many have died and the graves are plentiful. We can only hope this letter finds you. The children are safe. You must come home.*
Salali

HOME.
His cousin had used the word twice. A word that had no translation in Tsalagi. For him, the reservation was never a true home, and it was a place that, to him, he had never felt a part of. When he and his twin had come of age, they'd left their parents' house. Cary had left two years earlier, at ten and six. His brother, Garmin, had gone to live with their mother's people and only went by *Sequoyah*, the nickname his mother called him. Sparrow. His brother, the social one of the two who thrived living among the large group of their mother's people, had married within months and had been happy.

He and his brother may have been identical in looks, but they were as different as the sparrow and the eagle. *Uwohali.*

"I must leave."

"You sho this is sometin' you wanna do, CB?" Rufus asked him as they sat outside of the workers' tent.

"Yes." Cary hadn't really been speaking to his friend, a man a few years his junior. The two of them had worked for years doing back-breaking work on the rail line.

"Things have been better since both us got on this company with the union," Rufus argued.

"True. This is not my end, Rufus. I've stayed too long." He held the letter tighter in his hand. It was a testament that he'd focused more on earning funds than planning ways to start his life. A piece of himself was now gone, now that his brother had passed. A brother who had lived, loved, produced a family, and died.

Yes, he had been away from his own dreams for a lifetime.

Night had descended around them and it was cooler than in the day while they worked under the heat. The snow would come soon in Utah Territory. "If I am to make it, I must go now, before the snow."

"I understand. Let me know where ya end up, CB." Rufus was an ex-slave, and once he was freed in Alabama, he'd high-tailed it away. He'd told Cary that he'd been sold or traded so many times, he had no family to keep him in place. Rufus confessed that to his knowledge, he'd never been given a last name, so once the chains that bound him were gone, he took on Abraham Lincoln, the full name of the president who had set him free.

"I will, my friend." Cary glanced over at the man, who was just as big as he was. It was a reason they never had a problem with getting hired on with different rail companies and were paid better wages then most. Wages Cary had taught his friend how to save and plan instead of squandering it on char-women who cooked and cleaned for the company, those women who followed camps, or on drinks in the towns they passed through. "Take care of yourself, Mr. Lincoln."

Cary stood and embraced the man he'd been happy to call friend. There were others he'd worked alongside, immigrants, and foreigners, with whom he'd built a bond. Each of them had been there for different reasons but had been good, honest workers. Even as a loner, he'd miss the camaraderie. Going into the open space tent, he found his bag and began to pack away the few belongings stowed under his cot.

Other men, who were roused by his actions, sat up or came over to him to say their good-byes or offer him well wishes. Cary headed to the temporary office the crew had constructed and torn down at every location. The company's chief of operations used it to work, sleep, and issue out the pay at the end of each month. Knocking at the door, Cary waited for a moment before the door pulled open.

"What brings you round 'bout, Cary?" Mr. Sheffield's Irish roots showed rich in his speech as he inquired while standing in the doorway, the lamp from the room setting his face in shadows.

The man standing before Cary had always shown decency to all those under him. He judged each man by his work, not by race. Others in the rail industry hadn't, and they had been blatant about their dislike for people of color, be they ex-slaves, Asians, or Indians. Even a half-breed.

"I've come to tell you I'm leaving the company."

"What ya' say now?" Mr. Sheffield stepped back into the room, pulling the door wide as the light showed the confusion on his features. "Come in."

Cary crossed the threshold into the warmth of the room. There was a big fire outside of their tent, but it never quite made it back to his cot. It wasn't freezing out yet, but the heat from the roaring fire seeped into his skin and eased the aches in his muscles some.

"So, what were ya' goin' on bout? You're leavin'. Has someone done ya' wrong? If so, point'em out and I'll fix'em." Mr. Sheffield stood next to a table that was both his desk and the place he took his meals in the one room lodge.

Taking off his hat, Cary met the fair man's gaze. "Nothin' like that. I've had a family emergency. I can't take care of it on route."

Mr. Sheffield dragged a hand through red-brown hair he kept cut short. "Is there no way ya' could finish out the season?" He held his hands open in plea.

Cary shook his head. "If there was a way I could, I would. But once the snow sets in, travel will become slow and impossible in some places."

Sighing, Mr. Sheffield moved behind his desk and pulled a ring from his pants pocket that was connected by twine to a short leather strap that was buttoned at his waist. Those keys opened the black powder sticks container, the main office, the chest that held the money box, and the money box. Once his boss had the box pulled out from the chest under the table, he said, "You're one of my most consistent workers, big as an oak and strong as one too. I'm goin' hate to see ya' go."

Cary knew he was bigger than most of his mother's people, however, it was his father, a Scotsman, who was responsible for the size and build of him and his brother.

"I wasn't ready to part, either." It was true. He'd figured that he had one more year working the Transcontinental Rails before he had all he'd wanted saved to put his dream into action. Now, he'd have to make do on what he'd already earned.

"But family is family." Mr. Sheffield's family, a wife and four kids, had followed him from New York and usually settled in the closest town to their camp. He spent the winter months with them, wherever the work stopped. In early spring, he'd assemble everyone back together again and pick up where they'd left off.

"Yes, sir, it is." Cary took the folded bills for his months' pay. He flipped through the money and noted it was his normal pay and a little extra.

"I went ahead and paid you out the month and your Christmas bonus everyone else is goin' ta get in a few weeks." Mr. Sheffield snapped the metal lid of the strong box closed then locked it. "I don't want ta hear no argument. You'd have earned it."

"Thank you, Mr. Sheffield, it's been an honor." Cary held his hand out to the man.

Without hesitation, the boss man grasped it and gave a firm shake. "If ya' every need a job on the rails, you look me up. I'll even train ya to be an engineer."

Cary knew the honor in the man's words. Most of those positions went to Irishman and was passed down from fathers and uncles. It was true respect of a man's abilities in the older man's words.

"I 'preciate the offer." With a firm nod, Cary was out the door. Pulling his duster tighter around himself, he headed into the night toward town, to see a man about a horse.

TWO

"Well, hello there, Isabel. You're lookin' mighty fine today," Mrs. McCabe said, standing at the postal service window. She was a certified agent, along with her husband, who handled the large parcels and crates from the train and the stagecoach before that.

"It must be the nice spring evening. It's good to finally be able to get out of the house. I thought I'd go stir crazy through the winter months. I'm happy to get back to my weekly teaching and helping out Miss Beadle." It was true; Isabel hated doing nothing and sitting idle for so long. She had enjoyed several books in the long quiet days, always looking to educate herself, but she genuinely enjoyed being on the go and doing something.

"The town has been practically buzzing all week." Mrs. McCabe smiled as she looked through the window up and down the busy road that ran through town, a testament to her words.

"Yes. Well, my papa said he hadn't a chance to check round for the post yet."

"Oh, yes, a large batch came by the agent on the train last

week. It took me until yesterday to get it all sorted out. It gets some kinda backed up through the winter months." She laughed as she went to the shelf that had boxes with names on them for each family in Grover Town.

Isabel watched as the older woman followed the boxes labeled in alphabetical order until she got to the Rs.

"Reynolds." Mrs. McCabe grabbed the bundle held together with crossed twine and brought it over to the window. "Here you go. Let your pa know he's got some shipments here, so bring the wagon round."

"I will." Isabel was only half paying attention as she stared down at the bundle of letters. She wanted to unfasten the tight knot and flip through the stack to see if anything had come for her from her aunt. However, her mother and father would be upset that she'd gone through the mail first. She'd have to wait until she got home to find out. Minding her manners, she glanced up and smiled. "Thank you, Mrs. McCabe."

She started back toward the buggy where Rachel, their family maid, sat waiting for her.

"No problem at all. You ladies may want to come into town Saturday and peek at the order book the Russells got in at the Mercantile. Also, Molly got some wonderful fabric in from Paris. You'd look lovely in a new dress," the older woman called out after her, half hanging out of the wide window.

Isabel only smiled and waved back at the postal agent but continued up to the small horse and buggy. Her father had outfitted it for her mother. It only fit two adults, so when her mother came into town with her and her sister, they took one of the wagons. Using the snapper on the hindquarters of the horse, she got it moving toward the schoolhouse on the east side of town, across from Doc Clarkston's clinic up from the livery.

"A new dress may be pretty. Something fresh for the spring," Rachel commented. It was just Rachel, her mama, and her sister, since her father died from a sore that festered on his foot that he'd never had the doctor look at. They all had jobs working around town. Mrs. Morrison, Rachel's mother, ran the kitchen at the big brothel on the outskirts of town, but she refused to let her two daughters work there. So, Vera worked for Mrs. Livingston at the boarding house and Rachel worked for Isabel's family.

"Well, how about I let you go with my mama and sister in my place," Isabel told her.

"No, that wouldn't be right. But one day, I'll get married and hopefully my husband will let me get a new dress each spring." Rachel's wistful voice about marrying didn't surprise Isabel.

Rachel had worked for them for three years now, and she was only a year younger than Isabel. They'd spent many days talking and laughing on the weekly trips to town. She got along better with Rachel than she did with her own sister. Even though Rachel had dreams of getting married and having a family, she believed in the value of work. Unlike Sophia, who had already gotten their father to promise that when she married, he'd gift her with a maid and cook.

Since Robert was a deputy sheriff, he surely wouldn't have the funds to give her sister the kind of lifestyle she'd grown accustomed to living at their parents' home. If Sophia hadn't fallen for the deputy's dashing good looks, her sister may have chosen better from a financial standpoint.

For Isabel, none of that mattered. She wanted a career and independence, and she only hoped that the answer to her prayers had come in on the last train.

She pulled the buggy up beside the schoolhouse then climbed down with her satchel slung crossways over her body.

Rachel followed, and when she got to the steps, Robert came out of the schoolhouse.

"Good day, Deputy Nelson. How many men have arrived tonight to learn?" She smiled at the man as she ascended the stairs.

Robert was a tall, lanky young man, with hair so blond, it appeared white. He had deep blue eyes and a broad smile. He had just turned six and twenty, and even though he was just a deputy right now, most talked about him being smart, one of the best shots in town, and expected one day he'd take over for the sheriff when the older man retired.

"Hello, Miss Isabel. Four men showed tonight. Three of 'em were here last fall; they say they want to show you how well they doin' now."

That warmed her heart. She liked to see the joy of learning, no matter what the age. "And the other?"

"Don't know much 'bout him. He's a new month hire over at the Harvey Ranch. Says he was told about the teachin' you do?" Robert's face was scrunched as if he wanted to say something else about the man.

"Excellent." She spoke first, not wanting to hear disparaging remarks about someone she considered a pupil of hers. She knew most people in town tried to discourage her papa from letting her teach grown men, but she didn't think anyone should walk around ignorant if they had a chance to learn. Normally, she only got two at a time, and most only stayed long enough to learn the most rudimentary levels of reading and arithmetic. At least that was something. Four was her biggest tutorial session yet. Feeling lighthearted, she started to reach for the door.

"May I inquire as to the well-being of Miss Sophia?"

Isabel wanted to sigh but swallowed it down. Turning, she gave him her attention, briefly, just to keep him from drilling her later. "My sister is doing well. Feeling a little cooped up over the winter, like the rest of us. However, I'm pretty sure with the dress shop getting in some nice bolts of fabric; she will be in town for a new spring dress this week."

Even though she just found out about the material, Isabel was sure that tonight when she passed the information on to her sister and mother, they would rush into town.

His joy at the news was evident in his smile that showcased all his teeth.

"That sure is good news. I'll be on the lookout for her. I'd like to ask her to have a meal with me at Drummonds' on Sunday after service, maybe go for a ride.

Oh, no. She groaned. That would mean *she* would have to go too. "We'll see." She started away, catching the man's slight frown at her words. Not wanting to put her issue on his shoulders, she sighed and glanced over at him, holding the door open. "I'm sure Sophia would like that."

Not staying to see the light she was sure had shone in his eyes, she entered the schoolhouse. The men were spread out, for space and comfort. Most of them were usually uncomfortable at their level of ignorance and being unlearned, even though she repeatedly told them that not being able to have schooling was nothing to be ashamed of.

"Good evening, gentlemen. Nice to have a few of you back, and even a new face among us."

There were grumbles in response to her greeting. She knew they didn't like her calling them gentlemen. Their trades were varied so she didn't know what else to call them; besides, they all showed polite manners toward her and that made them worthy of the title in her sight.

She strutted toward the front of the room and Rachel silently claimed the bench along the back wall behind the newcomer.

Isabel didn't move toward the elevated area by the board yet. She liked to stay on their level for as long as possible. These were men not children. All of them were older than herself, some by a few years. The new man looked to be more than ten years her senior.

She recognized the three returners, but the other man had on his hat, black, and pulled low over his eyes. There were shaggy brown hair cut ragged and blunt at his shoulders. "Welcome. Are you new to Grover Town?"

His head turned toward the other men around the room then glanced over his shoulder to the deputy who leaned against the backside wall. When he swiveled back toward her, he said, "Sumpin' like that."

"What property or business are you workin' with?"

"Do ya have to be workin' to learn?" There was bite to his words.

She felt the tightness in her spine, one vertebra at a time, but she held herself still. There was something about this man —maybe because she couldn't see his eyes clearly, or the fact he gave short clipped responses. However, he wasn't the first rough rider she'd had to win over. Hopefully soon, she would be headed away to school and she'd be able to have her own schoolhouse and educate children.

Pulling her lips back into a cordial smile, she responded, "No. Some come to help them find work or do something while they look for work. All are welcome."

The silence stretched and still, he remained lock-jawed. Then when she started to speak, he let a single word come from his parted lips, "Harvey."

She could have figured as much. M.J. Harvey seemed to hire the roughest and at times most ill-mannered men in town. Her papa frequently warned her sister and her away from deals with them. She was going to try not to judge this man before she gave him a shot. Like she told him, all were welcome to learn.

"That's great. That means you'll be around a good amount of time hopefully." She forced another smile.

A curt nod was his only response.

"All right." She exhaled, hoping he didn't see the anxiety twisting her core. Most men who came were a little tight-lipped in the beginning. "Well, I'm Isabel, Isabel Reynolds. I'll handle the weekly instructions here. I offer all the people who come to meet another day during the week at Drummonds' if they need more one on one."

The other three men greeted her with hellos and grins. The man in the back didn't respond; he simply continued to stare.

Giving him the space to become comfortable, Isabel turned to the other men. "It has been a long winter this year. We're going to go over the sounds for each of the letters of the alphabet before I come around and see where you all are on reading." There were two stacks of books that Miss Beadle always left out for her on the nights Isabel used the building, and Isabel also brought some of her own. Being familiar with three of the men, she knew they were advanced enough to at least start the next level books, but with the newcomer, she didn't want to hand him a primer and single him out until she knew him better. Picking up the earlier readers from the corner of the desk, she handed them to Steve Calloway who sat closest to her at the front and was a hand at Spencer Ranch. She'd been working with him the longest of the three returning men. Jimbo Reece was also from Spencer's, and Lyle Joseph. Jr. was from Garret Rand's place.

"Take one and pass it back, Mr. Calloway."

Steve nodded and took the one off the top. She turned and walked up the single stair to the blackboard. There she wrote out each of the letters on the board. She turned back around and faced the class. "After we work on reading and writing, at the end of the class, we'll see how much arithmetic you all recall."

Three of the men nodded; one did not. She glanced over at Robert briefly and saw him arch a brow.

"Let's get started. Mr. Joseph, can I get you to start with the first five letters, please."

"Sure will." Eagerly, Lyle began stating the letter then making the sound.

An hour later, Isabel was both tired and eager to get home. She always loved teaching in any form, but having the extra man in the group who refused everything she tried took a lot out of her.

"Don't pay that one no mind. I'se seen him round town and at Manny's; he's always the same way," Jimbo told her.

"Thanks. I was thinking it was me for a moment," she teased. "Hopefully, he'll be back." The other men wouldn't need her much longer and if her aunt hadn't replied to her over the winter months, then she'd only have the days she helped Miss Beadle with the children.

"Maybe. Evenin'." He doffed his hat and walked the steps towards his horse.

When she returned inside to straighten up, Robert came over to her.

"You want me to look in on Harvey's and see if there's something up with the man?"

It was tempting, but she shook her head and grabbed the cloth hanging beside the board. "No. Learning to read isn't a requirement for employment. The man is welcome to come or not. I just wish I knew if he *could* read."

"It was strange that he left halfway through." Rachel

walked up the aisle and set the books the men had handed her on their way out on the desk.

Finished wiping down the board, Isabel frowned and faced her two companions. "It was, Rachel. But I've learned doing this that grown men's egos are more fragile than a little child's when it comes to them knowing the basics of reading, writing, and arithmetic. So, we'll see."

When everything was in order, the trio left the school-house and closed everything up tight.

Robert glanced up at the sky. "Dusk has already set in. I can let the sheriff know I'm escortin' you and Miss Rachel safely to your home."

"That's all right, Deputy Nelson." Isabel allowed him to hand her up into the buggy. Once settled, she collected the reins. "That's not necessary. The house is not too far outside of town. Rachel and I will be there before the land is dark."

Rachel didn't wait until he assisted her; she was already in the seat beside her.

The deputy looked a little forlorn not to be able to ride out with them. She knew he just wanted to take a chance to see Sophia if he could. However, Isabel would already be roped into spending a large portion of her afternoon with them and she wasn't feeling any more benevolent.

"Well, until Sunday, then."

She gave him a smile before she snapped the leather leads and called out to the horse.

"Do you truly like all that teachin' and repeatin' yourself?" Rachel rocked along beside her and stared out over the road as they headed out of town.

Glancing over at her friend, Isabel saw the frown on her brow before she turned her attention back to the road. She didn't want to strike along some new crater in the road. "I do like it. There are not many things women can do on their own and independently in this world. Besides, I'm right good at it. You saw those men...well, the three. They were able to read both those books and do basic adding and subtracting of numbers. I taught them that. Their own hard work too, of course."

Isabel wasn't sure if it came off as prideful or not. However, she did feel pride at seeing how well those men and at least ten others had learned with her assistance and patience.

"It is somethin'. Before I started coming and sittin' with you, I haven't seen grown men learning. Either they know, or they don't."

"You're right. A lot of men have learned to just get by on their wits. They're usually really observant, like watching what bills or coins other people give for things and do the same, never knowing truly how much money they have and just living life on handshakes, no written contracts."

"Hearin' you put it like that, I figure it must be scary for those men. Takin' on new jobs or buying things."

"Don't feel sorry for them...they get on just fine."

"S'pose so." Rachel remarked, then they both fell silent as Isabel's family home came into view.

Once they arrived at the house, the darkness had already fallen around them. In a couple of months, the days would be longer and winter fully shaken off. She was greeted by her father on the porch and the stable man, Peter, who sat on the stairs, both waiting on her return. Her father was stern but a good father. He was tough when it came to business and managing his properties, but she never doubted his love for her mother or her and her sister. Sometimes she wished he could have had a boy; he needed someone to follow in his footsteps and carry the legacy he'd started in property owner-ship and management. Neither she nor Sophia were interested. And Robert was sweet and smart, but even if he and Sophia ever married, his passion was the law. The man didn't have a head for farming, ranching, or property owning.

"Good evening, Papa." Isabel grabbed her satchel filled with the mail and allowed her father to assist her down from the buggy.

Peter gave Rachel a hand before he took charge of the horse and walked him toward the stables.

"Isabel, it always bothers me that you stay out late with those rough hands." He guided her up the four steps to their home washed in pale green paint and brown trim. Most didn't color the wood of their house, except with white-wash, but her mother had ordered large tins of it from the Sherwin-Williams Company in Cleveland, Ohio. It had been one of the first things on the train from the US Mail Agent her mother had ordered when it ran through Grover Town. Another way he spoiled their mother.

"Most of them are nice fellas and real respectable. You know Mr. Spencer and Mr. Rand only take on trustworthy sorts." She kept her arm wrapped around his as they moved in tandem. She wouldn't tell her father about the silent man from that night, or he'd surely forbid her from going back. However, that man wouldn't be the first grumpy Gus she'd won over with her charm and smile.

"Well, I still don't like it." At the door, he paused and looked at her. The light from the two large windows on the side of the door illuminated the porch even with the front door shut. "Why can't you settle down like most of the young ladies in town? Do you know the richness of your land I've set aside for you? Wasted, year after year."

She heard him sigh and watched the shake of his head.

"What if I never settle on it? Just lease it out, like the other acreage you own. You're losing money with it simply sitting there collecting moss and dust." She smiled at him, hoping to ease the truth of her words.

Once, years ago, when she'd turned ten and two, he'd driven her over there in the wagon and showed her the property. It was wild and massive. For a moment, she'd thought of it briefly and what it would be like to build a house there and raise a family, however, even then it had been fleeting. She'd already become Miss Beadle's star pupil and had more schooling on her mind.

Sophia had a completely different response a few years later when their papa took her out to her land. She came home brimming with ideas about a big house on the land and how her husband's ranch would be the biggest in all of Grover Town boundaries. When she met Robert, the ranching spouse had changed but not the big house, which her father had commissioned built on Sophia's ten and sixth birthday.

Since then, she'd only half listened when her papa talked about all the changes he'd made out on their properties. He wanted to take her out to see her land a few years back, however, Isabel had not been interested. It had angered her father and he hadn't spoken to her for a week, grumbling every time they were in the same room together.

"Isabel, you're young and you don't see the blessing in what I hand you. If I had a papa who could have given me even half what I've set up for you, ahh...nothing could have stopped me."

She saw the sincerity in his pale green eyes like hers as they held hers intently. She would have liked to give in, but she felt choked in this town. There wasn't a life for her here, not in the way her father devised. "Nothing did stop you. You came here on your own from North Carolina and took the opportunity. You spent all your money on buying two plots of land, one you built a house on, where we are standing, and the other you leased to a man to farm. Then you continued to buy more land with anything extra you had and leased those too. I just want to make my own way in a different manner."

"My father was a builder, a wise carpenter. What I learned from him, I hammered and nailed this house together." He patted the thick column securing the roof and porch before he placed a kiss on her forehead. "My smart girl. Your drive to prove you can be something other than a landowner's daughter are making the steps to ruin the path before you."

She never had a chance to respond. Her father moved away from her and opened the door and let her enter as he looked away.

It broke her heart to know she was hurting her father with her career plans, but she had to step out and hope one day he'd understand. Once she was in the house, she removed the bundle of mail and handed it to her father.

"There are also crates for you at the post, Mrs. McCabe said to tell you."

He nodded and took the mail from her on his way to the room he used as his home office. She would have liked to follow him and watch as he went through it. However, she knew he'd question what she was looking for, and the last thing she needed after their conversation was him questioning her about a letter she was waiting for from her aunt. Instead, she went to the spacious living area and sat in the Queen Anne style chair. Her mother sat in the other, drawing together squares of fabric, most likely for a gift for someone's upcoming nuptials or a new babe for someone in town. Her mother's quilts were highly sought after. It was how she made money when she and Papa first married, to help him buy food or save for more land. Now, her mother gave them away as special gifts.

"Don't sit there!" Sophia fussed and waved her away with

her free hand not holding the paint brush, as she sat across the room on a stool.

"Why not? I've had a long day." Isabel didn't move as she eyed her sister.

Sophia had seen a painting book in school when she was nine and swore, she'd become the next John Singer Sargent.

"I'm painting the chair and fireplace." This time she pointed the brush at her, its bristles covered in a brownish color.

Her sister was good, and many homes and establishments in Grover Town held her works of art on their walls. It was only for that reason that Isabel rose and moved to the clawfoot couch. "Fine, Sophia."

Sophia grinned as she dipped and swirled her brush into the palette of watercolors before brushing along her canvas.

"Mrs. Turner will bring tea momentarily. It's nice to have you sitting with us. I would have thought you'd be cloistered in your room reading or learning some bit of fact." Her mother rolled her eyes and exhaled.

Sitting there and trying not to fiddle with her fingers or tap her heel as she waited for the sound of her father's footsteps coming out of his office, she replied, "I'll read later. It's just been a full day. Can I just sit here and enjoy the company of my mother and sister before retiring?"

Her mother tilted her head, her dark blue eyes seeming to access her from across the room. She picked up another square from the basket beside her chair and began to thread it to the others. "What's on your mind, Isabel?"

"Nothing." She looked away from her mother, to the low fire. There was still a little chill in the air in the late evenings, and even though the fire wasn't raging like during the really cold winter months, the warm glow was nice. "There was a lot of mail in. Papa has it."

"Good. A letter from my sister would be nice, since her daughter married last year, at barely ten and eight, to a restaurateur of some fancy place." Her mother paused, and Isabel didn't have to look back at her to know she was staring pointedly at her. She continued, "Josie was in hopes that her daughter would be swollen with child by spring. I would like to have beaten her in becoming a grandma first, but that doesn't seem a possibility in any near future."

"If Papa allowed Robert and me to marry, we would put forth the effort in seeing you had a leg in the race."

Isabel did look over at her sister, who was shooting daggers at her. It was Isabel's turn to roll her eyes. She glanced at her mother and grinned. "I hope Aunt Josie has written as well. It would be nice to have news."

Long moments later, when she had practically given up waiting, the heels of her father's brogans were heard thumping along the wood.

"There's mail for you, ladies." He walked to their mother and gave her a stack of catalogs and letters.

"Thank you, James." Her mother's eyes lit up when she stared up at her father then kissed him on the corner of his mouth.

After caressing her mother's shoulder, their father walked away.

"Did Teresa send me a letter?" Sophia set down her brush and palette then wiped her hands on a rag as she rose and crossed the room to their mother. Teresa was her sister's closest friend who had recently married last fall, then she had gone to Oklahoma with her new husband for a honeymoon trip to visit his family. Since Teresa's wedding, Sophia had become touchier about not being able to marry the deputy.

Isabel was anxious for a correspondence of her own. She

slid to the edge of her seat, closer to her mother and the stack of mail, with bated breath.

"Yes, you have three letters, and one of them is from Teresa." Their mother passed over the envelopes to Sophia.

Smiling, her sister flipped through the letters then walked to the empty chair she had been painting just moments ago and tore into the first letter.

"Anything for me?" Isabel turned back to her mother.

"Yes. Looks like you got a letter from your cousin. I got one from your aunt. We will compare and see if either of them mention a coming arrival." Her mother smiled as she passed her the one piece of mail with her name on it.

Downcast, Isabel forced a smile on her lips. "Nothing else?"

"Hmm..." Her mother flipped through the items in her lap again. "No. I believe that is it."

"Oh." Isabel slipped back in the seat and stared down at her cousin's bold rounded script. She didn't even feel like opening it and hearing any type of happy news from anyone, especially if none was coming her way. However, her mother would want to know what Mary Agnes had to say.

"Wait. I must have missed this one. However, it is just from your Aunt Josie. I am not sure who you are expecting a message from." Her mother gave her a curious stare.

"No one. I love getting letters from Aunt Josie. You know she always has the most vivid tales." She pulled the mail from her mother's hand quick, unable to restrain her excitement. However, when she saw that the address on the envelope was to both her and Sophia, her smile dropped. She doubted if her aunt had answered her about sponsoring her through school. Aunt Josie would not have sent it to both her and her sister. And if she did, it would be disastrous. She would not be able to keep Sophia from knowing what was in the letter.

On cue, her sister looked up and paused in her giggling from the words her friend had written. "What has Aunt Josie said?"

"I don't know. I have yet to read it. Let me see what Mary Agnes has said first, then I will look." She quickly read through her cousin's letter. "Apparently, there is a child on the way. She has been sick most of the winter months and is hating life. Only three months along, well, five by the date of this, and she is ready for the young one to come."

"Fiddly sticks." Her mother said as she started opening her own letters. "I know now that when I open Josie's, it will be filled with braggadocious things."

Folding the letter and placing it back in the envelope, she grinned and said, "If it is any consolation, Mama, Bradley is already a nervous wreck and jumps up at every movement she makes, ready to call upon the midwife."

Her mother laughed. "Thank you for that, Isabel. This shall make the weeks until the babe arrives trying for Josie. Sweet justice."

Isabel could not help but smile.

Sophia pouted. "Robert shall not be in such a state when I am with child. He's a deputy and used to unpredictable situations. He'll be steady as a rock."

Isabel glanced over at her mother whose lips were rolled inward as she fought back either a big smile or a giggle at her sister's words.

Ignorant of the humor at her expense, Sophia recounted a few things from the long letter from Teresa. "You all will be as happy as I am to know that Teresa and Michael Joe will return in two months to Grover Town. She was not pregnant yet when she sent this letter. Perhaps it is because we both always wanted to be belly round together."

Isabel shook her head. She tore along the side seam of her

aunt's envelope and slipped out the letter. It smelled of lavender and there were crushed petals within the two pages.

Mrs. Tucker, a heavy bosomed woman with hips as wide as her smile, came in with a tray of her mother's grandmother's delicate tea set and a plate with three molasses cookies and set it down on the low table between the three of them. "Anything else you need for the night, Mrs. Reynolds?"

"We are good for the evening, thank you for today, Mrs. Tucker."

"Wishin' you all a good night and I'll be off to my home."

They all called out a mix of good night, see you in the morning, and tell your family hello. Once Mrs. Tucker went back toward the kitchen to head out the back to her home, which was across the field on their property, the same place Rachel rented a room, Isabel and Sophia snatched up one of the three small rectangle shortbreads.

Their mother poured tea for herself and Sophia; Isabel shook her head at the offer.

"Read it aloud." Sophia nibbled and demanded of Isabel, referring to the letter.

"I will." She finished off the last of the delicious cookie quicker than she would have liked. Taking a deep breath, Isabel began. In some way, she hoped that maybe she was wrong and her aunt had mentioned about the teaching academy. Something, even if it caused a disturbance in the household, was better than nothing. She went through the two pages and recited all the information her aunt had given her about Philadelphia in the winter, ice skating, and the winter Governor's Ball. At the end, she added a postscript for her specifically, about all the women's movement that were beginning to happen around the city and how she had joined in the new state level of the American Woman Suffrage Association, because it was more inclusive to all races, to include both free man and ex-slaves, as well as Native Americans.

Isabel thought about how, if or when, she moved to Pennsylvania, she'd be in such causes as that. Grover Town was small, but it was also unique in that it was more about the hard work of each person being accepted in the community and not race. However, it was still outdated when it came to what affluent men like her father believed women could, more like should, do.

Isabel stuffed the letter back into the envelope then rose. "Well, I have some reading to do, and I need to make an entry for today's literacy session."

"Really, Isabel, how you can stand being in the schoolhouse and sitting with dusty cowboys, I'll never know. I was so happy to finally get out of those four walls, I'll never return. Unless it is for special events for my own children."

That was her cue. When Sophia started talking about veil or crib things, Isabel took it as a point to excuse herself. She picked up her satchel and moved toward her mother. "Well, we each do what makes us happy. I could never sit for hours at an easel, but you do it so well. Let alone stitch together fabric to make quilts and coverlets."

Her mother smiled as Isabel leaned down toward her to lightly kiss her cheek. "You were always a bright and energetic child in school, Isabel. I'm sure the men and employers are grateful you assist their workers. Just like those around Grover are very delighted to possess a painting of yours, Sophia."

Lillian Reynolds, always the consummate broker of peace.

"I guess so," Sophia uttered half-heartedly as she opened another letter, a response from a Belgium company that held a small sample of their lace. "Oh, look, Mama. It is just as fine as the catalog claim. I'd love a yard for my front room table or even to make a fine doily trim."

Not even responding, Isabel went to her room. She would not even be missed when discussing home or clothing fashions between her mother and sister. In her room, she went to her desk and sat. The drapes were already pulled over her window before it, thanks to Rachel. Isabel was glad about that; the last thing she wanted was to see her reflection in the glass, caused by the burning lamp on her nightstand. She knew it would be etched in disappointment with similar shadows in her green eyes.

She pulled her leather-bound journal out from the drawer then opened it to the next blank page. She couldn't even draw the energy to write the date on it. As she sat there staring at the stacks of books, pamphlets, and an atlas, she could feel the walls closing in on her.

She flipped to the back of her journal, where she kept the brochure for the Young Ladies' Academy of Philadelphia that her aunt had brought to her a few years ago during her visit.

Isabel's father had ranted about it when he saw it and had ordered her to toss it in the trash, but it had been her first act of disobedience when she squirreled it away in her journal.

As she stared at it, the academy seemed farther away than just the seventeen hundred kilometers in travel but fading away in her dreams as well.

With renewed purpose, she pushed her journal aside for later and removed a fresh sheet of wood pulp from her drawer to pen another letter to her aunt. This time, she would emphatically express the urgency of support she needed from Aunt Josie.

"I will not give up," she vowed.

THREE

"So, what do you think about this plot of land, Mr. Brown?" Mr. Reynolds got off his horse.

Cary reined in Silver, his white stallion. It hadn't been the horse he'd purchased when he left his position on the rail. No, the big, strong horse had belonged to his brother. Along with his niece and nephew, Silver was also left for his care.

He heard the older man in the expensive suit's question, but he never was one to rush to respond. Staring out over the area, he thought what the land could produce for him. He took one step, then another, and felt the rocky hard packed earth below him. There was flat land, but there were trees... lots of trees that would hinder the size of area he could farm. He also noticed that the prairie grass, not yet fully bloomed from the winter months, was mere patches around his feet.

He could hear the birds in the trees enjoying the midday and his sharp gaze caught a few animals scurrying through the land, weary of humans. However, there was no sound of flowing water.

Fifty or so steps away from the property owner, he squatted down. Removing his hat, Cary rested it on his knee.

There was a soft breeze that ruffled a few strands of his hair, kept longer than most. The removal of his hat was his way of paying homage to the earth, seeing if it was for him. He believed if he farmed on land not meant to be his, it would be hollow ground, his crop meek, never truly yielding its fullest because the land was meant for another. He was seeking his land, fertile ground that would yield healthy, bountiful crop every year for him.

Using one hand, he dug deep through the topsoil. It was drier than he would have liked. Lifting a handful up to his nose, he closed his eyes and inhaled, filling his nose with the rich scent of the earth. He rubbed it into his palm with his finger and inspected it for weeds, rough pebbles, the animal's decay and waste, and dirt. It wasn't bad soil, but it wasn't the best.

"It's farther away from the water than I would like." Allowing the soil in his hand to drift back to the ground, with his free hand, he placed his hat back on his head and stood. "I will be honest; your properties have been the best I've been shown."

"Glad to hear it. Spencer Ranch is about four miles west of you and he's a good sort. There's a healthy creek on his land, and I'm sure he'd be willing to negotiate your use of it." Mr. Reynolds came up beside him, having kept his distance earlier and allowing him the space to survey the land. The man was average height and build, which only brought him around Cary's shoulder, like most men. The man seemed a pleasant sort who was straightforward and courteous.

Other men, like Bellmore, was pushy, and Harvey had sneered at him and tried harder to get him to come work his cattle ranch than to really lease him a piece of his land.

Reynolds hadn't given him the speech about Indians not being able to own or buy land. They were still regulated to the property the government handed out to them. Grover was the third town in Kansas he'd stopped in, looking to lease some land. Currently, he didn't have enough saved to outright buy the land and get all the needed supplies, animals, and wood to build a home, so leasing was his best option.

However, because Cary straddled the fence of race and his father was the white side, if he pushed it, people would give him a little more clemency. He never did. His pa loved his ma. Cary loved his mother and her people, even though living among them wasn't in the path for him like it had been for his brother.

Shaking the dust from his feet in those other narrow-minded towns, he'd come to Grover Town. He'd been a part of the team who'd laid the tracks through here a few years back, and it had always called to him. It was the farthest from his family he had traveled, but if it all worked out, it would be worth it.

"Good to know about the creek." Knowledge of the water source was helpful; it meant that if he dug deep enough into the soil, there was a possibility the earth would provide a well of water. It wasn't always true, because underground water created its own path, just like the rivers and streams above it, unless man steered it another way.

"I'd say it's not the best, but it's a good starter piece I have for leasing, for the pay we'd discussed."

Cary nodded. He knew his options were limited. Most likely, he'd have to take it. He wouldn't be happy about it, and he'd pray to the good Lord of his father's people, The One True God, and to *Unetlanvhi*, the Great Spirit, maker of all things, of his mother's people, that they would grant him mercy on the land if he chose to take it.

"May I take some days?"

Mr. Reynolds held his gaze with odd green eyes. "Take

time. I'll not lie to you. Grover is growing and land doesn't stay free for long. I've had others inquire on it."

When he lifted one side of his brow at the man's words, Mr. Reynolds continued. "I'll still give you your time. I don't believe in rush deals myself. Just like you want the right land, I want the right people on my land." After a brisk nod, he finished with, "A week should be enough time for us both."

"I appreciate you taking the time today to show me your properties."

The older man held his hand out to him. The hand was wide, and his nails were clean, not freshly cleaned as Cary maintained his hands when he wasn't working, but the sign of office work, not hard labor.

Cary grasped the other man's hand and was surprised to feel old calluses and cuts along his palm. They had known hard work in a time before.

When the quick but firm shake was over, the two of them parted ways, heading to their respective mounts.

"You need to follow me back to town?"

"No," Cary called out. He was good at finding his way and he wanted to see as much of the new county before the sun fell below the horizon.

Mr. Reynolds waved him off as he kicked his horse off into the direct direction of town.

Cary went the other way, toward the Spencer Ranch. He wasn't set on the man being his neighbor, but he was interested in meeting him. He never took anyone's words on someone else's character. There'd been too many times the nature a person showed one person was different than what they'd given to him.

The pressure of needing to find a place soon was mounting on his shoulders. He'd take the week Mr. Reynolds had offered him. If he found nothing else at the end of the time, he'd claim his piece of Grover Town.

AN EAGLE'S screech snared her attention. Isabel leaned back against the wagon Robert had rented from the livery in town, to escort her sister from church then to Drummonds' for a Sunday supper and, finally, for a ride through the countryside. They stopped at an expansive field of fresh new prairie grass that was just starting to force its way up through the ground. In a few weeks, the grass would be tall, vivid green, and waving, and other fields would be full of flowers and bumblebees gathering pollen. She tilted her head up and caught the eagle's majesty in flight as it soared through the late Sunday afternoon sky. She'd rather watch the eagle than think about the stolen kisses of her sister and Robert behind her. The eagle soared high in the blue, cloudless sky, wings spanned wide as it flew overhead, seconds before it dove toward the grassy knoll off in the distance. She observed its speed and focused intent. She figured it was after a rabbit or field mouse.

There was giggling behind her and she figured it was safe to glance back at them.

Her sister's arm was looped in Robert's and she was beaming up at him with adoring blue eyes, entranced at his every word. Robert was settling his brown hat, with the deputy sheriff's star reflecting the sunlight, back on his head. Isabel wasn't sure if he'd removed it to kiss her sister under the tree or if it had gotten knocked off somehow during the act. Isabel was ignorant when it came to the acts that went on between a man and a woman, besides the few things she'd witnessed between couples around town.

Once, she'd come across one of Mrs. Kitty's ladies, who was lip-locked with a cowboy on the side of a building, when she'd walked along the dusk streets during last fall's Harvest Barn Dance. It had been warm and stuffy inside because of all the people gathered and the energy put off by the foot stomping jigs and line dancing. The desperation in the couple's kiss, or mauling, had the man's hands tight on her waist, the woman's hand buried deep in the man's hair, and her garter was showing because the woman shockingly had her leg raised high along the man's side. It had been her gasps of shock that had pulled the two apart.

The woman, with her face full of rouge and kohl, had blushed and whispered something about the man just having proposed and her moving off to Wyoming Territory with him. Isabel had mumbled a congratulations and hurried on her way, apologizing for her interruption. She'd thought about that couple a few times secretly during the winter months and wondered if they'd truly married and had made it to Wyoming before the snow fell.

Even though the thought of what she'd witnessed had stuck with her and made her face heat at the memory of the frantic passion of their embrace, Isabel knew it was not a path for her. She'd be a schoolmarm, getting her joy from educating the young, never to marry.

Now, she watched Sophia and Robert making strides away from the big Bur Oak. She wondered if her sister felt that same frenzied emotion in Robert's arms. Isabel knew she could trust Robert with her sister's virtue and that he wouldn't let them go beyond a few kisses. Sophia, eight and ten now, was who she didn't trust. Her sister wanted to marry so badly, if she was courting another man, she'd let things go as far as she needed to, to force their papa's hand in allowing them to marry, dropping his archaic rule of the older sister must go first.

"Sorry we've kept you, Miss Isabel." Robert's eyes were bright and his smile twenty acres wide.

"No worries, Deputy Nelson. Papa will be looking for us. Sophia, it's time for us to head home," she instructed her sister as she climbed up into the wagon.

Robert was quick as he disentangled himself from Sophia, then he rushed to her and supported her up into the seat.

"I know. It's just that Robert and I get so little time to see each other." Sophia pouted and was quick to link her arm through the deputy's again once he'd stepped back. "Especially, since he can't officially ask Papa for my hand yet."

Isabel knew that barb was for her, even though Sophia hadn't taken her mooning blue gaze from Robert's face.

"It's no worries. I'll wait as long as needed for you to be my wife." It was Robert who offered Isabel a kind, supportive smile.

It wasn't news to anyone in town that Isabel saw her life in the schoolhouse. She'd been telling any and everyone who would listen since she was ten and two.

The pair walked around the back of the wagon to the other side, so that Robert could assist Sophia up into the wagon.

"You always say the sweetest of things, Robert." Her sister placed a quick kiss along the man's cheek before she got up on the wagon. Sophia slid and wiggled her hips over until she was occupying the middle seat, giving the deputy enough room to sit on the other side of her and handle the reins.

Once he was settled, Sophia scooted close enough to just barely give the man room to maneuver, instead of Sophia seating closer to her as was proper and courteous. Robert had to lean his elbows onto his knees to make sure he could safely drive the wagon and keep from bumping Sophia's small pert bosom every time he moved his arm.

Sighing, Isabel looked over the side of the wagon and chose to ignore the situation all the way home. When the wagon began to roll and jostle over the rocks and uneven ground as Robert steered it back toward the wagon-tracked road, a movement drew her gaze back toward the knoll where the eagle had disappeared after his prey.

However, the figure was too big to be an eagle, but a man. She could not make out who the man was as he sat proud, straight-backed, and large on a white horse just as imposing as he was. He was too far away for her to tell if the man was looking at them or just off into the distance. She continued to observe him. His hair was longer than most, and the ends of it were moving in the breeze as if held and controlled by some mysterious hands. If it weren't for his size, breadth of shoulders, even noticeable from the distance that grew between them, she would have thought it was a woman. She didn't know but a few men who grew their hair to such length. Some kept it as short as her papa's neat trim and others, to their collar. However, by the length of the man's strands waving, it had to stop at least across the back of his shoulders. Not nearly as long as her sister's and definitely not the extended length of hers, but still impressive and bold.

A shudder ran along her spine as she wondered how the man would look up close. *A mountain.*

"Well...are you?"

It was the hard nudge of her sister's shoulder against her own that snatched her attention away. Looking at Sophia in confusion, she clarified, "Am I what?"

Sophia exhaled loud and cast her eyes to the heavens as if in a silent prayer for Isabel. "Going to bake a pie for the Founder's Day gathering this summer."

She didn't say to her sister that she hoped to be gone before the celebration a few months away; instead, she simply responded, "No."

As if she didn't expect any other answer from her, Sophia continued her babbling. "There will be so many contests and games."

"I plan to enter the target contest," declared the deputy, who was fully engaged in the conversation with Sophia.

Isabel turned away again and glanced back toward the place where the horse and rider sat against the horizon. It was farther away now, but she could clearly see that both man and horse were gone. It took a long moment before she turned away and set her eyes on the road before them. She tried to push the thoughts of the mysterious figure away, but the image and questions nestled in the back of her mind as the wagon rolled them toward home.

Their parents were on the porch when they pulled up, sitting together on the swing. Their mother had a glass in her hand, most likely lemon syrup diluted with water, while ribbons of smoke circled over her parents' heads from their father's pipe, which he only smoked on Sunday evenings.

When the wagon rolled to a stop, she heard Sophia's sigh that was only drowned out by the sound of horse hooves behind them. Her parents stood to their feet on the porch as the three of them turned in the wagon to look back down the road.

For a moment, Isabel's heart leaped as she wondered if the figured man had followed them.

"I wonder what brings Mr. Spencer around?" Sophia asked as she got down from the wagon on Robert's side.

Isabel recognized the rancher as well as he drew near. She should have known it wasn't the man from the hill; that man was on a white horse and Spencer rode a black one. As he drew closer, Isabel could see that his four-year-old son was in the saddle before him. The little boy's hair was as red as his mother's now, and he had a smile filled with glee that stretched from ear to ear.

"Evening, Chance. You and junior out for a ride?" Her father had come down the stairs and was walking along the dirt to meet their guest.

Chance Spencer didn't get down as he tipped his hat and greeted everyone. "We were. Workin' on a few lessons."

"Would you all like a refreshment?" her mother called from the porch, where she leaned against the rail.

"Mighty kind, ma'am, but we need to be gettin' back." Chance offered her mother a smile. "We only came by because a piece of your mail got mixed up in ours. The missus meant to hand it off, but I guess the women got to talkin' with Mrs. Morgan 'bout how Serenity and the minister are fairin' in New Mexico and the sketch they sent of the new grandson and that was that."

Her mother blushed and made a comment about how adorable the baby looked in the artwork.

"S'pose he was, since my wife keeps talkin' about him too, as she coos at our new baby girl." Spencer reached into his saddle then removed the letter and handed it over to her father.

"Our names are close in the alphabet. I'm sure McCabe's had tons of bundles of mail to get separated from winter. Thanks." Her father nodded. "You sure we can't get you both somethin' before you go?"

"I'm sure. You all have a nice evenin'." Making a sound deep in his throat, Spencer commanded the big black stallion away and back up the drive.

They all waved them away.

"It's about time I get back to town." Deputy Nelson led her sister toward the porch where their mother stood.

"Nooo. Can't you stay a little longer?" Sophia's voice had a whining tinge to it.

"I'm on duty tonight, so I best be gettin' in some rest," Robert was explaining.

Not wanting to hear the pitiful show her sister was about to put on, Isabel headed toward the house.

"Seems this letter is addressed to you."

Hearing her father's words, Isabel paused in stride. She turned to her father, who was only a step or so behind her. "For me?"

"Looks like Josie had a few more things to say." He handed over the letter and kept on by her.

Isabel stared down at it. This time, the letter only had her name on it. It was still the same sweeping, elegant scroll of her aunt's, nothing else different. No hint on the outside, to give an inkling about what was inside of it.

It must be an answer to my request.

She hadn't posted the second message yet; the post wouldn't be open until Monday. She clutched this letter tight in her hand as she headed into the house. At the moment, she was grateful for two things, that the letter didn't come in with the bundle from the other day, because then she would have been forced to sit among her mother and sister and read it while they asked questions. Finally, that her sister Sophia was whining and pouting about how it was not fair that she can't be with Robert, even as the deputy thanked her for a lovely afternoon and said how grateful he was to her parents for letting him have supper with her.

Isabel was practically invisible as she moved up the steps and into the house. The soft breeze greeted her warm, tight skin. All the windows in the house were open, and they had created a wind tunnel. She inhaled deeply and allowed the air to fill her lungs and relax her some, but she didn't halt until she was in her room. The letter felt like fire in her hand, she was squeezing it so tight. Once there, she closed the door quietly, cutting off the coolness from the rest of the house. The window was open over her desk, but without the cross breeze, the room became stifling quickly.

She saw that a butterfly had come into her room and perched on the single fresh flower Rachel had placed in the small narrow vase early that morning. Rachel and Mrs. Tucker only worked Sunday mornings before service. Isabel didn't want to believe that the butterfly was any kind of sign, but she had hope.

Sitting down on the bed, she sent up a quick prayer then ripped into the envelope and removed the letter. It wasn't long. She read:

MY DEAREST NIECE ISABEL,

I hope this letter finds you well and not in too much poverty of spirit. I have received your letter. Your papa can be stubborn in all the right and wrong ways at times. However, I know he loves you and has the interest of your welfare at heart. For me, I find it difficult to support the women around me and not show the same courtesy to my niece when she needs it. Know that whenever you arrive, you have a place here. I have inquired at the academy for a slot for you. A new training class begins in a month, and they will allow your name on the list once you arrive. If it is needed, I can have funds wired to the bank there in Grover Town for your travel.

In fondest regards,
Aunt Josie

.   .   .

ISABEL DIDN'T REALIZE she was crying until the first two tears splashed onto the paper, smearing part of her aunt's name. Her heart felt full and overwhelmed with joy and madness. It was beating so fast, and all she could think about was talking to her father and laying her position out before him. He would be upset, but now that she had her aunt's support in writing and a timeline for her to start her training at the Young Ladies Academy of Philadelphia, he just had to listen.

She folded the letter and placed it into the pocket of her dress then left her room in search of her father. However, as soon as she stepped into the hall, she could hear that Sophia was in one of her full fits about the injustice of her not being able to marry the man she loved.

Seeing the scene played out before her, with her mother seated on the couch, her sister's face buried in her lap as she wailed, and their father pacing and waving his arms around as he barked out why the good Lord didn't give him a houseful of boys instead of two girls to turn all his hair white, even though only his temples were gray. He went on spouting about how Sophia marrying first would put a taint on Isabel, and folks would start thinking something was wrong with her.

"Is that what you want? For people to think Isabel ain't good marriage material?" When her papa was angry, he began to speak as the carpenter's son who only had six years of schooling, instead of the self-made property owner he had become. "You're still young, Soph, it's fit for ya' to wait."

"I don't want to wait." Sophia's voice was practically a screeching level.

"Shh...shh. There now." Her mother rubbed Sophia's back. "James, the girls know you want what is best. Don't get upset."

Seeing the writing on the wall and realizing she'd have to

approach her father once he'd calmed, she turned to head back to her room.

"Isabel."

Hearing her father call her name froze her feet in place. She'd lingered too long. Turning, she widened her eyes and set a smile to her mouth, hoping to calm his ire. "Yes, Papa."

Standing between the two Queen Anne chairs with one hand on his hip, he pointed the finger of his other hand at her. "I won't spend 'nother of the Lord's days in a mess like this. A man's home should be a place of peace."

Isabel swallowed then licked her lips. Dread was seeping into her pores from the tension filling the room. She wasn't sure what to say. Nothing came to mind that would not anger him more.

"You like ta write so much. You get in there and write a list."

"A list?" She frowned as the confused words came out.

"Yes. You modern women like a hand in who you'll wed. So, I'll give you a chance. Make a list of what men in this here town you want ta be lawful with, and I'll see that one of them is yours."

"But...but..." With a lexicon of words in her mind, she couldn't think of any of them to string together in a sentence, something to get her father to see reason and understand there wasn't a man in town who could make her dreams any different. "Papa."

"Get to it, Isabel. You got 'til week's end." With that, her father stomped out of the house.

The floor dropped from beneath her feet, and Isabel felt dizzy and shaky.

Sophia was still sniffling, but she was now sitting up with a tear-streaked face, staring at her, her gaze full of pleading.

Shifting her stare to her mother's face, hoping for

sympathy and understanding, Isabel, began, "Mama. Can't you talk to him? I want to go to Philadelphia. Aunt Josie has given permission for me to stay with her."

Sophia gasped.

Lillian Reynolds' gaze filled with hurt. "Was that what was in the other letter from Josie? Are you conspiring with my sister?"

Isabel realized too late that she had played her hand. "Um...it wasn't like that, Mama. I just wanted to talk to someone who understands."

Her mother rose from the seat tall and proud, with her chin high and her shoulders back, a posture Isabel had never seen before on her.

"You think because I don't choose to live in a big city, since I enjoy being a wife and mother in a small town of folks who care when someone among us goes hungry or has a bad crop that I lack in some way?"

Isabel rushed forward. "No. No. Mama, that was not what I meant," she entreated as she clutched at her mother's hand. "Grover Town is a wonderful place. I just don't think it's for me is all. And marriage..." Isabel shook her head.

"How do you know, when you haven't given it a try, not once allowed a young man to show a bit of kindness to you."

"You've always told us how you felt the first time you saw Papa. That we'd know it was right when we feel something special. Sophia even goes on and on about Robert causing a mess of butterflies to erupt in her stomach." Isabel looked at her sister, then her mother, and placed a hand on her stomach. "That has never happed for me. Not with a single man in Grover. But it does when I teach. I have gotten excited and happy every time I walk in those doors, since I was little. That's all I can think about."

Her mother cupped her cheek, but there were shadows in

her blue eyes as she stared at her. "You were a willful child, charging ahead like a bull in only the direction you wanted to go. If you ever set that energy on someone instead of something, you will know true happiness."

Moving away, her mother walked toward the door. "Now, my husband needs me."

In the wake of her mother's exit, she looked over at her sister, who still sat on the couch shaking he head slowly as she stared up at her. "Sophia—"

Her sister rose in silence, mimicking their mother's posture, and walked out of the room toward her bedroom.

Isabel stood in the center of the room and wondered how she could have come in there feeling elated and been deflated and crushed in a matter of minutes. Her eyes burned and she wanted to wail and cry. She didn't let herself give in to those useless emotions. Instead, she considered her options and knew what she had to do.

Leave Grover Town.

FOUR

Cary sat on the bench at one end of the rail station awaiting the Santa Fe line when he saw her. She came rushing from the side of the station manager's building with her bonnet and heavy outer garment. It was cool out, as spring started to spread across the land, but it was almost noon and the sun was heating things up for a warm day. Maybe that was what drew his attention to her.

When she occupied the end of the bench where he sat, he could barely make out more than the very front part of her face, like her forehead, nose, and lips. The bill of the bonnet was long and obscuring most of her face. What he could see of her was glistening with sweat. He feared that the darkness of her clothing was drawing more heat to her and she wouldn't be well.

Not my concern.

With the silent warning to himself, he turned away from her and glanced down the line in the direction the train was coming. He had a little less than a half hour if there was not any trouble on the line. Things that could happen that could cause a train to be delayed weren't good things to think about, so he shoved them out of the way. Today, there wasn't a reason for him to be at the station. He'd posted a couple letters in town that day, and he planned to make another pass through the properties he was deciding on. He knew what times the trains came and went, and since one was close, he came to sit, watch, listen, and think. There were two things that he enjoyed, being out in nature and trains.

Working on the lines and learning about the locomotives fascinated him, the speed, sound, and look of them. If it weren't for the thirst to farm and own his own land, he'd have taken his boss up on being an engineer. The first for his kind. It hadn't been the first time the boss had made mention of once the railway labor was complete that he could see a position for Cary in his family's railway company. It was a strong possibility he'd have taken it if not for the urgent letter. Now, he had mouths other than his own to feed, a duty to family, and following the line was no place for children. Especially small ones with no ma.

So, he'd returned to his first love, the land.

The tapping of the woman's foot beside him and her fidgeting on the seat drew him back to her. Glancing her way, he found himself poleaxed. The look of her knocked him off balance as she gazed over her shoulder toward the main section of town. From where they sat, much of the boardwalk or the various places could not truly be seen, but it would be the way that most, other than her, would come to the depot. He didn't need to follow her gaze. He'd already eyed the crowd of people milling around the area. The station manager, a middle-aged white man with the brightest red hair and red spots on his face, was smiling and chatting with people buying tickets or waiting on cargo or people they knew to arrive.

Her dubious gaze darted from left to right as if she were looking for someone or maybe ensuring someone wasn't there.

She was lovely.

Maybe it was because the only thing he could see was her face, surrounded by the long bill of her bonnet and underscored by the high-dark collar of her outer garment. She wasn't a classic beauty. Her eyes were too round and her lips too full for that; most might find them too striking and apparent. A man could drown in eyes so pale, vivid green. They were usually only seen in the first leaf of a new crop or the first blade of spring. The color alone brought joy to fill a person's blood. In the eyes of a woman, it sent the same bubble of excitement, followed by traces of heat that drove his blood to one specific place.

Heat that could only be incited when a man took in the fullness of her lips. They looked as if she were in a permanent pout. He wondered how they'd appear if she smiled. As if she'd heard him, they moved, not in a smile, but she rolled the bottom one into her mouth as she continued to stare at those around them.

He held his breath. He had to. The sight of her even white teeth and lips so red, they were like bright red cherries straight from the vine. He liked cherries, but this woman wasn't for him. Too bad his loins weren't getting the message.

The urge to see her hair assailed him. All of it was well hidden inside of her bonnet, it tied securely under her chin. The only thing he could tell by her eyebrows and long sweeping lashes was that her hair was dark in color, sable maybe.

He began to turn away from her when she shifted, and for a moment their gazes met. She assessed him quickly without recognition and turned back toward the tracks. The disregard didn't bother him; he was used to most people discounting him. His split nationality was an oddity, and most didn't want to ask questions of how he appeared not all together native and not all together white. So, it was easier to ignore him than to ask the question hovering in the air. His hair and style of dress caused a war in his own image.

There were others like him and his twin he had lost—half-breeds. Most of them didn't have the parental story that he did. He wasn't created from rape built of hate or revenge, but just the old tale of man meets woman and falls for her.

Still captivated by the woman, even though he warned himself not to be, he took in other things about her, like her thin, long fingers that she held together so tightly that her knuckles were a shocking white in her pale skin. There was a soft leather bag at her side on the seat between them. It was almost bursting at the seams, the buckle over the top strained.

It was clear she waited on the train to leave. By the second furtive glance she made over her shoulder, it was a moment that couldn't come too soon.

This time, he did glance over toward the others on the platform, not sure what he was looking for but just taking stock of his surroundings to see if he could see anything out of order that could cause such a pretty face to be drawn in worry.

When he faced her again, she was looking down the track, her heels still making a rat-a-tat sound on the wood boards below their feet. Her covering was so long, he couldn't see the kind of shoes she wore, just hear them.

"Ma'am, you in trouble?" Even though he'd been sitting there telling himself not to get involved with her, he was getting involved. One thing he couldn't abide by were men hurtin' women. If she was on the run because she was escaping an abusive husband, then he'd have to step in and offer the woman whatever assistance and safety he could until she was able to get away.

He believed that a man had a right to discipline his wife, when she'd placed her own safety or health at risk. Women tended to act too quickly on their emotions and could rush headlong into danger or a reckless situation without always thinking it through. Men were guilty of it too, but most men could handle themselves physically. It was their job to protect their women and children. However, being violent and causing such worry and angst as he could see and feel coming off this woman was unacceptable.

"Ma'am? I'll help if I can." He'd had to repeat himself to get her attention.

Appearing startled at his words, the woman glanced at him with questions shadowing her gaze. She looked at him, seeing him this time. She was silent as her new-grass green eyes glided over his face. Something flickered in her eyes and then it was stifled, and she glanced more beyond his shoulder than looking at him. "Pardon, me. Are you speaking to me?"

Not looking away, he nodded, not sure if she could see the small gesture as she was trying not to look at him. "Seems you're in a bit of distress."

She glanced at him, glanced away. "Um...no. I'm just waiting for the train."

He could hear the heavy exhale and the pull at the corners of her lips as she attempted to appear calmer and relaxed. It didn't work. He could see the clouds of distress in her gaze that made her deportment a façade.

"That might be so, but you don't look...well." It was the best word he could come up with that wouldn't possibly cause an offense to her situation.

"I'm fine. No need to concern yourself." She turned away

again, her head turning so far that all he could see was the back of her bonnet.

Not forcing the issue, he turned away too and stared over at the single set of tracks, remembering when they came through Grover Town to lay them. It was easier to think of his past hard work than the young lady beside him.

The folks in the town had been kind to them when they'd camped some distance away but came in for meals, looking for something different than the hearty beans and bacon from the women cooks who followed the line. The job had just been to fill the belly, not cater to any want or need for variety in foods. Thanks to them, he'd never gone hungry. While in the town, his friend Rufus had taken a couple lessons and learned the basics of readin' before they'd moved too far northwest for him to make it back to the town by dusk to learn more. Cary had aided Rufus on occasion if he stumbled or struggled.

It was heavy stomps of a man's feet that drew Cary's attention toward the milling people, and he saw a bellowing man.

"Isabel!" When the crowd parted, he recognized the landowner, Mr. Reynolds, as he looked around.

He wasn't sure who he was calling or looking for as he glanced around. Even from fifty feet of distance between, he could see the anger in the man's face. A young woman, with her brownish-blonde hair pinned in a style of twists and curls in a small fashionable bonnet some millinery owner had created of feathers and flowers, was with him. It was a sight to behold. However, the young woman, appearing no more than ten and eight, began pointing in his direction.

"There she is, Papa."

Cary realized she was gesturing toward the woman down the bench from him.

"Oh, no. No!" the red lipped, green eyed woman murmured. The words had barely been audible. "So close."

He glanced back at her. Her head was bowed and her chin lowered to her chest in a defeatist's posture. He wanted to shield her, shelter her from whatever storm she felt was coming her way.

"Isabel Reynolds." Mr. Reynolds and the young fashionable woman, who didn't look like either the older man or the young woman on the bench, crossed the platform beside him with a proud smile stretching her thin lips in a smile.

Cary figured the willowy young woman was impressed with herself for finding the other woman.

"I'm ashamed of such behavior," Mr. Reynolds chided in low tones as he stood behind their bench, speaking to the seated woman. "Your mama and I have taught you better than to run off and leave without word. Do you know how worried and sick your little adventure has made your mother?"

Exhaling, the woman took hold of her bag, glanced wistfully at the tracks as the train barreled forward, then turned to face him. "Papa, I can explain."

It was the mist in her gaze that had Cary rising to his feet. He wasn't even sure what he could do in a situation that was clearly between a father and his wayward daughter. For a moment, Cary wondered if he'd misjudged the property owner. Was he a cruel man at home to his wife and children? What would cause his daughter to flee without the traditional good-byes?

Seeing Cary for the first time, Mr. Reynolds nodded in his direction.

The hatted young woman gasped as he rose to his full height. She appeared startled and shuffled back behind her father.

Cary wasn't sure if it was his size or his long hair and features below his hat that made wariness flash in her blue gaze, which he didn't care.

"Is there something I can help with, Mr. Reynolds?" He kept his voice low too, not wanting to attract attention their way. Thankfully, the train's arrival and the normal hustle and bustle that went on with people pouring out and others rushing on kept the little family scene from notice, mostly. Some gave them a cursory glance.

"No, 'preciate the offer." Mr. Reynolds shifted his gaze back toward his daughter, who resembled him in coloring, and took hold of her bag. "Know that there'll be further talk at home, Isabel."

"Yes, Papa." Downcast, Isabel rounded the bench and followed her father and the other young lady across the depot.

Every step she took revealed her dejection. Wherever the woman had plans to go, she was heartbroken not to be on the train that would soon be pulling away from the station.

Isabel. Cary willed himself not to think about the young woman with the green eyes and full red mouth. She was Mr. Reynolds' daughter; the man wouldn't take too kindly of the enchanted thoughts Cary had been having of her as they'd occupied a bench for mere moments.

No reason for him to stay, Cary headed toward town to get Silver from the livery and ride his prospects of land one more time. Tomorrow, was the deadline Mr. Reynolds had given him to make his decision. Cary had already made it before the situation at the depot and had planned to go by Mr. Reynolds' office later in the afternoon, one day earlier, and confirm he'd take the land. It wasn't the best, but it was exceedingly better than the others unless he wanted to live farther away from town. With the kids in his care, needing schooling, it would be wise to have them not have to travel too far. Now, he had concerns that he would be lining a man's pocket each month who may be abusive to his family.

He'd go out one more time and see if he could convince

himself to take another stretch of land. Maybe change the crops he'd planned to plant. Potatoes and onions could grow even in the harshest of soil.

Isabel. The woman's name rang again in his mind, and he shoved it away. That road of thought was one best not taken.

"ISABEL CARRIE—"

She sat on the loveseat as her father paced along the low table before her, angry. It had been the fourth time he'd said her name without going on. She'd never seen him so upset that he was practically speechless. They had ridden home in utter silence; even Sophia didn't say a word. However, her sister had still maintained a haughty attitude then and now.

SHE AND HER mother sat in the two Queen Anne chairs at the ends of the seat she was in. It was as if everyone wanted to be in attendance for the show, but no one wanted to align themselves beside her for a show of support. She'd never really had support in her own home when it came to what she wanted; her own family saw her wish to remain a spinster and teach as a sort of illness, one her papa was determined to treat.

He stopped pacing and stared at her with dark green eyes filled with mixed emotions, none of them good.

"Isabel..." He shoved a hand through his hair, which had long since lost its sleek pomade style from the moment he'd started to pace. With his coat and tie off, he'd loosened two of the top buttons of his stiff shirt collar and he just stood there in suspenders, shirt, and trousers, appearing undone. He looked more like the carpenter's son he was than the self-made property owner. It was as if her actions had stripped him of his identity. "The utter humiliation—"

"I'm sorry, Papa." They were the only words she thought to say to help the situation. They hadn't so far.

"Sorry, Isabel? Ya think that word is goin' remove the...the scandal of it all?"

She shook her head once.

"How 'bout the hurt of ya mama?" He arched an eyebrow at her.

She started to move her head again.

He cut that action off with his words. "I'm sorry, Isabel Carrie, I cain't seem to hear you. You're so good at teachin', open your mouth and teach us all about how a young lady, raised well with good things and clothes and food and a family who loves her...can...can...run away from home. Come on, girl, teach us."

She continued to stare at her father, now through a watery gaze. She could feel the looks of her sister and mother, but she didn't look away from her father. Hearing his rough, broken language hurt her heart, knowing it was a sign of the distress he was in.

"I wasn't trying to hurt anyone, Papa. I just wanted to go to the academy in Philadelphia. Aunt Josie would have helped—"

"Josie!" he raged.

"James," her mother said softly, caution and concern in her voice and gaze.

Her father took a deep breath, closed his eyes, and took another one. When he opened them, he glanced at her mother instead of her.

When her mama nodded, seeing that he was a little calmer, her father continued. It was times like this that she could see how her mother was her father's center. He may run the home, but her mother could always calm him, get him to smile or see the better side of an issue that upset him.

Isabel didn't see any hope for herself on the latter.

"Another thing. You went behind your mama's back, and mine, to embroil your aunt's aid in all your foolishness. You think for one moment, Josie would take too kindly to your mama helpin' her girl without her knowing it?"

"No, Papa."

"We didn't raise you and Sophia to be sneaks, dishonest, disrespectful, connivin'...is that enough words for ya, teacher?"

Isabel rolled her bottom lip into her mouth at her father's mocking words.

"What do ya have ta say for yourself?" He folded his arms over his chest and stared down at her.

When she'd set her plans in motion on Sunday night, it had seemed like the best option. As she'd secretly gathered her things and hidden her bag in her closet until today, it had felt genius. And deciding that Tuesday was the perfect day, since her papa would be away until after supper, surveying his properties, she thought it was the best solution for everyone. Once she was gone, her papa would know she was safe with her aunt, her sister would be able to marry, and everyone would have what they want. Admittedly, in her selfish actions, she had not considered her mother, who even in her calmness, sat with tears in her eyes and tension around her mouth.

"I just wanted to take the opportunity to attend the school. Aunt Josie said they had a place for me there that they would hold if I could get there in a month's time, before it started." Honesty was all she had.

"So, ya lied to your mother about havin' a headache and set out to deceive us all?"

"Yes." She glanced over at her mother now and waited

until she met her gaze. "I'm sorry for the untruths. I'm sorry if I hurt you, Mama."

"Well, your actions did wound. If Sophia hadn't gone in to inquire on your health, and instead, she found you gone and that letter..." Her mother's words drifted away.

Isabel groaned silently. At the time, the letter had seemed a thoughtful good-bye.

"Is that truly how you see your mama and papa, Isabel? That we'd be happy to have you 'relieve us of the burden of you and the disappointment of your dreams not in line with our path for you' dribble?"

It stung now to hear her words given back to her. "Well, you all act as if my wanting to teach is the worst thing, while I see Miss Beadle's life as fulfilling and exciting."

"You think it's excitin' for a grown woman ta have to live off the generosity of townsfolk? A town council or board tellin' you what you can and cain't do? That you get a single room in a boardin' house to live alone all ya days? If a man thought kindly toward you, you couldn't even let him take ya to the Drummonds' for supper. That's a fulfilled life?"

When her father put it that way, it sounded constraining and lonely.

"I don't know." She was sweating under the outer garment and bonnet she had yet to remove since her father and sister had taken her from the depot. "I like teaching."

"If the good Lord blesses ya, you'll have plenty of young'uns to teach *at home*."

"But what if I don't think marriage is for me?"

"I ain't askin'." He threw his hands in the air in exasperation.

"Fine, you want me to marry, but have you even realized that no one is offering? Letting me teach solves this issue—"

He sliced a hand through the air. "No, Isabel. No more of

this nonsense. The Lord saw fit to give me two girls. And me and ya mama have worked hard to give ya a good life. I won't see all my efforts be washed down in a ditch. Ifin' ain't no sons to carry on what we've built," he pointed between him and her mother, "my daughters will damn sure reap in the benefits!"

Tears fell onto her cheeks and ran down. Isabel swiped them away. She knew how hard her parents had struggled to create a better, more prosperous life for themselves and for her and her sister. She'd heard stories, and she recalled the days her father didn't get home until nightfall, working and saving. She still had her own hopes and dreams, but they gave her no ammunition to fight his words.

"What do you expect me to do, Papa...change my dress and ways to be more like Sophia, to attract a husband?"

Her sister preened.

Isabel rolled her eyes.

"Your mama and I don't need two Sophias." Her father glanced over at her sister and shook his head. "You leave the husband gettin' to me. Before this week is out, you'll be settled."

"The end of the week?" Now, she looked to her mother for assistance.

Her mother rose and went to him. She slipped a hand around one of his arms. "James, at least give Isabel time to draft a list of men she'd like you to approach on her behalf."

He covered her hand with his own and appeared more eased by her touch. "Wife, I already gave her that opportunity. She chose to plan an escape instead. I know Grover Town, and I know men. I'll find someone who won't take the good land and sell it off for the money it would bring. A good man for her, Lillian." He fixed his gaze back on Isabel. "Maybe even someone to tame all those farfetched ideas from her head."

"Papa, I don't see wanting to educate the youth fanciful or

farfetched. It's a noble profession for young, single women," Isabel explained.

"Well, that'll soon count you out," he declared.

Isabel gasped at the vehement words.

He patted her mother's hand and placed a kiss along her cheek. "Since you like to plan and plot in that room of yours so much, you'll keep to it until I find you a spouse."

"B-but, Papa." She rushed to his side as he headed toward the door. Taking hold of his arm as he reached for his hat, she pleaded, "Please, don't do this. I'll do better."

He didn't pull his arm away as he stared at her. "You're not a child anymore, daughter. In life, we all have responsibilities. I've allowed too much slack in the leash for too long. No more." He set his hat on his head. "Until I find you a spouse, you won't leave this house, Isabel. Mark my words, if you test me in this, it won't go kindly for you. Old man Rivers, out by the creek on the north side of town, has been bellowing how he needs him a new wife in his old age to care for him, help with his gout."

With that threat stated, her father tugged his arm away and left the house.

She stood there, frozen, watching him walk off into the midday sun as he went to the wagon before the stairs Peter stood beside. He called out instructions, and Peter unhitched her papa's horse from beside the other one. Minutes later, her father flung himself up into the saddle and rode off, galloping away to seal her fate.

"You best be off to your room as your papa stated." The click of her mother's kid boots sounded behind her.

When Isabel turned around, she saw her mother head off toward the kitchen, not even sparing her a backward glance. Having nothing else to do but close the door and head to her room, Isabel pushed it behind her.

She didn't see her sister in the front room any longer, and she felt relief not to have to deal with Sophia. When she arrived in her room, the sliver of joy was short lived. Sophia was standing inside, a pleased grin on her perfect, bow-shaped lips.

Groaning, Isabel met her gaze. "Why did you do it?"

There was no need for Isabel to explain what she was talking about. Sophia knew.

Sophia stared at her, not responding. She crossed her arms over her small breasts. "I had to."

Isabel shook her head and moved deeper into her room.

"You think you are smart, Isabel. That you know so much."

"I know that you would have been free to finally marry Robert and stop having to wait around for me to go first." The chortle she let out was dry. "We both would have had what we wanted."

Sophia answered with a guffaw as she took hold of her arm, when Isabel would have brushed past her to go to her desk, firm and desperate in the same way Isabel had held their father. "No, Isabel. You think you could have just run away without Mama and Papa searching the area for you. When they didn't find you, or if you would have made it onto that noon train, they would have followed. *We* would have followed, because I would have been dragged along for the chase, my hopes of marriage and a family dashed."

She had never considered that her parents would come for her.

Her sister's gaze was wet with unshed tears. "I have never been as smart as you, Isabel. You know how much I leaned on you to help me study and learn. I struggled."

She could not discount her sister's words. Isabel wasn't sure what was going on with her sister's brain or why things had been so confusing for Sophia when it came to letters, but it had pained the entire household to watch Sophia struggle night after night. When her parents' patience had worn thin in knowing how to help, Isabel had gone to Miss Beadle and asked her to teach a way to help Sophia at home. Sophia had become Isabel's first pupil. It was then that she had decided to have a lifelong career in her own schoolhouse. Now that was gone.

"But you did learn, Sophia. Now, there's so much more you could do."

Shaking her head, Sophia continued, "The only thing I have is my style, beauty, and painting. Robert cares for me beyond that, though. No...he loves me. I would do anything...*anything* to be his wife. Even tattling on you."

Isabel picked up on the determination in her sister's voice. She gave her a sharp nod. "I understand. Now, you will have your dream."

The words Isabel didn't say hung in the air between them.

Sophia appeared contrite. "It wasn't my intention to hurt you. I was afraid."

"I'd like to be alone now."

Her sister walked to the door. When she got to it, she turned and stared at her a moment. "Isabel, you may see marriage as something awful. Remember that when you marry, you have true freedom from Papa and Mama. The rules change, and you become the head of your household and rule your destiny."

With that said, Sophia closed the door behind her.

She and Sophia had never been close since the hems of their dresses had lowered beyond their shins. However, now there was a wide, expansive gully between them, and Isabel wasn't sure if it would ever be bridged.

Sighing, she felt the stifling heat and the oppressive four walls surrounding her in her domiciliary prison. When she went to the window, the way now cleared of her desk for her to walk right to it, she took hold of the bottom and lifted it. It didn't budge. She tried again, with a loud grunt.

"Mr. Reynolds had Peter nail it shut from the outside."

"What?" Isabel turned and met Rachel's gaze. "Why?"

The maid stood there in her simple calico dress, light brown hair, and pale skin, holding a tray with a pitcher and a glass of water and sandwich. "When your papa realized you'd escaped through it, he told Peter to fasten it shut."

Isabel was both embarrassed and ashamed. She stepped back and sank into her desk chair.

"I thought you may be hungry. You left after breakfast, and I figured you must have walked more than three country miles getting to the depot."

Her stomach growled as Rachel set the tray down on the nightstand. However, Isabel didn't feel like eating. Her fate was sealed, literally. In days, her papa would be marrying her off to some man. Her plans had not worked out the way she'd expected.

"Just leave the tray, Rachel, I'll get to it." Isabel wasn't sure if she was telling the truth, but she just wanted to be by herself.

"I'll go. If you need anything or just wanna talk, call me and I'll come sit with you."

"Thank you." Isabel turned and looked out the window. She saw the vast prairie land stretch out before her and the copse of trees alongside it, the same trees she'd walked along to keep from being seen from the road. Her throat was tight, and her eyes burned as the ominous cloud of her fate moved in on her, but she refused to give in.

Now, the parting words of her sister returned to her. Marriage would give her freedom from her parents' control. Just a fraction, the burden on her shoulders and the tension in her body eased some. Her papa could make her marry, but he could not force her to give up teaching. All her life, she'd watched her mother cajole her father into allowing her to do things or purchase things he'd originally said no to, with a simple look or mysterious phrase that only the two of them understood, Even, at times, she'd led her papa to their room or, strangely, out to the barn for a private discussion, and somehow he would be convinced by morning.

Evidently, husbands were more amenable and open-minded in discussions than fathers were. That bit of knowledge gave her hope.

FIVE

"I'm here to see Mr. Reynolds."

Mr. Brown, he's been expecting you." The thin, short man with black hair stood, dressed in another black suit and starched white shirt and collar, as he had been a few days ago when Cary had first walked in looking for property.

Cary gave the young man who couldn't be older than two and twenty a firm nod.

The clerk's desk was in the front part of the town office that was wedged between the tanner shop and the postal service office. The man walked to the open door of the only other room in the place.

Cary strolled to the wide window with the company name painted on it and stared out. There was another property firm across the way, but down the other end of town, next to the saloon, Bellmore Property Management. Cary had gone to that one as well, but that man had been more interested in getting Cary to open a business in town, touting how he could help him manage it and make a lot of money. The man and his office were both decorated with the high quality of furniture and clothing that was evidence the man was successful. When Cary had been firm on his desire to have a farm, the man had taken him out to survey a few available properties that were pitiful. He'd broken rocky ground to create paths for the train in better soil than what Bellmore was offering.

One of the properties already had a small home on it and a small area right in front of the house where someone had farmed. The dry earth was tilled, but when Cary had dug his hand into the earth to see what lay beneath, it was a lot of half split seeds that had never even started to sprout, a testament to bad soil and low natural minerals and sediments. It would take a person too much work and hauling in good topsoil and manure for at least a year, with continued tilling, to get it to yield only crops that could grow in harsh lands.

Those properties were out, and so was Mr. Bellmore. The man smiled too much, with hands softer than a women's that made Cary leery of him.

After he made a deal with Mr. Reynolds, he'd have to head over to the sawmill and inquire on the cost of planks of wood to start on the house he'd need. His parents couldn't keep the children indefinitely. They were too old to be running after young ones. The place wouldn't be anything fancy to start out with and maybe no bigger than the single room shack on the property Bellmore had shown him. It would have to do for now. Cary had saved quite a bit, not as much as if he'd seen the rail line through to the west, but enough. However, his funds would be substantially lower after he paid Chance Spencer the funds for the two oxen he was holding for him and the mule he was getting from the livery. The local blacksmith, who was also a wainwright, had an older busted wagon he'd found and had taken some of the cost off the repair, since Cary had offered to lend a hand refurbishing it.

Grover was shapin' up to be the town for him once he signed his name to the property.

"Mr. Brown, I'm hoping you've made a decision in my favor."

Turning at the voice of the older man, Cary spotted Mr. Reynolds standing in the open doorway and the clerk already at his desk working again.

"I have," Cary sighed. Decent land was better than no land at all.

"Well, come on in. Let's talk." The older man waved him over.

Cary followed the man inside and was shocked when he closed them into the room. The last time he'd come over, Cary and the man had discussed what he was looking for with the door standing open.

Shrugging, Cary took the seat across from the big desk that took up most of the small room.

Once Mr. Reynolds was seated, Cary saw no reason to belabor the discussion with haggling, as the man before him was offering a fair price. "I'm going to take the last property you showed me, Mr. Reynolds. The one a few miles down from the Spencer Ranch line."

Mr. Reynolds nodded but wasn't saying much as he simply stared at him with his odd green eyes. Feeling a little disconcerted by the man's appraisal, Cary clenched his teeth and felt the muscle flex in his jaw; however, he remained still in his seat. There hadn't been a man he'd ever come across who could flap him. So, Cary kept his own direct gaze on the older man.

For a moment, Cary began to think he'd possibly misread the integrity of the man. Tired of waiting, he grumbled, "Do we have a deal?"

"Mr. Brown, you seem to be a good man. Honest, not

afraid of the hard work it would take to make and keep land prosperous."

Uneasy, Cary wasn't sure where the man was going with his observation of his character, so he remained silent.

"May I ask you a personal question?"

Arching a brow, Cary continued to stare across the table at the man. "Is my answer going to change our deal on the property that you'd agreed to hold until today?" He reminded the man of his word.

"Not in the way you think. It could work out even better for you."

Better? Had the man hidden away some of his better property, held it back from Cary's viewing because of his mixed race? Cary had gotten that in other towns but hadn't seen Grover as such a place. It was the reason he was pretty set on bringing his family up to join him. The kids would be safe growing up in an area that accepted all people, native, white, and the freed. "Ask."

"Are you married? Got plans of a wife, perhaps, joining you on the land?" Mr. Reynolds settled back in his chair and waited.

Cary hadn't expected that. Most people wanted sordid details about how he'd gotten his mixed race. People had even been so vulgar as to suggest that his father was Indian and had raped a decent white woman on one of those long wagon trains, headed to Utah or Wyoming Territories. None ever suspected the truth of the matter.

"No wife. There will be children, though, who, in a couple years, will soon attend the schoolhouse in town. Would that be a problem?" He wondered if the man was warning him off bringing a family. That maybe a lone half-breed was one thing, but a family that would fold into the fabric of the local culture was not welcome.

"Oh? Did your wife pass?"

"No." Cary felt the tension in his shoulders and fingers as he fought against balling his fists. He didn't want the property owner to see him as a threat. Cary couldn't stop the fingers of his one hand flexing around the brim of his hat that rested on his right knee. "Why all the questions, Mr. Reynolds? Is it because you have changed your mind about selling to me?"

Mr. Reynolds offered a smile as he sat calm in his seat. "Nothing like that. I think I have another offer for you."

"What is it?"

"I own another piece of property. Something more substantial and lucrative." Mr. Reynolds told him the acreage and where it was located, not too far from town but on the opposite side of the other properties.

Cary shifted in his seat. "Did you not show this to me, because you suspected I couldn't afford to pay or handle the size?"

With a firm shake of his head, Mr. Reynolds began, "I didn't show it, because it is not for sale."

His face drew in as his frown deepened. "What game are you playing, Mr. Reynolds?"

The older man let out a harsh and heavy sigh, as if the man struggled with a great weight. "The property that I split into two identical parcels of land are not for sale. Inheritance —they belong to my daughters and their husbands. Rather, whomever they eventually marry."

"Then why mention them to me?" Cary didn't like to waste time in his day, and this conversation that, to him, continued in head spinning circles seemed like a complete waste of precious sunlight.

"I'm offering you the hand of my oldest daughter."

What? "What?" It was a good thing Cary was seated,

because he'd have fallen over otherwise. "I'm not looking for a wife."

"No. But you want land. Good land. I've got it to offer."

"But it is not for sale."

"No. More like in exchange." Mr. Reynolds folded his hands over the slight roundness of his vest-covered stomach. "I'll tell you, Mr. Brown. Children are a blessing from the good Lord, but a lot of work. Which I'm sure you know."

Cary really didn't, since he'd only spent a little time with the two children in his care. He didn't respond.

"When a man has only sired daughters, it's years filled with both joy and grief. You worry of the men they will choose, men not out for their good or who may hurt them. I see you as an honest man. I will be truthful with you. Isabel, my oldest, is smart but willful. Kind, self-aware...but selfish at times. She'll need a man who is loving, perhaps firm in hand."

Meeting the man's stare, Cary understood the man's meaning. He'd heard a lot of men on the line grumbling about their wives trying to lead instead of following and having to take a hand to them. Some of those men, he would have liked to take a fist to their jaw for how they talked about beatin' their wives to keep them in line. Cary was all for discipline when it was due, but not striking women and children in violence or anger. Cary didn't get that impression from Mr. Reynolds.

"There are plenty of men in Grover Town who are looking for wives." Away from the east, women were in short supply. It was frequently discussed among the men on the line, who talked about settling west or in the frontier of wild Texas and New Mexico, where they would set up accounts for mail order brides from the east. "Why me?"

"Why not you?" countered the older man.

"Hm," was Cary's gruff response.

"You said you have children, but no spouse to help you raise them while you farm your land. You'll need a house. This land already has one...fully outfitted, thanks to the missus and my youngest, who enjoy emptying my coffers."

The man made a valid argument. Cary would be able to afford more grain seed to harvest, wood for a coup, and fencing to have a few chickens for eggs. True, Cary hadn't been in the hunt for a wife, but having one could benefit him in several ways.

"You don't know if your Isabel will have me. Perhaps her eyes are set on another." Cary didn't ask but could not help but wonder if the woman had been running away with someone. When she'd been glancing around in haste, maybe it wasn't her pa she was in fear of catching up to her before the train, but some lover who'd promised her escape and another life. The last thing he wanted was his wife pining after another. Especially one residing in the same town. Even a wife of convenience, he would expect to be faithful, someone he could trust.

As a farmer, he didn't have time to whittle beside her to keep her from wandering to another's bed.

"She has no choice. Both my girls understand they have a responsibility as far as their inheritance is involved."

Such arrangements were not uncommon. Since before time, men and women were placed together in holy matrimony to fulfill one bargain or another.

Cary ran his thumb along the worn leather of his cowboy hat. "I refuse to agree sight unseen."

"Understandable. I'll have you over for supper tomorrow, to meet Isabel and the family."

"No, the land." Cary didn't much care what the young woman looked like, he convinced himself. Besides, he'd already got a glimpse of the girl if she was the one at the station. This was a deal for property, a way for him to have the kind of farm and home he'd planned and saved for. If it was as good as the older man went on about it was, he would not be able to refuse.

Mr. Reynolds raised a brow at him but nodded. The man may not approve of Cary's words, but he remained silent. The older man couldn't argue, when he'd been the one to set the terms on the table.

"I'll get my hat. We can head over to the livery for horses and ride out."

When they both rose, Cary decided to confess some things to the older man who would be entrusting his daughter's life and well-being to him. "The children are those of my deceased brother and his wife. They are now in my care. If we make this deal, I will not mistreat your Isabel."

"Thank you for saying so." Mr. Reynolds let out a breath and his shoulders appeared to lower a bit. "Just so you know, she was the young woman I got from the depot yesterday."

"Figured." Cary doffed his hat and walked out of the room before the older man. He didn't need to be good with numbers in order to put it together that Mr. Reynolds would be attempting to saddle his runaway daughter with a man, instead of the thin blonde who surely had all the men in town chasin' her skirts.

Isabel. To his chagrin, he hadn't been able to forget her name or face, a face that had been more memorable than Cary had liked it to be. The captivating young woman from the depot had caused his body to respond in ways it had rarely responded in many years. Since leaving his home at sixteen, he'd kept himself refrained and focused on his goal. He wasn't a priest, and there had been times he'd given in to urges same as any man, but they had been mutual situations with understanding it would go no further. There had been plenty of women along the way who had hidden fantasies about lying with an Indian. Since he was a half-breed, he was safe, a way for them to live out their lusty imaginings.

There had been no emotional connection with those women; they had seen him as an instrument to use for their need, and it had been the same for him. He had been a young man, without discernment of how such situations could lessen his spirit. He'd matured, changed, and kept to his goals.

Now, before him, lay a possibility his ambitions could be fulfilled through marrying one woman. One woman, with beguiling eyes and a sensual mouth, who caused him to lie awake in his bed in the boarding house most of the night and fight the urge to take his cock in hand like a randy buck who couldn't control his need.

Isabel. The only things he knew of her looks were her face and her small, delicate hands that had clutched the handle of her bag. Everything else had been hidden from his view under an oversized bonnet and hefty, thick cape. Having seen the other young lady who had been with the older gentleman, pretty but slim, he assumed the man's older daughter was made the same.

He was a big man, and a slip of a girl wasn't to his liking. If he was going to be saddled with a woman for the remainder of his days on this side of land, he would prefer not to have to temper his lust.

"Sooner, I can let you see the land. Later, I can let the missus know we'll have company for supper."

"Your confidence is such that you believe I will agree to your offer?" Cary walked in step along the boardwalk with the man until they took a set of stairs before the tanner shop, to cross the road to the livery.

"It is. I know the value of the land. No smart man can resist it. Even knowing you a short time, Cary, you're no fool."

Silent, Cary continued beside the older man.

"GOOD EVENING, sir. Mr. Reynolds will be right out."

Isabel laid her worn copy of *Little Women* by Louisa May Alcott on her desk at the sound of Peter's rough voice coming from the front. She'd moved her desk back before her window since there was no way of escape anymore through it. Getting up, she wedged herself in the small space between the wall and desk's edge and tried to see toward the front of the house. Her room had never offered much in the way of the front road. She could barely make out the muzzle of a horse. From the distance, it was even obscured, and she could not tell if it was gray or white. If Peter decided to take the long route around the house, she would be able to get a view of the horse and that would clue her in to who was coming for supper.

At noon day, her father had sent a message to her mother that the family was having company for supper, for Isabel to make herself presentable. It had been two days since she'd been sequestered in her room. The night before, her father had sent Mrs. Turner into her room with a supper tray and she had not been allowed to join the family.

Now, tonight would be different. Her mother had ordered Rachel to draw her a bath in the bathing room in preparation for that night. Her mother had insisted she use her fragrant soap for her hair and body.

Through the day, she'd kept her room door open for air circulation, hoping for a chance to hear something of her fate. An hour ago, her father had come home from his office in town and had walked up to her room door to approve her apparel. The only thing Isabel wore that was not high collared and serviceable was the indigo dress she'd worn to the End of Harvest dance last fall in Mayor Snead's large barn, located at the end of town. It had never really been a barn, just an old mill that the mayor had cleared out and used for events. It was the place Sophia always talked about having her wedding dinner so that more people than just the family could come.

She hadn't done much dancing in the dress and had spent most of her time in the corner or walking through town. The memory of that walk brought the recollection of the couple, and she shoved it away. The last thing she wanted to do now was think about men and women canoodling, with some strange man who would most likely end up as her husband only steps away from her.

At the window still, she heard her father's greeting, and the other voice was too low and deep for her to identify, even when she pressed her ear against the glass.

"What are you doing?"

Caught, she turned and saw her sister standing at the foot of her bed with a frown, as she observed her.

Isabel had been concentrating so hard in seeing or hearing something of the visitor, she had not heard her sister come into her room. Heat filled her face at being seen in such a position. Now, wedged in between the desk and the wall, she struggled a little to right herself. Once again at her full height, she moved away from her spot. "Nothing. I was just seeing—"

"Spying." Her sister giggled. "Well, you don't have to press yourself through the glass any longer. Papa sent me in here to fetch you."

Stepping to her sister, she took hold of Sophia's hands. "Tell me, sister, who is it?"

"I don't know. Papa and Mama went to the porch to greet him when he sent me back here." Sophia smiled and squeezed her hands. "It has to be someone good, because you didn't see how Papa came into the house tonight. He was practically whistling."

"Whistling?" That bit of knowledge made Isabel nervous. There wasn't a single man in Grover Town she could conceive of who would have her papa pleased to take as a son-in-law. Most, he believed, would simply be after her and Sophia for their land and to sell it off. Others, he would say, didn't have the know how to get themselves out of a burlap sack, let alone handle a large farm.

That was most important to her father. If he could not have a son to take over his business, then he'd have a son-in-law who could turn the massive acres into a profit.

"Sophia. Isabel." Their father's baritone voice called them from the front room.

"I hope he is someone as handsome and tall as my Robert." Sophia released her hands then headed toward the door.

"I hope he's smart." Isabel really didn't care what a man looked like; appearances faded over time. If she was going to be stuck with a man in holy matrimony for the rest of her life, she wanted him to be able to converse with her on various topics.

With a deep breath and running a hand along her hair that, for the first time in a long time, was fashioned in a riot of twists and curls where the loose ends brushed her shoulder blades, instead of in her usual tight chignon. She joined her sister in the hall then journeyed along it toward the front.

"Girls, Mr. Brown will be joining us for supper tonight."

Sophia gasped.

Isabel envied the sound her sister made because she didn't have the air in her body to make a sound as she stared across the well-lit room at the man beside her father. The man was massive. It was the first thing she noticed, how his size dwarfed her father. The stranger had to be over seventy-five inches because her father was at least sixty-eight inches. It had been where she got her height, while her sister and mother were shorter in stature.

It wasn't just his size, but his face, that appeared as if it had been carved from a desert mountain, both in the pale reddish brown of his complexion and the strength in his brow, nose, and jawline. His mouth, thinner than hers but perfect in shape, wasn't smiling. The man's mouth was set, and his eyes stared back at her, intense. His hair was so dark and long, it looked like ink was forming two rivers from the part at the center of his head and continuing until it passed beyond his shoulders, longer than most men she knew, even the cowhands and wranglers, who didn't keep their hair cut about the collar like her father and other men who worked in town.

His shirt was blue, with white stitching along the crest of his wide shoulders, down along the bottoms in front, and around his wrist. He wore brown, fresh trousers and a well-worn pair of brown boots.

His features and style of dress clued her in to the fact this man wasn't all native nor all white. He was caught somewhere in between.

"Come forward and meet Mr. Brown, Isabel. He has agreed to marry you." Her father's words helped to unstick her heeled boots from the floor.

She wanted to apologize for her rudeness and staring. However, there wasn't a drop of moisture that had returned to her mouth for the words to come out more than a squeak as she approached him.

Lucky me. She felt like a piece of her father's property that he was showing off and angling for someone to purchase. Pretty much, it was exactly what was happening. She wondered how much Mr. Brown had paid to own her and the land she came with. What kind of man came into a town and bought a woman? The thought angered her.

"We meet again." The man had taken a step toward her.

As they met in the center of the room, keeping a respectable two feet apart, she frowned. She had to swallow to speak. "We've met?"

His gaze held hers, and now that she was closer, she could see the slate gray color of his eyes. The sight of them gazing down at her, unusual and odd, assessing her, caused her pulse to kick up. She'd never seen eyes that color before, and they almost didn't seem to fit in the face with his coloring.

"Yes. The train platform yesterday." His tone was clear and matter of fact.

Her anger turned to embarrassment as a flush of warmth spread over her skin from her face to her toes. The man had been a witness to her humiliation. She wracked her mind to recall if he was someone in the crowd, then it struck her. He had been seated down the long bench from her. He'd inquired if she needed assistance.

Yesterday had been such a whirl of emotions and moments, she had forgotten him.

How? Nothing about this man was remotely forgettable.

"Forgive my rudeness. You're correct."

He held his hand out to her. "How about we put that situation behind us?" His voice rumbled.

It reminded her of the 1867 earthquake that happened while her family had taken Aunt Josie to join her husband, who had been finishing up his education at Kansas State Agricultural College in Manhattan, Kansas. Her papa had also been going to listen in on a few lectures about some newfangled ideas around soil and crop growth. At the time, her father was still farming the land around their house.

The earth had shaken under her feet then and sent her body reeling, and this man before her was doing the same.

When she slipped her hand into his wide callused one, the sensation of being knocked sideways didn't ease, but intensified.

"Yes." It was the only word she could think of to respond.

One corner of his mouth twitched; it didn't really lift or begin to curl into a smile, just moved like a wink of the lips.

"The table is set if you all are ready for supper, Mrs. Reynolds." Mrs. Turners' voice broke up the tension she felt touching this man.

Isabel pulled her hand away and stepped back.

"Perfect. We're ready." Her mother's voice was practically singing as she smiled at her and Mr. Brown. "Isabel, why don't you escort Mr. Brown into the dining area?"

"Yes, Mama." She wanted to tell her mother that their home was large, but not so grand that the man would not be able to find his way since the rest of them were headed in the same direction. Having been raised with proper courting customs, even though it was something that she never used herself, she knew she was supposed to slip her hand around the bend of the man's elbow. However, she was still wobbling from just touching him a moment ago and wasn't sure how her body would respond if she did it again so soon. "This way, Mr. Brown."

Taking his cues from her, the big man simply fell in line beside her. His heavy footfalls caused more shockwaves to journey up from the base of her feet.

How would she be expected to share a home with someone so massive and all-consuming of the air and space around her? She thought about her father's threat of marrying her off to Old Man Rivers, with his chronic gout. That man was a wiry fellow, and if she chose to sit across a room from him to keep her distance, she would have felt as if she could breathe.

With Mr. Brown, she was finding each breath and thought a struggle.

There were some big men who worked out at the Spencer Ranch, those who could wrestle down a bull in a contest, but still none of them competed with the man beside her.

Proof on just how spectacular of an image the man made was in Sophia's gaze. Her sister kept looking over her shoulder every few steps, to assess the man with a look of trepidation in her blue eyes. She and her sister weren't raised with a narrow-minded view of natives, to fear them. So, it had to do with the mountainous appearance of the man that had Sophia appearing anxious. Or maybe Sophia was simply piqued because Deputy Robert Nelson could not hold a candle to the man entering the dining area beside Isabel.

Robert was handsome, almost to the point of prettiness, with his round face and smiling eyes. However, Mr. Brown was striking and imposing and would never be considered comely in any way. That bit of knowledge made Isabel smile inside as she sat in her usual seat across from her sister while Mr. Brown held out her chair.

Their father first assisted their mother at the end of the table, then Sophia. Mr. Brown claimed the place beside her.

As he took his seat, their elbows bumped briefly, and she caught the small gasp before it left her mouth at the electric contact.

Mr. Brown cleared his throat, causing her to glance up at him. He was staring at her; his gaze seeming a darker gray, like the charcoal color of burned wood. It smoldered too.

She looked away quickly, least she find herself singed.

Her father requested for them all to bow their heads as he said grace. Usually long in verse, her father started by thanking the good Lord for not only the provisions before them but their guest who joined them at the table.

Isabel tipped her head down but didn't close her eyes as she usually did. She used the chance to glance at the man beside her without his intense gaze on her. His hands were curled and resting on his thighs, barely constrained beneath the material of his britches. The tablecloth covered him from the knees down, but she suspected that he sat with his feet planted shoulder width apart, as most men. She let her gaze travel up the tuck of his shirt beneath his belt and noticed there was no protrusion of his belly; it seemed flat. She didn't allow herself to consider how he looked beneath his clothing. She'd seen a man or two shirtless as they swam in the creek, while the woman had to settle on dipping their toes in to cool off in front of mixed company.

As she allowed her eyes to travel up, she noticed the strain of the fabric of his shirt across his wide chest. It looked crisp, and she wondered if he'd just purchased the shirt at the Russells' store before coming to meet them for dinner. She inhaled to see if she could pick up the scent of the dye that was always in new colored fabric until after the first few washes. However, instead of the chemical odor, her lungs were filled with sandalwood, the deep, rich, woody scent with a soft hint of sweetness at the end.

Her heart rate kicked up as she inhaled a second time and she had to swallow twice. Unlike when she'd first seen him and her mouth had gone dry, she was practically salivating as her mind considered all the ways a man could smell like sandalwood. Was it infused in his cakes of soap, or did he dab the imported oil on like women and some men?

When she arrived at his face, she breezed past his lips, too nervous to spend too much time there, and the aquiline shape of his nose made her want to reach out and run her finger along the sloped bridge. Mostly because it wasn't her way, but the fact that his lids were open, and she found him staring at her.

Had he been assessing me as I had been doing him?

"Amen," her father ended the prayer.

"Amen," they all echoed around the table.

Mr. Brown's gaze held too much mystery to unpack and she turned away from him, only to be greeted by the high arch of her sister's slender brow.

Had no one's eyes been closed as her father prayed.

"What is it that you do, Mr. Brown?" Sophia asked as she scooped boiled potatoes from the serving bowl onto her plate.

"Farm." One word, as he'd uttered before taking the platter of brisket from her mother and adding a slice to his plate.

Isabel took the platter from him and was careful to ensure she only grasped the edge of the dish to keep from brushing fingers with him. His hand was flat below it as he easily balanced the platter and allowed her to remove a piece of meat.

"What brought you to Grover Town?" Sophia continued with her questions.

Isabel was grateful for her sister's inquisitive manner; it kept her from having to ask, and she could simply sit back and focus on eating. She was hoping that the meal would not last long.

"Mr. Brown worked the rails. He actually was through here, putting down the tracks." Her father answered first before sinking into one of Mrs. Turner's fluffy yeast rolls.

"So, you weren't a farmer before you came here?" Sophia put a small piece of potato into her mouth.

"Sophia?" The warning tone came from their mother, who didn't abide rudeness.

Isabel offered an apologetic smile to Mr. Brown when she received a bowl of peas and onions from him.

"Well, Mama, if Mr. Brown is going to be marrying my sister, I would think we all would like to know who this man is. Why would he even agree to marry Isabel, sight unseen?"

Mortified at her sister's blunt but truthful words, Isabel clenched her teeth and felt the flex of muscles around her mouth.

"I know who he is. He's a decent man." For the first time since he'd arrived home that evening, her father appeared annoyed. The corners of his eyes were beginning to draw in and tighten as he met Sophia's gaze.

"I do not mind the questions, Mr. Reynolds. Isabel," she could feel his gaze as he paused, "or any of the members of your family can ask me what weighs on their minds. What would you like to know?" He picked up his glass of cider and drank.

Isabel continued to keep her head down and eat, not sure if his question was directed at her or the invasive Sophia.

"Where are you from? You can start there."

"Wichita Falls, Texas, borderin' Oklahoma. My ma and pa raised my brother and me there, on the same farm my pa was raised on. My uncle, pa's older brother, inherited the land that he too lived and worked with his family. I left at sixteen, to find my way, doing odd jobs until I got a position on the line, and I've carved out paths and laid wood and eventually steel tracks from Pennsylvania to Utah all while savin' up for my own farm someday." When he finished talking, he sliced into his meat, resuming eating.

Isabel noticed that unlike the rest of them, Mr. Brown had forgone pouring gravy on his meat or potatoes.

"Have you never married?" It was her mother who asked,

holding her fork midway to her mouth with four peas balanced on it.

Normally, Isabel didn't give much thought to the dainty portions her mother and sister ate compared to her own fork-fuls, but sitting beside the man who would be her husband at some point, she felt inelegant. There was a marked difference she was sure he noticed in her fuller frame compared to her sister's and mother's slim ones.

She tried to cut smaller bits, but she just ended up raising her fork more often to feel as if she had a mouthful enough to chew.

"No."

That shocked Isabel, as the man appeared to be at least more than ten years her senior. Most men had settled down at least once or twice if their wife died young.

"Workin' and movin' around a lot, I just didn't see it as a place for a wife and kids to be happy."

"That's understandable and admirable even." Her father, who was seeming to be Mr. Brown's champion, smiled.

To Isabel, her father appeared incredibly pleased at his pick.

"When do you think you and Isabel will tie the knot?" Sophia plucked a small piece of roll off and placed it gingerly on her tongue.

"I've asked your pa for at least two weeks. Time enough for my family to arrive."

Two weeks? Stunned, Isabel glanced at him.

"Two weeks?" Her mother spoke her words out loud as her fork clanked against the edge of her plate. "I'm not sure if I can plan a wedding in such little time."

"I don't see any need to stretch it out. Isabel has never discussed anything fancy," her father reminded them.

She'd never discussed a wedding at all. It had been some-thing she'd refused to entertain a discussion about.

"Wouldn't you like something nice, Isabel?" Sophia's eyes were practically aglow with the thought.

Isabel knew her sister would love a reason to shop or deco-rate. In her mind, she could just see the many trellises weighed down with every flower from Grover to Topeka, Sophia would design.

Finally, finding her voice, before her mother and sister ran away with arrangements, Isabel swallowed the half of potato she'd just chewed and used her napkin to wipe the sides of her mouth to ensure no thick gravy rested there. "No. If this has to be done, the simpler, the better. The sooner, the better. If we must wait for his mama and papa, then we will delay it only until then."

"Fine, but I insist that we decorate your lawn for the wedding meal." In her excitement, their mother put two small pieces of roll in her mouth.

Sophia's brain was practically ticking loudly as she started putting together ideas. "Besides your papa and mama, Mr. Brown, who else would you like to have there?"

"Only the children." He scooped up peas then ate them.

Isabel looked from him to her father as she set the other half of her buttery yeast roll back onto her plate. "Children. *Your* children?"

SIX

"Now. Yes."

"I don't understand." Had her father been so anxious to have her married off that he would have saddled her with a man who had born little ones out of wedlock? Were the young ones even from the same mother, or had he collected them along the way, at each new rail line stop?

"My brother and his wife died last year, from cholera. At some point, a few barrels of water supplied to the reservation where they lived had been rancid. Many became sick, and some passed before aid was brought in and fresh water replaced the bad. Garmin and Adsila were with those who did not make it."

Isabel's heart sank at his words, and she felt guilty over her silent obloquy of his moral character.

"That is very noble of you, taking on the care of your niece and nephew," her mother responded, reaching along the table then covering Mr. Brown's hand.

He glanced at the place where her mother touched his wrist then over at her. "I just hope to honor my brother and his wife and not fail."

Her mother offered him a kind smile, her gaze soft and filled with comfort. "I have no doubt you will."

Mr. Brown had just won over her mother as he had apparently done to her father.

The big man didn't respond as her mother moved her hand. He cut more of his meat then speared it with his fork. Before lifting it, he glanced at her. "Are the children a concern for you?"

Yes. "No." It was the right thing to say, she knew. Her hands shook a bit at the thought of being an instant mother. She placed them in her lap for a moment, to keep their trembling from view.

His gray eyes held hers, and she was sure his perspective gaze had caught her nervousness, but he didn't question her response.

"What are the children's names?" She wanted to distract him from reading her; the man made her too unsettled in many ways.

"Atohi, he is the oldest at four. Ama, my niece, is three."

"They're very young." Isabel had hoped they were of school age and she could take them with her when she helped Miss Beadle. Since she couldn't get her own training, she still planned to assist at the schoolhouse and teach the uneducated adults in town. Like Sophia had reminded her yesterday, this marriage would be her ticket to freedom.

"Very brave as well. Having lost both their parents at such a young age." Her mother had a hand over her heart as she shook her head at the story. Her mother always knew the right words to say.

"Yes, brave," Isabel parroted, not wanting Mr. Brown to feel she was insensitive. She wasn't. She was around children all the time at the schoolhouse, and she had witnessed how often they dealt with adult grief and pain, things their young minds could not process yet, but they still soldiered on better than some grownups. Yes, children were remarkable.

As dinner drew to a close, Mrs. Turner came into the dining room to collect the dishes. "Anyone care for dessert? I've made a pound cake." When she stepped closer to Mr. Brown, she greeted him by saying, "Well, now. You're the type of man a cook enjoys feeding. Instead of a houseful of women who eat like birds." Mrs. Turner punctuated her words with a wink at her.

Isabel felt heat fill her cheeks.

Their guest didn't fully smile, but the corners of his mouth twitched then slightly curled. "Thank you. My ma didn't always feel that way with me, my twin brother, and Pa. She used to say good thing we were farmers, because it took half a field to feed us."

Mrs. Turner laughed and shook her head as she balanced the plates. "I grew up with older brothers and that sounds 'bout right."

Once the cook had passed the archway, her mother said, "Mrs. Turner makes the best pound cakes."

"I'm afraid I don't do desserts. I've never really had a sweet tooth."

"I'm having coffee. How about sharing a cup with me?" her father offered.

"Another time if I can," Mr. Brown suggested.

"That's fine," her father agreed before he slid his chair back and rose.

When Mr. Brown stood next and assisted her with her chair again, Isabel stood beside him and her core quivered as his size. Mrs. Turner had been correct; it would take a lot to feed this man. She was glad now for all the years she'd learned beside the cook. Then she'd told herself she needed to know how to prepare her own meals since she would be living alone and would not earn enough to pay someone to cook for her. That skill would do her well.

She wasn't sure if she would ever become used to her body's overwhelming response to his size.

"Mama and I will get started immediately on the wedding plans." Sophia came around the table. When her sister noticed Mr. Brown glancing at her briefly, she giggled. "We'll get some input from Isabel, but planning all that is involved with social events, no matter how small, is not something my sister does."

Isabel lifted a shoulder but didn't apologize.

"Isabel does have many other qualities," their mother assured their guest as they all started toward the front room.

Mr. Brown gave a nod as he moved in step with her, not offering her his arm this time.

It was Rachel who came back in to gather the platters and bowls.

"Rachel, please inform Mrs. Turner that we'll have that dessert in the front room."

"Yes, Mrs. Reynolds," Rachel called out behind them.

In the front room, Mr. Brown shook hands with her father as the older man told him to come by the office the next day so that could settle some things.

"I will." Mr. Brown looked toward her mother next and thanked her for the meal.

"You're welcome at our table anytime. You'll be family." Lillian smiled as she settled herself on the loveseat.

"Isabel will show you out," announced her father, who took up the chair closest to her mother.

"Of course." Isabel started toward the door. It had not been her plan to spend any more time with the man tonight. She looked forward to having some distance between them so she could process the odd feels she had experienced through the evening.

"Wait!" Sophia's voice stopped them.

Since Isabel had already stepped back while pulling the door open and Mr. Brown had moved forward to remove his hat from one of the pegs beside the door, their halting placed them oh so close. The heat of the big man was seeping into her back through her clothing. For a moment, his breath tickled the wisps of hair that didn't make it into her coiffure.

She glanced over her shoulder at him, her heart pounding at his nearness as she witnessed the shadows of something darkening his gray eyes.

He uttered a word that sounded like 'forgive me' or 'excuse me', she could not be sure because the blood pumping fast in her through her heart was thrumming in her eardrums.

Either way, Mr. Brown stepped back before he cut his eyes toward her sister, waiting.

Sophia, who had already fetched her planning journal, was seated in the chair by the low fire in the hearth. "We never got your first name, Mr. Brown. If we're to put up an announcement about the nuptials at the postal office and mercantile, it must state your full name."

Isabel knew, like everyone in town, those were the two places to post any type of announcements, even if a person was buying, selling, or declaring a new infant arrival, because everyone in town went to those places often.

"Cary." His deep voice rumbled as he said his name.

Shocked, Isabel looked at him.

"That's Isabel's name." Sophia let out a giggle, apparently delighted at the discovery.

Frowning, her intended looked over at her.

Isabel nodded. "Isabel Carrie Reynolds. C-a-r-r-i-e." She wasn't sure why she spelled it, and she chalked it up to the fact the man made her so nervous, she instantly did what was comfortable to her—instructing.

He seemed to find humor in something she said. His eyes lightened to the steel gray color again. "Mine has a y."

She let out a slow breath and turned away from him. "Do you think you have everything now, Sophia?"

Grinning, her sister nodded.

Isabel continued out the door and into the night. She saw that Peter had already brought Mr. Brown's horse around. *Cary*.

She found it kinder to her senses to concentrate on the horse instead of the man on the stairs beside her. The light from the windows made an arch around the front lawn and made it easy to see the horse. The stallion was all white, tall, with sleek powerful muscles shifting under his beautiful coat.

The horse neighed at the site of the man as they started down the stairs.

"What's your horse's name?"

"Silver." He continued down to the last step that brought them almost at eye level. "He belonged to my brother; Garmin trained him from a foal."

There was both pride and grief in his voice as he stretched his left hand out and caressed the horse's muzzle.

"It seems your brother left everything he valued in your care."

He took his hand from the horse and faced her again. "Yes. It is nothing less than I'd have done if the situation were reversed."

"Of course." Isabel and Sophia were like two sides of a half-cent, but if something happened to her sister, Isabel would be there for her.

They stood there in the amber glow of the house lights keeping the night at bay. With his hat on, it shadowed half his face, and she could no longer see his eyes.

"May I?" he asked in a low voice.

She nodded, not sure what she was even agreeing to. However, with her parents just in the front room, she had no concern that the man would do something untoward.

He reached up with his right hand and ran two of his knuckles slowly along the underside of her jaw.

The touch was so light, she could barely feel it. What she felt was the heat that followed in its wake. It made her yearn to feel his caress along the side of her neck or her arm and other places she shouldn't be thinking about.

At her chin, he paused and stroked his thumb just under her full bottom lip.

It wasn't possible for her to see his gaze, but she could feel the intensity of it as he focused on her mouth. His stare caused her lips to tingle.

She wanted to roll it in, embarrassed of its dark, plump size. His finger was callused and abraded her skin. The feel of his touch didn't disgust her. No, it was doing other things to her.

He pulled away, and she was all too grateful for his retreat.

Without a word, he turned and closed the gap between himself and his horse.

As she watched him pull himself up in one fluid, confident motion onto the saddle of the horse, she stared at him. He made one impressive figure on such a powerful mount. Her mind filled with the image of the lone man on the grassy hill. She now knew who it had been. Cary.

Her heart thumped faster, and the air rushed out of her mouth in a sigh she prayed he could not hear. She'd mused more than once since Sunday evening about the obscure man. He'd appeared so free when her life was anything but.

The stranger's existence before her was proof of that. He'd be her husband, her permanent tether to Grover

Town, one sealed by the good Lord that she could not break.

Night was falling, and there were too many shadows now around Cary, even with all the lamp light coming through the two large windows on both sides of the front door. She couldn't see his stare, but she could feel it. It was like a caress along her bare collarbone and the length of her arms.

Her nipples tightened, even though she doubted the stoic man had taken any wayward glances toward such an intimate part of her person. Yet, her breasts still felt heavy in her corset and something again stirred deep in her core, filling her lower region and limbs with heat.

"G'night, Miss Reynolds." He tipped his hat.

"Evening, sir. Rest well," she bid him.

He made a clicking sound accompanied by some word she didn't understand, as the horse turned and headed down the road.

She leaned against the banister along the stairs as she thought about the whisper of words she swore she'd heard before he galloped away. *No hope of that, Carrie.*

Those words to her rest well entreaty didn't make any sense to her. The man should sleep like a log, with a smile on his face. He'd not only have a wife but land to boot. If anyone had a right to a disturbed sleep, it was her. Cary Brown was one disturbing man in many ways.

There was a quiet intensity about him, the passion in his voice as he'd spoken during dinner about his love of farming. He'd talked about his pa working alongside his grandfather when he was younger. She'd learned that he'd already sent a wire to his parents to let them know to bring the children up.

Children. She would become a wife and aunt, mother figure type, in a couple weeks. She had no experience when it came to young ones who weren't in school yet. Thankfully, he'd stated his parents had plans to stay in Grover Town, to spend the remainder of their days. They wanted to be around their son and grandchildren, Cary had said.

What he had left unsaid was *and any others that came along.*

She placed a hand on her belly as shivers spiraled along her spine and out to her limbs. There'd never been a remote possibility in her mind that she'd be swollen with child. Or married.

Or conceived of a Cary Brown in her life.

"Has he left, Isabel?"

Startled out of her own musings by her sister's voice, Isabel turned and exhaled. "Yes. Just."

She moved up the few steps to her sister's side on the porch. "Did you leave me any pound cake?"

Cary wasn't one for desserts, but she loved them.

"Of course. Mrs. Turner left you a covered slice on the table."

When Isabel would have gone past her sister, she felt the soft touch on her elbow. Pausing, she glanced over at Sophia. There was a tightness around her mouth and worry in her gaze.

"What is it?"

"Are you sure you will be okay...with him?"

Her sister's words caused a rod to slide along her spine. They had been raised not to have bigoted ideas. Their pa came from carpenters, farmers, and sharecroppers, during a time when life wasn't as easy as they had it now. People of all types had worked the land and shared all that they had, so everyone had a chance to survive. "What do you mean, him? Because there is Indian blood that runs through his veins? Don't forget, Sophia, there will be some of that same blood that is in any children we have...your kin."

Sophia understood her words and gasped. "No. Oh, no, Isabel. Not his race, his *size*. He's so...so...." Sophia waved her hands up and out so many times, it was comical.

"Yes. Mr. Brown is impressive in height and width." His size may have caused disquiet in her sister's mind, but it caused trepidation in her body for another reason, one she tried to tamp down.

"And intense."

Looping her arm through her sister's, Isabel smiled to put her at ease. "He'll need that to get at least one crop going so late in the planting season this year."

"You're probably right."

Pulling her back toward the front room where they had all taken their dessert and tea, well, coffee for her father, Isabel teased her sister, "I am always right; I'm oldest."

Her mother and Sophia both laughed at her words. Isabel caught the small smile her papa offered her. The shadows that had been in his eyes for months and the light that her actions had seemed to snuff out just days ago was a spark in his eyes again, green eyes that matched her own.

As she took her seat beside her mother on the loveseat, while Sophia took her place in the chair beside the fire across from their father, Isabel felt some of her worry ebb away. She still had doubts about becoming a wife instead of a school-marm, but not having the cloud of disappointment hanging between her and her father was better.

"HELLO, CAROLINE." It was early, all the shops barely open one hour, and she hadn't expected to see many people.

The young lady her age stepped onto the boardwalk from the Russells' Mercantile shop. As normal, the young woman's gaze was downcast, but she looked up at the sound of her name and smiled.

"Isabel?" There was question in Caroline's voice. The other woman was rarely seen in town, and she and her father never attended any of the town's community functions.

They had been in the schoolhouse together until thirteen, when Caroline's father wouldn't allow her to attend anymore. She had been Isabel's closest friend and confidant.

"It's good to see you." She closed the gap between them and hugged her old friend. Isabel's heart ached at her sight and the feel of Caroline's slight form under the worn yellow calico dress that was no more than a drape on her.

Strong but thin arms embraced her back. For a moment, they stood there, and Isabel could feel the almost desperation in the tightness of the hold from her lost friend. However, it was fleeting, and soon, the other woman stepped away first.

Releasing her, Isabel asked, "I hope you are dropping off some more of your lovely soaps."

"I had a few cakes to bring by, and I got some eggs as well." Caroline resituated the basket on her arm that had a few towels gathered inside, to protect the eggs she claimed to have picked up from cracking on the journey home.

Isabel would never be so crass as to ask how many eggs Caroline was able to get and if more than two or four were under the towels. All Grover Town knew of the plight of her friend, caused and made worse by Caroline's father. "Wonderful. I am here to busy myself with soap smelling and purchasing, to keep away from been fussed over and poked at in Molly's dress shop."

"Ah. Yes. I recall how much you hated new dresses when we were younger, claiming they were stiff and itchy." Caroline laughed and fingered a lock of her chestnut colored hair back behind her ear, it having slipped loose from the simple tie at the back of her hair. Her ribbon holding her old friend's hair back appeared to be a strip of material matching the dress she wore.

Isabel didn't look down at the hem to see.

"Because Mama thought that because Sophia loved lots and lots of lace everywhere and I would never pick out my own dress, she decorated it in the same fashion. To this day, I swear lace gives me a rash on sight."

Caroline's laugh became a little louder.

Isabel laughed at her own expense. It had been so long since she'd genuinely smiled or laughed over the last few months. However, Caroline had always done that for her, could make her smile.

"Is the reason you are being tortured have to do with this?" Caroline tapped the posting pasted to the glass on the inside of the shop window.

Groaning, Isabel didn't even have to look at it to know it was the dreaded wedding announcement. In Grover, posted announcements and word of mouth were the only way people got news. It was nothing like The Pennsylvania Inquirer that her Aunt Josie received for her news. "Yes. And it was all anyone who came into the shop wanted to talk about. I see no need of a new dress for a wedding my father should be having, not me."

Insightful, and understanding how things worked in a time when women had extraordinarily little rights in their own life, Caroline nodded. "Have you decided that teaching is not for you?"

"Papa has." Isabel stepped closer to her friend and lowered her voice. "However, it is a dream I refuse to let go completely."

"No one should have to put aside all their dreams to satisfy their pa." There were shadows in Caroline's eyes.

Isabel didn't have to ask the other woman what dream she was missing out on. Her friend had always wanted to be a wife and mother. Unlike Isabel, Caroline was interested in farming or raising animals and seeing what she could produce in the land, as well as watching her little ones grow and understand the same blessings of nature. But Caroline's father kept her fastened to his side. It was just the two of them, and the man had lost everything coming to Grover, so he held to Caroline that much tighter.

She wondered why the man didn't see that he was suffocating his own daughter with his hold. Then she realized she had no place to think such things. Her family wasn't poor or destitute in any way, but her own father held the reins to her life in an iron grip too.

"Who is the man your pa has saddled you with? I didn't recognize his name."

Before Isabel could answer her, heavy, booted feet echoed onto the boards of the walk. Beyond Caroline's shoulder, she saw the big figure of her intended.

A gasp slipped from her mouth before she could catch it.

Hearing it, Caroline turned in the direction she gazed. "Oh, my. Is that him?"

Isabel's mouth had gone dry and she couldn't seem to find even enough moisture to swallow. She could only nod.

It didn't help that Cary angled his head to the side and locked his gaze right on her. She thought about stepping into the store, running from him. The man caused too many quakes to go off in her lower belly and muddled her brain. She'd never been a fawning, simpering female, but around the large man, she wasn't herself. The places he'd touched a few nights ago started to tingle again.

He moved down the boardwalk toward them, and the few people about appeared to part or step aside as he walked by. The man had a strut that was more animal then male.

When he arrived before them, his gaze broke away for a moment as he offered a polite greeting to Caroline, "Ma'am."

Her manners kicked in, and Isabel introduced the two. "Caroline Douglas, this is Mr. Cary Brown."

She knew she should have said my intended at the end, but those words would make her feel as if Cary already obtained her. Technically, he did, since he had her father's blessing and Isabel was sure that they had already signed papers placing her inheritance in his name, final on the day of their marriage.

"Miss Douglas." His gaze shifted back to Isabel again.

"Mr. Brown. Welcome to Grover Town." Caroline was looking from him to her. "I must get back to the farm. Pa will be wanting some eats after being in the field so early."

"Maybe we can get together soon." Isabel turned away from the imposing man and watched Caroline take the steps to the buckboard parked there.

"Maybe." The other woman didn't expound as she climbed up into the groaning, rickety seat of the vehicle, the end tatters of her hem revealed. The small wagon was more seat on four-spoked-wheels than anything that could be used to haul anything. The boards in the back were warped or broken and in great need of repair. It looked too dangerous to even carry her old friend away as Caroline settled the basket of eggs in the seat beside her. In seconds, she had the bleached and thin leather leads in her hand and had the single swoop-backed nag on the move.

"Your friend?"

She looked away from the leaving wagon and back at the man beside her. She noticed there seemed to be concern in his gaze. That touched her. A person didn't have to be a genius to see that Caroline was in bad straits. Most in town had become used to it and no longer expressed concern. Especially since it was how Caroline's father chose to live. The man was too stubborn to allow anyone in town to help.

The soaps Caroline made were most likely their only source of income, small as it may be.

"Yes. She was. Now, we are barely more than strangers."

"I am sorry. Maybe things will return one day."

"Maybe." Isabel offered the same lack of hope in the one word as Caroline had. "You're up and about early."

"I like to get things done." He held her gaze. There wasn't a smile on his face, but there was a light in his gray eyes as if he was pleased to see her. "Most ladies are not in town before the sun has made its crest."

"No. My mother and sister are a testament to ladies of leisure. However, they were up to ensure we could accompany Papa into town. Apparently, our wedding is cause for a new dress."

His gaze traveled along her body, perusing her attire, something she had refused to do to Caroline. Isabel felt uncomfortable as he took in the high neck of her dark green gown, with its three-quarter length sleeves and the many layers of her skirts. Unlike most women in Grover, she also wore a corset, not giving in to the new-fashioned apparel that Molly and her daughters had designed. A schoolmarm had to be respectable and above reproach, even if the heat was oppressive. Besides, her curves were so substantial, she needed something to reduce the size of her breasts and hips.

When his eyes lifted and met hers, they were darker. "You don't like new dresses, I take it?"

"No." Her words came out wispy, so she inhaled and started again. "I like to keep things simple and serviceable. As long as something is well tended, there is no need to continue to add to one's wardrobe."

"Maybe," he uttered in a low rumble; however, there was something in the one word when he said it.

Disapproval? Disappointment? She couldn't decipher.

"You came from Preston Tanners?" She needed to get the topic off her.

"I needed a better saddle. I was told Mrs. Taylor does good work."

"Eileen Taylor's skill is amazing. All Papa's saddles are made by her, or older ones from her father. She learned from her father. When he passed, she inherited the shop and runs it successfully." Isabel envied the woman, more than seven years older than she was, and Eileen's independence. Even having been married more than four years, she still lived her life in her own way. Her husband Roy, the bookkeeper, left her to run everything else.

"That is what I've heard. If your ma and sister are in the dress shop, why is it you are here?"

Isabel shrugged and looked toward Molly's. She doubted anyone had even noticed her walk out. "They have my measurements. I will not be needed again until the fitting, a week from now. I'd rather occupy myself than sit around the shop for hours, discussing patterns and material."

"Then you have some free time?"

"Sort of." She glanced back at him.

"Mr. Reynolds gave me keys to the house. I'm building a barn. I need some place to move the animals to, once we have married. Would you like to ride there with me?"

She should have said no. It was proper for her to say no. Especially with her sister in the shop with their mother. There would be no one to chaperone them. Even with their wedding a little more than a week away, it wasn't done.

"I can bring you back to meet them."

"Yes." Her response was impulsive, but she didn't let herself care.

The curl at one corner of his mouth let her know he was pleased by her response. "The wagon is at the sawmill, loaded."

"Okay. Just give me one moment."

When he nodded, she went inside of the mercantile.

"Morning, Isabel." Mrs. Russell glanced at her with a grin as she continued to dust the shelves that held ornate paraffin oil lamps.

Isabel returned the greeting of the older woman as she moved to the display at the end of the counter of soap cakes. "I needed to pick up a few new bathing soaps."

"Oh, there are some wonderful scents. I have an orange and thyme from Paris that came in last Monday that smells wonderful."

"Oh, that does sound wonderful." Even as Isabel said it, she was turning over the squares and rectangles, instead of the ones carved into fancy flowered shapes. She knew Caroline didn't have any equipment to make her soaps so fancy. Her friend's were more provincial and simpler in smells. She found eight of the classic rose scents, with CD carved below the single word *rose*.

Her mother and sister loved dabbing their bodies with some rose oil that was shipped in from Italy or Bulgaria that they found in one of the catalogues they maintained subscriptions with. Isabel didn't know nor did she care.

She set them down on the counter.

"Wow. I do believe that is all that Caroline brought in this morning." Mrs. Russell gave her a quizzical glance then looked toward the wide bay window where Cary stood with his back to the glass. "I guess a young woman set to marry wants to have a stock of smell goods."

Not realizing how it would appear with her intended at the store and her coming to buy bathing soaps. "I-I-I was running low. Nothing more."

"Mmhm." The older woman gathered the soaps together. "Anything else? I have some lamps, just arrived on the last train, that would brighten up a new home."

Isabel groaned. "No. This is all. Matter of fact, can you hold them for me?" Isabel pulled the correct coins from her reticule based on the price that had been above the display. "My mother and sister will come here looking for me. Can you give the items to them? Please, let them know I went to my property but will meet them back at the house shortly?"

"Is that Mr. Brown I see?" Mrs. Russell peered beyond her again. Isabel knew good and well that she'd probably already spied them together before the shop.

"Yes."

"A genuinely nice man. You're lucky to have scooped him up when he was fresh in town. More than one young lady has been eyeing him." The older woman was stacking and restacking the soaps idly as she spoke.

Isabel didn't have to stretch her imagination to conceive of the young and old women in town considering setting their cap for Cary. He was impressive in both size and mannerism. The stoic man of mystery drew people to him, trying to figure him out or catch his attention. Word would have gotten around that he was there looking for land to put down roots. That kind of stability would have most women blushing and sidling up to him.

She stepped away from the counter and rushed up the center aisle toward the door, feeling hot under the collar and tense at Mrs. Russell's words. "The property is close to town. So, I won't be long."

"Can't wait for your wedding day," Mrs. Russell's voice sang out behind her, blending with the ringing of the bell above the door

She blushed as Cary stepped to her, grateful that he had not been in the store to hear.

"You ready?" He angled his elbow out, offering her his arm.

"Yes. Let's go, please." Surprised by the gesture, it being so intimate and public, an announcement to all around that the two of them were together. With only a brief hesitation, she slipped her hand around his arm, settling her fingers in the bend as her thumb pressed into his thick bicep.

She could feel the strength of his muscles under her touch and swore she felt him flex before they set off toward the sawmill. Her heart started pounding and her cheeks and body felt warm, and the sun hadn't even begun to heat the day.

SEVEN

"I was surprised you didn't bring Silver along today." She sat beside him on the wide wagon seat. There was enough distance between them that another person would be able to fit comfortably.

He wasn't sure if she chose to sit closer to the edge because of propriety or because she didn't want to risk swaying or bumping against him as the wagon bounced on down the road. The road wasn't as rutty as some, newer than most. There were still patches of grass growing in the road, roots not yet ripped out by heavy travel.

She maintained her seat well; impressively, she rode with her back rod straight and her shoulders back. How she kept such a proper posture fascinated him.

"Silver's not built for pulling and hauling heavy loads, the reason I purchased this mule. They're bred for such. I'll keep Silver at the livery until the barn is complete." Cary glanced over at her, still stunned at his body's response every time he laid eyes on her.

When he'd gone to her family home for dinner a few days ago and she'd walked into the front room alongside her sister, the air had gone out of his lungs and every drop of blood and heat in his body had pooled in his core, in the hopes of filling his groin. It was only years of self-control that kept him from embarrassing himself before her and her family with a stiff cock in his trousers.

Her sister, the classic willowy beauty, may turn most men's heads; however, that had never been his inclination. He was a man of substantial height and width and looked for women who could take his weight and thrusting without him having to worry if she would break or was too fragile, especially if any children they produced followed his paternal side.

It was the women built with a full hour-glass frame, such as Isabel, he preferred. In the blue evening dress she had worn, her breasts appeared high and full. The dark fabric had obscured the shape of her breasts, but nothing could hide the swell of her hips. When he was close to her, the only thing he wanted to do was cup them in his hands and draw her forward, align her body with his.

Marriage had not been his idea, not for a long while, but since meeting Isabel, he looked forward to the moment she would be his wife, the moment he'd be able to claim her and feel her rocking and thrusting beneath him.

"How long do you think it will be before you complete the barn?"

Her voice pulled him away from thoughts of her body. However, it drew his gaze to her mouth. Her mouth, so full and red. On another, such lips may appear unbecoming, grotesque. However, accompanied by Isabel's round face and wide green eyes, her lips were a complement, salaciously becoming. The urge to kiss her mouth overwhelmed him. He wanted to show her the passion that could be found in a kiss, teach her the art of brushing her lips over his skin, and instruct her in taking parts of him deep in her mouth. The image of her vibrant colored lips circling his shaft, in harmony with the reddish brown of his skin, caused a groan to rise in his chest.

One of the wagon wheels hitting an unexpected rut jarred him back into the conversation at hand, squelching his wayward thoughts. He tightened his hands on the reins and refocused on the road, commanding himself not to look at her.

"It will be complete by next week now that I've gotten most of the lumber I needed. I hired a few hands lookin' for work to help get it done by the wedding."

"Oh." Her response was short, breathy.

He wondered if thoughts of their wedding, perhaps the wedding night, played in her mind too. He didn't ask.

They continued the last few miles in silence. When they came upon the first lush field with the long single level house painted yellow with dark green shutters and trim and a porch that went all around the perimeter of the house, sitting back from the road but clearly seen, he commented, "Mr. Reynolds said that house is your sister's?"

Isabel looked away from the view on her side of the road, toward him then beyond. "Oh, my. Sophia's home rivals our parents' one. She even put a swing on the front porch that she'd always talked about having."

He frowned at her words. It sounded as if Isabel had never seen her sister's house before. "I'm surprised she'd chosen to place the structure right in the middle of her property. If she ever farms the land, it will be a bit awkward to have the grownin' in front and behind the house."

Isabel shook her head. "Sophia has no plans to farm it. I'm sure she'll have a big garden in the front but not much else."

Seems a waste, he thought, but he kept his criticism to himself. He realized that not all people were like him, who hungered for the feel of the earth in his hand and the yearning to see something he planted grow. Mr. Reynolds had been correct when he'd told him he'd saved his best two properties for his girls.

"My sister has her bonnet set for the deputy," she paused as she looked away from the property, "she'll do whatever's needed to have her dreams of him and the house."

He picked up something in her voice, envy...regret...disappointment. He wasn't sure.

Arriving at two Bur Oaks that sat about forty-five feet apart from each other, he tugged on one side of the reins and steered the mule between them. The two trees sat like a gate to the land. As they drove through the thick, sweeping branches, his chest felt tight with emotions even as his shoulders eased from the tension that had rested there for most of his life.

"Oh. My sweet heaven."

The wonder in her voice caused him to pull the animal to a stop with the house to one side of the new path before them and the vast acreage on the other side. This section of land was larger than the first one they'd passed.

He glanced over at Isabel. Her face was filled with awe. Her lovely green eyes were stretched, rounder than they normally were, and her full lips were parted. She appeared shocked as she stared at the two-level house, then turned to look at the spacious empty field on the other side of the lane, then back again.

"Was the house not complete the last time you were out here?" Mr. Reynolds had told him he'd gotten everything installed inside before the first snow fell. The older man hadn't said when the actual house had been finished.

"I've never seen any of it." She closed her mouth then sent her delicious pink tongue between the seam.

He tracked the movement as her words settled into his mind. His brows drew tight as he looked up at her eyes, still focused on the house. "Never seen it? How's that possible? Your pa said he's had this land and the other across the road since you were seven or eight."

"Yes." She sat silent, and he thought she wasn't going to say more until she continued. "I never wanted to see it. I never believed I'd live on it."

He realized that he'd been wrong. If Isabel had been at the station expecting to run away with some man, they had not planned to settle back in Grover Town at any point.

"Never?" he confirmed.

"No." She shook her head and glanced down at her lap. Her hands were grasping the bottom planks of the box style seat of the wagon. Her shoulders were slouched some, even as her back was still straight, and she looked as if she was grieved, in mourning for something. Or someone.

"Why?" He felt as if it were time for him to know the truth of the woman who would soon become his wife.

She lifted her gaze to the house again. "I always saw myself in a schoolhouse, leading my own classroom of children. I never wanted anything else."

The passion in her voice echoed his when he thought about having his own land to farm. "The station. When I saw you, did your papa stop you from meetin' someone? Someone maybe that was goin' with you to find a place to teach?"

It was the question he didn't want to ask, but the thing that now he realized he needed to know. There was no way that he could plan to make a life with the woman beside him if he didn't know if there was another man in town she pined for, desired to be with. He knew that theirs was just a contract, an arrangement brokered by her father, and he truly didn't have any claim to what was in her mind or heart. Even if he lusted for her body greater than any other woman he'd ever seen or met.

"'There was no other, save my Aunt Josie."

"Is this aunt in Grover? Was she at the station?" He didn't recall seeing anyone else around her but her father and sister.

She folded her hands in her lap again. "No. My mother's sister lives in Philadelphia and was expecting me there."

"Is that all that is back east for you?"

"The Young Ladies Academy is there. They were holding a spot for my training to be a schoolmarm."

He now understood. "Is there a need for me, as your husband, to be concerned you'll hop the train at the first chance you get?"

She looked at him, holding his gaze for a moment, shadows in her gaze making her eyes as dark as the leaves on the trees behind them. "Having a husband eliminates me from the position. Schoolmarms are expected to be spinsters. Never married, no children."

In two strikes, he'd wiped out her option of fulfilling her dream. Not only in signing the contract with her father to marry her for the land, but by also cartin' in two children for her to help raise to boot. He had an urge to apologize to her, knowing how gutted he'd feel if he couldn't have his own farm. He didn't.

"Good to know. I'll not suffer a disobedient wife, and we won't have disobedient children." He offered her a firm nod, showing her he understood. Then he made a clicking sound and snapped the reins to get the mule moving along again.

"You can't be serious." She stared at the big man; he had to be jesting.

"If the occasion calls for it, Isabel Carrie, you'll find I'm very serious."

She wasn't even sure how she should respond to such a

threat. When she was younger, her papa always warned them off bad actions by showing them a switch. However, that was usually enough for them to keep on the straight path. It was more in the recent years she'd pushed her father, tested his patience. He had never struck her or Sophia; he would simply punish them in other ways. For a moment, she thought about what had happened with her last stunt, how he'd locked her in her room. She also thought about the times her mother had upset her papa with something she'd done, and he'd ordered her to the barn and sent Isabel and Sophia off to bed. The next day, her mother would be contrite, overly attentive to her father. *Had Papa taken a switch to Mama?*

"I doubt there'll be any of that."

Cary didn't comment.

As they pulled up before the house, he stopped. "I'll let you off here, while I take the load over to the barn. That way, you can take your time gettin' a look inside at the house."

"I'm glad they didn't go with yellow, like Sophia's house." She was staring up at the house with its sky blue coloring and white trim.

When he got around to her side of the wagon, she turned to him then reached to take hold of the hands he'd raised to lift her down. She used them to support herself as she got down on her own instead. He figured it was best, because the urge to put his hands on her was growing strong with every passing moment he was around her.

"Thank you."

He tipped his hat as he removed a key to the door Mr. Reynolds had given him then set it in her soft small palm. "Be back 'round soon."

She gave him a small smile before she walked away to the house. The shadows were still in her gaze. However, he was hoping that the smile was to tell him she was going to do her best in giving the marriage a go.

There wasn't a contingency in the contract if the marriage ended; it was 'til death they do part. He wasn't expectin' either of them to meet the good Lord no time soon. He watched her take the four steps up to the porch then enter the house before he pulled away. There was another oak between the house and the barn, and he planned to create a swing on one of the lower sturdy branches for the children. He didn't know much about raisin' little ones, but he figured with Isabel being so keen on being in a schoolhouse full of them, she had the experience to guide him along the way.

His parents would be here, wanting to be close to their grandchildren and any others who came along, but he'd work on building them a small house behind the main one once he got the first crop in the ground. He liked having his ma and pa around for support, but he'd create a home for his family as his parents had for him and his brother. He'd do the same for his brother's young ones. Maybe there'd be others.

He stopped before the barn, a little less than half complete. The men he hired would arrive right after daybreak to help him finish it. He'd need the barn done by the time his pa arrived with the corn seed. As he worked to get the load of lumber off the bed of the refurbished wagon, he told himself not to think about the woman in the house.

Isabel had a way of drawing his attention even when she wasn't around. Since meeting her, he'd lain awake long hours in the night in a bed at the boarding house, with multiple thoughts and images of her. He preferred not to remind himself how many times he'd taken himself in hand after sitting beside her at dinner with her family and feeling the softness of her face. He'd wondered about all the other soft places of her body. He went to sleep with her on his mind, only to wake in the morning with his cock hard from provocative erotic dreams of her.

Snatching off his hat, he lifted his forearm to use his sleeve to wipe his brow. He told himself he was sweating from the exertion of effort in pulling and hauling lumber to the stack by the barn, not because of any internal furnace stoked by the woman inside, the woman who would be his wife in a few days, the woman he'd be able to do more than caress along her chin. He groaned and grabbed at a slat roughly, thankful for the worn leather gloves covering his hands. Since his mind was elsewhere instead of on the job at hand, he was lucky not to shove a splinter the size of a spear in his hand from his negligence. He kept casting an eye toward the house, expecting to see her walking by one of the side windows. The front room was on the corner of the house closest to the barn, but with it being brighter outside than in, he couldn't see anything beyond the glass, but it didn't stop him from looking.

After the last piece of wood was unloaded and set aside, he strutted back over to the house, allowing the mule to graze on the sweet grass and dandelions. Too much of it wasn't good for the animal to consume all the time, but he'd fed well on feed before he'd loaded up the wagon, so Cary wasn't worried.

When he passed the water pump, he primed it then removed his gloves and shoved them deep in a back pocket and washed off his hand and splashed some on his face, enjoyed the cooling of his skin. He considered dunkin' himself down at the river about five hundred yards past the barn. Yes, Reynolds had been right; this was prime property that only deserved to be handed down through family.

He continued to the house. Each step of the way, he worked on convincing himself he was only going in to check and see if she was ready to go or maybe wanted to take a stroll through the field where he'd start tillage next week after the 'I dos'. He'd already placed markers down and would walk through the acreage again today and remove debris that would hinder his work or injure the oxen. Until he completed the barn and the small corral around it, he didn't want to bring the animals to the property.

He took the steps one at a time, giving himself a moment to inhale the fresh spring air and use it to fill his lungs and stabilize his need. Once he'd reached the door, he felt level-headed and focused. When he pushed open the door, all his focus sent his blood flowing toward his cock. He caught the profile of Isabel as she stood in the front room before the large window with the early afternoon sun surrounding her in a ray of sunlight.

Her eyes were closed as if she was absorbing the warmth into her being, or perhaps simply thinking. Her dark brown hair seemed to absorb the sunlight, drinking it in and making it dark as fresh brewed coffee. A few tendrils were hanging loose around the back of her neck and from the ride over. He barely stopped himself from stepping forward to blow gentle breaths over them and watching them dance along her skin. Pale, creamy alabaster skin was a testament as to how much time she spent within doors.

Her round nose and full lips were on display. His mind traced the outline of those plump lips. For once in his life, he longed to have the skills of an artist so he could sketch them over and over. He must have made a sound, possibly a groan, because she opened her eyes and turned toward him.

"Done with the lumber?" Her voice soft, husky, almost a whisper.

Or maybe he was imagining it, because his mind was thinking about all the things he'd have liked for her to croon in his ear as he thrust deep inside of her. He cleared his throat. "I have. You get your fill of the house?"

He closed the door then the space to her.

She smiled, and her cheeks showed a pink tinge. "I've not made it beyond this point yet. The sun...it's nice right here."

For a moment, he wondered about the reason she hadn't made at least two walk throughs of the house in the time he'd been out at the barn. For a moment, he considered the spot she'd been standing when he entered. Yes, the seat in front of the large bay window was long enough for at least three people or four children to sit side by side, and there was a view of the front of the house and the field. True, that just like now, the sun shone in just right. However, he shifted his gaze to the smaller window on the other wall, the way her body had been positioned, and he could see the unfinished barn, the wagon before it and the pile of lumber—where he'd been working.

Had she been watchin' me?

Instead of asking her, he returned the conversation to the house. "Was it your mother and sister who picked out all the furnishings?"

"Yes. They love shopping and decorating spaces. It seems they truly have a knack for making things and people look lovely." There was something in her voice, but she moved past him and continued to comment on the wall hangings and curtains. She headed into the direction he knew the kitchen was located.

He followed. In the kitchen, there was a high table in the center to be used to prepare food, a deep copper sink before a window, and shelves on both sides of it, already laden with various dishes. The counter was littered with large, open mason jars filled with utensils for cooking and eating.

He watched Isabel open the pantry door and look inside.

"There wasn't much here. I'll have to pick up supplies from the mercantile before the wedding if we plan to eat." It was the first time she'd voluntarily spoken about them marrying.

He held a position at the wall, balancing his body on his shoulder as he observed her picking up things and opening cupboards and drawers. "Can you cook? If not, we can live off dried meat for a while. I'm fairly good at that."

While he'd been over at the Spencer Ranch, he'd ordered a side of beef from his next slaughter for just that purpose. With farm work and being out in the field, it was good to have pieces in the saddle bag to keep workin' and not have to stop.

At the four-eyed large stove with its wide round pipe crawling up to the ceiling, she turned and faced him. She laughed. "I think I have skills enough to provide more at the table then hardtack and dried meat."

He gave her a lopsided smile. "Good to know."

"I learned from Mrs. Turner, our family cook. A school-marm has to be able to feed herself."

Schoolmarm. He was raised to believe in education by both his parents, seeing it as important in the burgeoning country, but the thought of the beautiful woman before him spending her nights in some one room place alone didn't settle well with him. A pretty woman, with such a lush form, deserved to be loved well by a man and have her supper table filled with a passel of children who looked just like her.

"There's supposed to be four rooms in the house if I recall my mother and sister discussing color pattern choices." She went past him, her hip brushing along his as he stood still with his shifted to the side from where he had been leaning against the entranceway. Electricity shot through him from the contact.

She gasped and stumbled.

Shifting quickly, he reached for her as her body pitched forward. Catching her by the waist, he held her, feeling the frame of a corset under his grip. He now knew how it was she'd ridden beside him so ramrod straight in the wagon. Evidently, she didn't hold to the custom of most women in Grover who had forgone the tradition of corset wearing as most Mid-west towns. It was constricting and oppressive to work in the heat. The men who flowed through Manning's, the better of two local saloons, had a lot of dirty talk about the feel of a woman's body beneath her clothes instead of steel boning.

"Whoa there."

"Oh." Her hands held him on one arm at his wrist and forearm. As he righted her body and pulled her closer to him, she glanced up at him. Her gaze was a vivid green that flashed with awareness of their moment alone, their attraction—him.

Drowning in her gaze, he was unable to resist pulling her closer. Her dragged her frame against his then held her closer as his fingers flexed in the constraints surrounding her from breasts to hips. He yearned to know what her supple skin felt like under his and against his chest.

He shifted his gaze from her eyes to her mouth, her full, plump, red mouth. He'd once had one of those exotic Mediter-ranean pomegranates; the seeds inside were sweet, tart and so deep red, he couldn't stop from sampling them. When he'd finished, the rare fruit had stained his fingers and mouth. He wondered what kind of stain on his person she'd leave after he kissed her. Because he *was* going to kiss her.

Hauling her closer and lifting her just enough to meet his mouth as he lowered his lips to hers, he warned, "Stop me if you don't want this."

He wasn't sure if this was the kiss, the marriage, or some-thing more...all he knew was that he had to have a taste of her now.

Her fingers moved, to holding his biceps, and clenched

deep into his muscles, but she didn't voice any objections. With a groan, he seized her mouth. Feeling those pillow soft lips under his with their tentative movements but pressing firm along his, confirmed she wanted him too.

As he nipped at her bottom lip, he heard her intake of breath then the whimper she let out. He then drew the beguiling flesh into his mouth and suckled it. She was more than a delectable morsel, but so much more. He sealed his lips on to hers and drove his tongue deep. He should have been kind, kissing her softly, letting her ease into it and ensuring he didn't frighten her away. He should have allowed their first kiss to be nice and gentle. However, he wasn't nice and gentle, and he wanted her too much. He'd known her less than a week, but his lust for the bookish beauty was overwhelming.

His desire for her had his body beckoning hers, wanting to take more than a few stolen kisses. His cock was hard as he tasted the sweetness of her mouth. She was warm and soft inside as he brushed along her tongue then curled his over the sensitive roof of her mouth.

She moaned and clutched him tighter as her hand crawled up to his shoulders.

Feeling how the fury of her passion matched his, made him want to walk them toward the nearest wall and lift her skirts. He wanted to discover everything about her that was hidden behind all the layers. The thought of plucking apart each of the tiny buttons that coursed down the front of her blouse from her neck to her waist and revealing the bounty of her breasts made his heart pound harder.

Learning quickly, she kissed him back. Tentative touches of her tongue flew across his then became bolder as she slipped into his mouth.

Fuck. His mind was exploding with one dirty, raunchy thought after another. Things he should not be considering now, while she was not yet his bride. Hell, his body was more than willing to consummate the marriage before the vows.

A part of him wondered if it had just been too long since he'd last bedded a woman, or if it was all Isabel that exploded inside of him and caused the avalanche of lust that tumbled down his body. Continuing the passionate onslaught of her mouth, he lowered his hands from her waist to her ass and palmed the two round halves. Practically bursting through the front of his breeches, his cock was hard and throbbing as he felt the abundance of her curves.

She flexed beneath his grasp and the movements in him caused a frisson of heat to zip down along his spine. His pulse kicked up and his heart swelled as it beat harder in his chest.

"A-yv a-dan-v-do." The words of his mother's people sailed along the breath he exhaled as he pulled his mouth from hers. He didn't stop to analyze the endearment but trailed kisses along her jaw. Her scent was the same soft, sweet, and delicate of a rose. He wanted to discover all the places she smelled of roses and all the places her musk was rich, spicy, and sweet to the taste.

"What? Cary..." She was moaning and squirming against him as she tilted her head to the side and provided him with more access to the skin above her collar.

He pressed his lips to her ear and growled, "Say it again."

"Wh-at...say what?" She was panting, just as caught in the storm as he was. Her hands had become buried in his hair at some point and she was raking her short nails along his scalp.

If she didn't stop her grinding and needy caresses, he'd find it impossible not to bury himself balls deep inside of her. The wedding be damned.

Already, his hands were fisting the fabric of her skirts and it was taking all his willpower not to hike up the layers and get a feel of her bare, warm, supple flesh in his hands.

"I need..." She tipped her mouth toward him again.

He fused his mouth to hers again, taking command of her mouth, and allowing her to feel his passion for her unleashed. Ripping his lips from hers again, he inquired, "Tell me what you need, Isabel?"

Lord forgive them both if she uttered the words that drove them straight into lust's arms.

Slowly, she opened her eyes and he saw the depth of desire radiating out from her now emerald orbs. How such pale green eyes had become so darkened, he could not determine, but he was awash with satisfaction to see such raw cravings that matched his own.

"I need—"

The sound of wagon wheels coming along the path before the house was like a snowstorm drift collapsing the roof of their passion paradise.

"Isabel! Isabel!" Sophia her sister called from outside.

Shock removed the yearning that just a breath before had her quaking against him. She shoved out of his arms before he could release her. She stumbled again but caught herself before he could get hold of her.

Isabel's gaze was pale and shadowed with trepidation as she glanced around the room at anything but him. She smoothed a hand along her bonnet, shirt, skirt and then pressed her palms on her cheeks as if her touch could remove the flush that resided there. It didn't. Her lips were more swollen and redder than normal and her eyes and mouth both held telltale signs of being kissed thoroughly.

"Isabel," he uttered her name as he took two steps toward her.

"No." She moved farther away. "I should not have come here with you. It's not proper."

With a frown, he watched her try to compose herself.

However, when she reached for the door handle, he spotted the trembling in her hands. He wanted to believe it was still some evidence of the passion they had shared.

Frowning, he watched her hustle outside. He stood there taking one breath, then another, as he stooped over and swiped his hat from the floor. He hadn't removed it when he came in, forgetting himself as he'd been captured by her beauty. Continuing with slow strides to the door, he was happy to feel that his cock had receded to something more respectable by the time he stepped onto the porch.

"If you wanted to come see the house, why didn't you wait for me and Mama, Isabel?"

Isabel was already on the second step, anxiously putting distance between them. She shrugged a shoulder. "It was spur of the moment. You and Mama were busy in the shop, and I knew we would only be out here a moment."

"Still," Sophia pouted.

"Hello, Mr. Brown. I see the barn is coming along." Mrs. Reynolds glanced from her daughter to him, her gaze more perceptive than her youngest daughter's. It was filled with knowledge of what they had possibly been up to in the house alone. There was a sly smile on her lips.

If he and Isabel didn't already have a wedding date set in just a matter of days, he was sure that the smiling mama would have had him and her daughter before the Methodist preacher in a blink, with someone dispatched to Mr. Reynolds as well. However, as it was, it was improper for them to be here, still unmarried, without a chaperone, but since they could clearly see no harm had come to Isabel, there wasn't any need of a change of their plans.

"Yes, it is. When it's done, there'll be enough room for about four horses and a back section for the oxen if the weather is bad, with a loft above that." His modest structure was nothing compared to the large barn at the Reynolds' place, but it would do nicely for what they needed it for.

"It's good to know. I'm looking forward to seeing it finished at the family meal following the nuptials."

He offered a nod.

"Don't you just love the house, Isabel?" Sophia sat on the wagon and beamed at her own handiwork, Cary was sure.

"Yes..." Isabel glanced over her shoulders at the house, her gaze meeting his for a moment before she turned back to her sister. "You and Mama have done a wonderful job setting it up. I'd have been lost if I had to do it in less than two weeks."

"It's a good thing we didn't wait for you."

Isabel didn't respond; she simply looked beyond her sister and mother to the field across from them.

Cary thought Sophia was an energetic young lady and nice for the most part, however, he didn't care for the absent-minded way she put down Isabel's lack of interest in the house or shopping. The young woman was too immature to really understand that just because someone had different interests then hers, it didn't mean they were lacking.

Isabel wasn't lacking in a single area he could see. He didn't evaluate his protective thoughts toward the woman who would become his wife.

Sophia continued, "It's good we came out here today." The blonde looked from left to right around the front of the house. "Mama and I have started on the menu and where to arrange everyone. Maybe we should go to the furniture shop and speak with Mr. Cleary about making a few long tables for the guests to sit out here on the lawn. You all can keep the tables in the new barn for other events you may have."

"I don't want long tables. I'd prefer one table with a light, traditional fare of tea sandwiches like tomato or chopped ham, pickles, deviled eggs, and nuts, also Mama's pear cider, nothing fancy. I'd like Mrs. Turner to make the wedding cake."

He could tell that Isabel's family was not used to her speaking up on such matters, because both the ladies, young and old, sat with their mouths gaping.

Isabel descended the last two stairs then turned to look at him. "Thank you, Mr. Brown, for bringing me to see the house."

He offered her a wink. It was both a praise for her deciding not to allow her mother and sister to run like unleashed bulls over her and to simply tease to remind her of what they had just shared.

When her cheeks pinkened, he knew she'd understood his indication.

"My pleasure, Miss Reynolds." He followed her down the stairs. By the time she reached the other side of the wagon, his long strides had him there beside her. Taking her by the waist, he lifted her with ease, enjoying the full weight of her curves in his hands again.

When she was settled on the seat, he tipped his hat to her then the other two ladies. "Y'all need me to follow you home, make sure you get there safe?"

"That won't be necessary, Mr. Brown. I'm sure there are things here you'd like to take care of." Isabel distracted herself by taking the leads from her mother's hands.

She was erecting a wall between them. He didn't like it.

"That is kind of you, Mr. Brown. We'll be able to navigate the roads fine," Mrs. Reynolds added with a kind smile.

"Then I'll bid you ladies good day." He glanced from the mother to his intended one last time, but Isabel kept her eyes trained on the two horses before the wagon. So, he stepped back so that Isabel could bring the team around.

Once the wagon had passed through the trees and the

women were out of sight, he went over to where his was still parked by the barn. There he got his rifle, just in case he came upon any snakes that were ornery about him trapsin' over their home while he was in the field clearing out debris. As he started making his way through the marked land, he hoped that the hot sun would bake out the fiery thoughts and memory of what it had been like to kiss and hold Isabel. Just maybe he could exhaust himself to the point of delirium and sleep without images of her disturbing his rest.

Doubtful.

Already, as he looked at the verdant prairie grass, he thought of the rich hue of her eyes as they filled with passion.

Yup, he'd have to be out here for the next week before he'd be tuckered out enough not to think of the soon to be Mrs. Cary Brown.

"IS the sight of a locomotive old for you, having worked around them so much?" Isabel was beside him. Over the last week, he'd spent more than a few suppers at the Reynolds' home. Each time he came, he arrived early just to take a stroll with Isabel on the property. He ensured they never strayed too far and kept in view of the house.

Not because he thought anyone would say something to them if they wandered too far, more like he didn't trust himself alone with her. Rachel had accompanied her today, to meet him in town.

Cary stood on the platform again. This time, he wasn't just sitting and thinking as he watched the train. No, he was watching for it to pull into the station and bring his family to Grover Town. He and Isabel were once again at the depot, but this time he had guided her to the opposite end of the platform from where they had first encountered each other.

"Never." He looked over at her, her bonnet offering shadow to her features, but he could still see her clearly as she stared down the railway like all others. Yes, he was still impressed by trains, but not more than the vision of her beauty. However, he wasn't a poetic man, he didn't spout such pretty words. Most likely, because in the past, his relationships with women were transaction based or need based. They weren't anyone permanent or bonded to him. Even though he knew things were different when it came to Isabel, he still could not find the words.

His mind taunted him about the words he had whispered to her yesterday. They had both shocked and soothed his soul. He was going to consider it a momentary slip in the heat of passion.

"I've worked the railways for years," he continued. "Mostly, I was in front of the train, unless the crew was assigned to repair broken tracks, but that was even rare. Others usually did that. I like to watch them. It helps me clear my head."

"Journaling is that way for me." She met his gaze and offered a piece of herself as he had done. "Maybe because I was always learning something or figuring out how to teach something and had a pencil and paper in hand. So, when something was on my mind, I wrote it down. I keep writing until I'm exhausted of it or I have solved the issue. Mama and Sophia are more creative. Not me, I've always been different."

She glanced away, not before he saw those clouds moving though her eyes again. Tomorrow would be their wedding. Silent, he made it his mission to remove every disconcerting thought she had of herself. His wife wasn't going to compare herself to any woman and see herself lacking.

"The good Lord even made blades of grass unique and different, why not us?"

Isabel eyed him again with a slight tip up to the corners of her mouth, but before she could comment, the train whistle pierced the air, heralding its arrival. Bellows of smoke from the tons of burning coal plumed high into the air, the first sight before the front of the engine of the Missouri-Kansas-Texas Railway coming up from the south.

Once the train came around the bend, people around him were oohing and ahhing, and some children made loud gasps. Train travel was a fascination for most, finding it hard to conceive of anything moving so fast. Particularly, when the fastest thing seen by most was a wild mustang. Few could catch or handle something that untamed, so harnessing the power of a locomotive was a hard concept to fathom.

When it finally stopped, smoke from the stack surrounded them on the platform and made it hard to see for a moment until it cleared. Then people began to exit the train at the commands of the conductor.

"Shouldn't we head back down the other way?" Isabel inquired as she looked down toward the first and second car, where men, women, and children, some dressed in fine clothing and others from the second car wearing more serviceable or worn attire, but all pale of skin, exited.

"No. My family will not be there. It'll also be easier for Pa and me to haul the seed to the wagon once it is unloaded."

He could see the bunching of Isabel's brows in the center of her otherwise smooth forehead as she tried to process his words. He didn't explain. Instead, he turned again to the door of the back car, the last passenger car. It was connected to the livestock and storage cars. He watched a man of color step off then aid his pregnant wife a few shades lighter than his soil rich complexion. After that, he reached toward the steps and lifted a small boy into his arms. When they passed them, the brown man nodded at Cary. Cary returned it.

He noticed Isabel was smiling at the small child who stared at her with wide eyes as he clung to his father's neck. They were given a boisterous greeting by another man of color who stood several feet behind Cary, Isabel, and Rachel. Cary had met the man a couple nights ago at the town's landowner meeting. Reggie Green owned a small soybean farm with his wife and kids. There weren't many people like him in Grover Town, but it was seeing those like Reggie and the new family smiling and accepted to set up life in Grover Town that made Cary's decision to not only settle here himself, but to raise his brother's children in such a blended place.

At the same meeting, he'd spoken with Mr. Pettigrew, the gristmill owner, to negotiate an agreement and price to have the harvested corn sifted and milled. The man had only managed wheat, the main product of Kansas, however, he'd been already looking into new advancements and was eager to branch out. Since most of the cornmeal was shipped up from Topeka, the venture would be profitable for both Cary and Mr. Pettigrew.

"Ah, there's my boy!" It was the deep, rustic, twang of his father's Okie-Texas voice that drew Cary's attention back to the passengers.

In a single breath, Cary was smiling, his boots thumping on the wood beneath his feet as he crossed to his father. "Pa!"

His father dropped the big satchel he lugged on the platform and stretched his arms out.

It had been almost two months since he'd seen them last, dropping off their grandchildren, then heading northwest to find land to farm. However, it didn't matter; he loved his parents. They had given all their strength and love in raising him and his brother. His father was a foot shorter than Cary, but still barreled-chested, with wide shoulders and strong arms, even if they did feel thinner than they had when Cary was younger.

"I never doubted you, my boy." His father gave him a hearty pat on the back.

"Thanks, Pa. I hope your trip was good. No mishaps." Train robberies were happening all too commonly, and more railway lines were hiring a U.S. Marshall to ride them, an attempt to squelch the thievery, especially around the trains pulling the United Postal cars.

"Are my two men going to help an old lady down from these high steps or keep cuddling?" His mother's raspy silk voice was still textured in the ways of her people, even after thirty years of being married to his pa and being around mostly those who didn't look like her.

"I got her." Cary stopped his father with a hand on his shoulder as he rushed forward to his mother. Scooping her at the waist and lifting her from the steps, he hugged her tight. "*U-ni-tsi.*"

"Ah *Uwohali*. I am too old to be so high off the ground." She kissed his cheek then swatted his back. When he set her down, she stared up at him from her short stature, her dark brown eyes gazing up at him as she grinned. "You are like your pa; he is always lifting me, making me dizzy."

"I like taking you to the clouds." His father winked at her.

His mother, even after so many years of marriage, still blushed at her husband's words. Cary couldn't help but wonder if one day, he and Isabel would ever have something close and intimate between them. He knew the difference was his parents had met and fallen in love; it had not been an arrangement such as he had with Isabel.

He and his father went to the train and helped the children off.

Others on the platform began showing their tickets and boarding the train before it left the station.

"Did you enjoy your train ride, Atohi?" Cary brushed his nephew's long dark bangs back from his face. Unlike the adults on the reservation, children's hair was cut shorter, more in style with white people who ran the schools and taught the Christian religion.

The boy stared up at him. There was a small smile on his lips, but his eyes still assessed him warily. The boy, at four, was old enough to understand that his parents were dead and would not return, and it made him and his sister shy, unsure. Cary had only met the boy once when he was only eight full moons. He'd spent most of the winter months with them at his parents' home, getting to know them before he set out to find a place for all of them.

He stooped down before the boy, who favored him and his brother only by the square of his jaw and the width of his shoulders. The boy would most likely grow tall and big, as they had. "I told you when I left, I would find us a home and land to farm."

"And that you wouldn't die," the small voice reminded him.

With a hand on the boy's shoulders, he held his gaze. "I have kept all promises."

Ama moved from her grandfather and came to him and stroked a hand down his hair twice then placed her tiny hand on his cheek.

Cary glanced over at her and knew that his hair, unlike his father's that was short, brown with sun bleached and gray streaks, reminded his niece of his brother, her father. It also helped the little girl that he was the exact image of the papa she had lost. It had taken her a few weeks to stop calling him Papa.

"E-du-tsi."

"Yes. Uncle." He took her hand and kissed her palm. He still wasn't sure if she understood that he wasn't her father, just with a different name.

"She is very lovely, *Uwohali?"*

Cary didn't have to turn around to know that his mother spoke about Isabel. His bride-to-be had remained back and silent, allowing him the reunion with his family. When he'd wired his parents about Grover Town and the land, he had also explained that he would be marrying upon their arrival. He urged them to take the next train to Kansas.

Still holding his niece's hand, he rose and faced the adults gathered. He moved to Isabel's side, to ensure his mother knew Isabel, not Rachel, would be his wife.

"Isabel, this is *U-ni-tsi*, Ma." He translated the term for Isabel. "Sunny is her name, and my father, Colby Brown."

"It is nice meeting you all." Isabel offered his mother a smile that could only be called awkward. The woman wasn't normally shy, but he wondered if the wedding looming tomorrow and who his parents would be to her had anything to do with it. Marriage and family had not been in Isabel's life plans.

His mother stepped closer to Isabel and held out her hands.

He was happy to see that Isabel did not hesitate in accepting his mother's offered hands. Isabel, taller than his mother's five and fifty inches of height, by at least a foot, slipped her hands into his mother's.

Sunny Brown held Isabel's gaze for a moment, silent, almost appearing unaware of the hustle and bustle going on at the station.

As they all stood there, respecting the inaugurated moment of his mother, Cary felt a soft breeze blow by, ruffling the ends of his mother's hair and the tempting tendrils at the base of Isabel's neck that refused to be restrained with the rest of her auburn locks.

With the wind settled, his mother's eyes lit with a brightness that seemed to come from within her. "You are the one. The bride for our Cary."

"Thank y-you." Isabel stammered, her eyes a misty green as his mother pulled her into a hug.

His mother was small in stature; however, her embraces were fierce. "Come and meet the family." His mother took his niece's hand from his and waved his nephew to them.

"Come, Pa. Let's get the trunks and seed loaded." Cary guided his father away from the women and children toward the area where the station workers were directing people to their items piled along the track.

It didn't take the two of them long to get the sacks of dried maize seeds and trunks loaded. Cary felt good that with the arrival of the seeds and his father; he was one step closer to not only planting his field, but a harvest by fall. Another reason that his marriage to Isabel would happen sooner, rather than later.

The ladies met them at his wagon, full and laden with the items.

"Mr. Brown, I know you probably want to get those items out to the farm and show your pa around the property." He watched the sway of Isabel's full hips as she approached him where he stood beside the wagon.

"I would. However, I can't take everyone until I get this stuff handled. I'm sure Ma and the children are hungry," he explained.

She glanced back over her shoulder at his ma and pa where they stood talking to the little ones and pointing things out around them. "Rachel and I can take your ma and the children to the Drummonds' restaurant. We can get to know each other while we wait on you and your pa to return."

He felt relieved to hear Isabel say she wanted to spend more time with his mother. His mother had always been the most important woman in his life. No other had come close to stealing even a corner of his heart. Then came Isabel. "I'd like that. I've got some jerky and hardtack to tide Pa over until I can get him a full meal."

"If they would like rest before you make it back?"

"I've got them rooms along with mine at the boarding house."

"I thought you were out at the house?" she asked, incredulity filling her voice. "Papa gave you the keys, and all the paperwork has been signed between the two of you for weeks."

He noticed she didn't say our house. It was hard for him to put a label to the place as well. "I completed the barn and marked the fields, but until we're married, it just didn't seem right. Not really mine to do more than that with yet."

"Oh." Her head was tilted just the slightest bit; the angle allowed the sunlight to rest in her eyes where they looked more of a golden green.

His gaze traveled to her mouth, but he quickly dragged his eyes away. Surrounded by so many people, he didn't want to get caught being calf-eyed. Being around Isabel drew him in and he always had to watch his response to her.

Tomorrow, she'll be my wife.

However, he couldn't let his mind play in those thoughts too long before his body was taking over.

With a brisk nod, he thanked her. Heading over to his parents, he explained the plan. In minutes, he was watching his mother and the children moving down the boardwalk toward the center of town. After he saw they were safely on their way, he and his pa climbed up on his wagon and started out.

"Thanks for not only bringing Garmin's kids, Pa, but for decidin' to make a home for you and Ma here, too."

The mule carried the two Brown men out of town in the opposite direction of the ladies.

"It was no bother. We want to be around you, the grands..." His sigh was full of unsaid words and thoughts. "There wasn't anythin' left for us in Wichita."

Cary knew what his father meant. *Now that Garmin was gone.* His brother's decision to move to the reservation with the woman he loved instead of making a home somewhere else was the only reason his parents never left his father's brother's land.

"I miss him, too." It was all Cary said about it, as they continued making their way and began to speak of other things.

EIGHT

"I now pronounce you husband and wife," Pastor Morgan declared before the packed Methodist church. "You may kiss your bride."

Isabel stood at the altar in a Queen Josie white-style wedding dress re-creation with so many ruffles, pleats, and ribbons, she could only groan internally at her mistake of telling her sister that she didn't care what it looked like. Instead of a high collar as she normally wore, keeping her style more spinsterish, her sister had the dress created with a wide-scooped neckline that rode along the curve of her shoulders. The sleeves of the dress were puffy bunched fabric, with lace trim hanging around her elbows. Instead of a wreath of flowers in her hair, Sophia had found her a small white bonnet with white daisies, braided green stems, and a veil attached to it. Leave it to Sophia to turn a request for a simple affair into some monstrosity.

She felt both bare and flabbergasted at the ensemble. Isabel had wanted to cry when she went for the fitting after she'd taken Cary's mother and the children to the boarding house to rest. It had been too late for any changes to be made, and once again she only had herself to blame for putting the final fitting off. It wasn't that she didn't want to marry Cary, she'd resigned herself to the situation, she just didn't care for a lot of fuss surrounding her. It amazed her how Cary didn't laugh the moment she entered the church.

However, he hadn't then, and he wasn't now. There was nothing but intense warmth in his gaze as he stared down at her as if he only saw her, nothing else or anyone else for that matter. Before Cary, she'd never had anyone look at her with such blatant desire. Those were the words to describe it. It wasn't the polite kindness that most men in town offered her, or the love from her father, or the fondness of the Grover Town pastor. The heat in his steel gray eyes made her feel bared, and she was always in a flushed state.

Now, he stood dressed in a black suit, crisp white shirt, and his hair was held back by a thin leather strap. She wished he had left it down; she liked his hair, the straightness of it and how it fell around his shoulders. It always tempted her to run her fingers through it. She recalled the dampness of it when it brushed against her hands last week.

Last week. The kiss. Since that moment in the house, her mind had no hope of focusing on anything else. Her body had ached for something; she wasn't altogether sure what. She knew that there were things that happened between a man and a woman but not fully all the mechanics of it. After the kiss, she had a clear understanding of the abandoned passion of the woman and man beside the building that one night.

Whether Cary was around her or not, all she could think about was the feel of his lips on her, the way he held her so tight against him that she could feel the pounding of his heartbeat vibrating along her corset. Her corset was the only thing of the dress that was hers. As uncomfortable as it may be, it was part of the respectability of a schoolmarm and she didn't know how to let it go, as she had to do to her dream.

Pastor Morgan cleared his throat, and there were chuckles and twitters that rang out.

"You're supposed to kiss her," Pastor Morgan whispered, offering a small, knowing grin.

Blinking, as if out of a trance, Cary leaned down and brushed her lips lightly with his. She felt a little disappointed with the chasteness of it all. It would have been foolish of her to wish for the same kind of all-consuming kisses from before, but this kiss was so quick, she had barely felt the warmth of his flesh on hers.

He looked away from her as he took hold of her hand and slipped it into the bend of his as Pastor Morgan presented them to the townsfolk gathered. Isabel saw her mother and sister wiping eyes with small linen and lace handkerchiefs. Even Mrs. Brown, who had both an exquisite and ethereal personality, had water streaming down the smooth red-brown skin of her face. Sunny showered gentle affection to not only her son and grandchildren, but on Isabel as well. Even Rachel could not stop talking about the older Native woman as they rode home.

As she and Cary went down the aisle, Isabel saw the swollen chest and proud look of her father. He was pleased at his selection of Cary whom he treated like a son already. Over the last two weeks, he had often started most of his sentences with Cary did this or Cary did that...or that's one smart and dedicated young man. Isabel realized that if her father had a son, then he would have never stood in her way of going to school.

Then you would have never met Cary.

She allowed her new husband to escort her out the doors of the church. They stood on the side of the stairs together as neighbors flowed out, congratulating them with hugs, hand-shakes, and a few kisses by the older generation along their cheeks. People deposited baskets, preserves, canned items, and other gifts into Cary's wagon, decorated with flowers and ribbons. Something else to thank Sophia for doing.

She was sad not to see Caroline, her friend, but most likely Mr. Douglas would not have allowed her to attend, too busy helping him with the farm.

"Isabel, you must come over one afternoon for tea." It was Elizabeth Clarkston, who still managed to look stylish and beautiful even with her protruding belly. The doctor's wife had only been in town for six months but had recently opened an etiquette school for young girls. The woman was educated, married, and independent. Isabel wondered if the woman had any tips for her.

Isabel wasn't sure if she was cracked up to be a good wife or mother. With the options of her teaching gone, she felt at loose ends. "I'd like that."

"Once you all get settled and the farm is going, you should bring the wife and family over. I've always got plenty chickens to roast," Doc Clarkston said to Cary before he escorted his wife down the stairs after Cary agreed.

As she stood alongside Cary, who kept her hand held in his as they spoke to people and received several invitations to suppers or events coming up, Isabel felt the hairs on the back of her neck rise. At first, she chalked up the reaction to the man beside her and how he always caused her body to go haywire, but it wasn't him. Then she just figured it was that so many folks were around, and she wasn't used to being the center of attention. However, the feeling wouldn't go away, and it wasn't until she and Cary turned to head back into the church, she noticed a man standing off in the distance alone. He was leaning against one of the trees dotting the side of the church. The sun was shining bright that day, but the man stood on the shaded side, making it hard to get a good look at his face. He was close enough to tell he was a burly man, dressed in chaps and a vest over his shirt and trousers, giving a clue that most likely he was a wrangler. He had his hat pulled so low that despite whether he was in the sunlight or not, she couldn't make out a single detail of his face. One thing she could tell from the shiver that ran up her spine, he was staring right at them. It rankled not being able to see his expression and tell if he was happy for them or not, so she marked it as simply a casual observer. Some people were like that.

When she stumbled on the hem of her bulky dress on the last step, Cary pulled her to him. "You all right?"

She leaned into her new husband's side, and staring up into his eyes gave her a sense of calm and safety. "Yes."

When he glanced in the direction of the stranger, she glanced back too. The man was gone.

"Did you know him?" Cary questioned, his voice cool and emotionless as he continued to hold her against him as they made their way to the back of the church to the pastor's office.

"No." She didn't have to ask him who.

"Ah, Mr. and Mrs. Brown." The conversation ended as they were greeted by Pastor Morgan, who stood before his office.

An hour later, she and Cary had their signed marriage certificate that they would present to the town clerk's office. The circuit judge reviewed all the town's legal documents and transactions when he came through town monthly from Topeka. After leaving the preacher's office, they followed her sister and mother's instructions to take the long route to their new home through town, so that those who could not attend the wedding could cheer and wave, offering congratulations.

As they passed people and places, Isabel took the time to

tell Cary about them, who they worked for, what they may have owned, how they owned, and if they were new in town or their family had been there since the founders put down the first stake in 1804.

"I'm impressed. You're so knowledgeable about Grover Town and those livin' here."

She flushed, a little embarrassed. She glanced away, not sure if her new husband saw her as a busybody. "I've always been a little on the outskirts of the social scene. Not talking, dancing, or playing games at gatherings kind of gives me a lot of time to watch people and hear things."

He held the reins in one hand and took hold of hers, pulling it onto his thigh. The gesture wasn't necessary since she was already touching him. She sat closer to him on the box seat than she had in the past. Now that they were married, it would seem odd there was a large gap between them. Every time the wagon jolted and rocked, she swayed against him. Her nerves were like short bolts of lightning in her body, firing off with every connection, causing her to feel winded and lightheaded.

"It wasn't a put down. You're observant. That's a good thing. In life, there are no guarantees, death can come for any of us..."

When he paused, she wondered if he was thinking of his brother and sister-in-law. The parents of the two children who were now Cary and her children. They both had a ready-made family.

"They need someone to tell their story. Know their history. Someone smart like you." He looked down at her for a long moment then winked.

She blushed, no longer from embarrassment but from the heat in her husband's gaze. Her mind went back to that kiss, not the chaste one in the church before staring eyes, but the one they'd had in private, in what was now their home. She'd never felt anything like it or imagined there could be such a blaze of fire in the blood from connecting her mouth to another. She thought about Sophia now. all the times she'd chaperoned her sister and Robert and how verklempt she would be after a few stolen kisses.

That night after she'd been kissed by Cary and her body had begun to have urges and aches like never before, she'd even secretly touched herself over her breasts and between her thighs to see if she could quell the need, but she had shied away when the feelings grew even more. They scared her. Cary scared her, from the emotions he stirred within her. She could understand why her sister, who'd had more than a few tastes of passion with the deputy, was raring to marry him as soon as possible. It was as if her sister knew there would be more...more kisses, more intensity, more passion.

Isabel had been grateful that if she was forced to marry, she didn't have to wait long.

"Tell me of your brother," she asked. They still had a few miles go until they reached their home, having gone the longest route. She needed something to take her mind away from what the night would entail once they were alone. By the intense looks Cary kept sending her way, if they didn't keep the tension at bay, she was sure he'd be pulling over the wagon to give her another toe-curling kiss.

Cary didn't say anything for a while. They continued to ride in the hot sun, with nothing but the birds screeching overhead, the groan of the wagon, and the clopping of the mule.

"If it's too painful, you don't have too."

"It is, but I want to." He squeezed her hand, not crushing it, but holding it firm as he began, "Garmin. My brother's name was Garmin and his wife, Adsila."

"Since he was already married, was Garmin older than you? Do parents have the same archaic rule for boys?"

He chuckled and some of the tension eased in his grip. "No. But even if they did. I am older by minutes."

"Minutes?" She frowned and glanced up at him. "Were you twins?"

"Yes. Identical."

Something else became clear to her. "It is why Ama touches you the way she does when you are with her. Like at the station." She recalled the little girl stroking his hair and face. It had seemed odd to Isabel since everyone in their family had the same hair except for Cary's father.

"Ama was so young when Garmin and Adsila joined with the spirits of my mother's people; she is still young. When I first came to the reservation, she screamed 'Papa', believed I was him. It took me and Atohi weeks to teach her *edutsi*, uncle."

"*E-du-tsi,*" she repeated.

"Yes." Cary smiled, and there was something in his gaze resembling gratitude. She figured that he liked she was learning something of his mother's people.

"If you all lived with your mother and father on a farm in Wichita Falls, Texas, how was it Garmin came to be at the reservation?"

"Love." There was a wistfulness to his voice.

She wasn't sure what drove it, but she wondered if Cary was like her. She envied what her sister had with Robert. The deputy and her sister had a love match; she and Cary did not.

"Every year after the harvest and before the snow fell, my pa would take us all back to Tahlequah, where the Cherokee Nation resided. When we were ten and six, our last trip as a family, Garmin met Adsila. She was ten and three and in her last year of school. He fell in love with her beauty and smile.

He talked about her all the way back to Wichita." Cary chuckled. "I even pushed him off the back of the wagon at one point, to get him to shut up."

Isabel gasped but laughed. There were times she had wanted to shove a babbling Sophia off the back of a wagon as well, however didn't.

"It was moving slow enough for him to tuck and roll, just a scrape or two. He ran and jumped back on, but his last words were that he would return and marry her and live where she lived." His sigh was heavy. "It was never easy for my brother and me. We were accepted more than *unitsi* by our pa's family because we were half him. The schoolhouse was worse. Garmin and I fought with white boys to school and back, daily."

"Did you all have family who went to school with you as well?"

"Yes. They never joined in, but they didn't stop it, either."

Isabel was horrified at his words.

"So, Garmin didn't need much excuse to live within the Nation. He married Adsila when he was ten and nine, and he left our parents' home on our uncle's farm. My family still went back every year, but I left three years before. I was tired of working another's land. I wanted to find my own way."

She could understand Cary's need to set out and have something of his own. It had been how she felt about teaching in the schoolhouse. She didn't want to remind him that he had filled his dream, but she had lost hers through their marriage.

"You all were treated so horribly, why would your father subject his family to such harshness?"

"He made a vow to his pa. His older brother became lame when they were in their youth. His pa also became sick around the same time. He promised his pa that he would not only help his brother work the land, but he would take care of his ma. Granny Brown was mean and surly; she never welcomed *unitsi* into her home once."

She understood the word for mother; it was what Cary always called Sunny. Horrified at his words, she asked, "How did your *unitsi* respond to such blatant cruelty?"

"With blankets, carvings, food, and kindness. My ma doesn't have a drop of meanness in her blood. As long as Pa's family treated Garmin and me well, she kept her peace. Our pa never let it go. He rarely took us to the main house. He did his foreman duties and taught my brother and me the ways of farming but remained distant from the others when he could. He ensured our home was always filled with love."

"Is your granny still living?"

"No. She passed two winters ago. My parents were making plans to move with my ma's people when we lost Garmin. Adsila succumbed to cholera first, and it was my brother's dying wish for the children to be placed in my care."

"So, your parents followed the children."

Cary nodded as he led the mule between the Bur Oaks to their new land and home.

When Isabel spotted their families on the porch and front lawn, her gaze was drawn to Sunny and Colby. Another revelation dawned on her and she was almost ashamed to shed light on her own ignorance. "The train. Sunny and the children, who are more Cherokee than white, would not have been allowed to ride in the forward cars because of their race. Your pa would never have taken a seat where his family was not welcomed."

Cary responded by lifting their joined hands and kissing the back of hers. Enough had been said. However, she vowed that if the good Lord blessed her and Cary with children, who would be more white than Cherokee, she would never allow them to take liberties that were not allowed for their cousins, who would be raised as siblings.

Finally, they had pulled up to the house where her sister had heeded her request to keep the family reception simple. There was one long table on the lawn with a light repast, a big bowl of cider and the iced cake that would be filled with dried fruit and nuts as was the wedding tradition.

They pulled up before the house to welcoming cheers. After Cary took her by the waist and helped her down, the family moved quickly in helping them unload the wagon of all the gifts before they ate, talked, and spent time celebrating their nuptials.

Isabel wasn't sure of the life that was before her and Cary, but as he settled her along his side while they socialized, for the first time, she looked forward to being his wife.

"HE'S A GOOD MAN. Cary's going to make you a fine husband, Isabel. He'll provide for you and the children. You'll be happy; you'll see." Two hours later, her father grasped her shoulders and stared into her face beside the wagon where her mother were already settled. His steady gaze that matched her own, reflected the faith and optimism in his words.

"I know, Papa." She only said the words to salve her father's conscience. Isabel didn't know how to tell her father that she wasn't worried about whether or not Cary was good to her in the future, if he would be by her side as they raised the children, or how well he could tend the farm and bring in a bounty of crops so that they would want for nothing. There were no appropriate words for her to explain to her father that at the moment, she only had one thought on her mind—that in a matter of minutes, when all the guests were gone, she'd become Cary's wife in the Biblical sense of the word, truly his. He'd unleash most of the onslaught of passion he'd allowed her to experience a sliver of in his kiss, in their house. That she was trembling deep and low in her core, for what she didn't know.

No, there were no words for a daughter to say such to her father. "I love you, Papa. I'll be happy."

Apparently satisfied with her words, her father gave a firm nod then climbed up beside her mother.

"I'll be by at the end of the week," her mother waved and called out to her.

"Yes, Mama." She lifted a hand and waved them off.

Last night, her mother had come into her room and had a talk with her. It hadn't been long, and she had simply told her that in the marriage bed, she would find beauty, pain, passion, and a connection to another that was bone deep. Her mother's expression had become enchanted with glazed eyes as if images of things were moving through her mind, then her mother had blushed and exhaled. Finally, she had taken Isabel's hands and stared into her eyes, blue meeting green, and entreated her to submit to her husband better than she had to her parents and to try to let go of some of her stubborn ways.

"It will go better for you, Isabel," her mother warned.

Isabel had smiled and nodded, because like her father, she knew it would assuage her mother's mind, eliminate her worry. However, Isabel knew that her parents never really understood her drive to have something of her own.

As they pulled away, and a second wagon followed, Isabel noted that Sophia, who trailed them seated beside Deputy Nelson, still held a pleased expression on her face. She knew her sister would turn all, what she saw as a joyous success of Isabel's wedding, into energy toward her own nuptials in the fall. A few days ago, her papa had finally allowed Robert to ask for Sophia's hand. Yes, Sophia was pleased as punch that all things were right in her world.

Turning back toward the house, she didn't find Cary there as she expected. Instead, she located him close to the barn. Her new husband was assisting his mother in the wagon while his father lifted Atohi up from the other side to scoot in the middle.

Confused, Isabel headed in that direction. Cary's family would be staying with them here at the house, until Cary and his father built them a place behind their house. So, Isabel wasn't sure why the Brown brood was packing onto the wagon and preparing to leave.

Ama spotted her and came running from where she stood next to Cary's leg waiting to be lifted.

Bending down, Isabel watched the girl, her reddish-brown face still holding a bit of chubbiness. The pretty yellow dress, with the white ruffles peeping from the hem at her shins, made the little girl look like a burst of sunshine.

"For you!" Ama held out her tiny fist, offering her six dandelions that must have been in the girl's hand all through the reception because they were now completely bowed over her fingers.

"Hello, Ama. Well, look at these lovely flowers." Isabel plucked them from the girl, one by one. She tucked them around the coiffure Rachel and her mother had twisted and pinned at the top of her head. The bonnet and veil were long gone, in the front room of the house somewhere.

"Ah, pretty." Ama smiled and giggled as she followed those words with some Cherokee ones Isabel was hard-pressed to decipher.

It was that way with the two children, they slipped in and out between their native tongue and English. Isabel hoped over time to learn enough of their language to understand or communicate at least on a basic level.

"Thank you, Ama. They are lovely, but not as lovely as you." She tweaked the little girl's nose lightly at the tip. She stayed there as Ama brushed a hand gently over her hair and the flowers there.

"Come on, little one, time to go." Cary's deep voice caused the air to stir around Isabel as he stepped beside his niece.

Their gaze locked a moment over Ama's head, and Isabel felt the breath leave her chest at his heated stare. He had not worn a hat for their wedding, and he didn't have one on now to keep the warm spring breeze from blowing his dark strands up around his shoulders. Her hands itched to capture them and feel the silk slide through her fingers and experience it over other parts of her skin.

His gaze darkened as if he could hear her thoughts. Did he growl, or did she imagine the sound?

The spell was broken as he shifted his eyes toward Ama. He scooped up his niece, and the girl's peal of laughter that filled the air broke the intense spell. Cary returned to the wagon with Ama in his arms.

Isabel rose slowly, trying to steady herself. The man had a way of making her body forget basic things like breathing, standing, walking, talking, even. After a deep breath, she followed his steps to the wagon.

"Pa, we'll see you all tomorrow," Cary was saying as he handed Ama up to his mother's outstretched hands.

"Sure thing, son. We'll probably have some fixin' at that Drummond place. Your ma heard from Mrs. Livingston they make the best biscuits so she's hankerin' to try'em. But we'll return after, and you and I'll get that soil turned."

"Thanks, Pa. You all have a good night." Cary must have

sensed her beside him because he glanced down at her, even though he didn't touch her.

"It is good to have you as part of our *si-da-ne-lv*." Sunny made a circle motion with her hand as she smiled down at her, the older woman's brown gaze brightened. "Good for Cary."

Isabel shifted her gaze to Cary's, who she found was not staring at his mother as she assumed, but right at her, his gray eyes dark. Swallowing twice to moisten her mouth, she stitched together the context clues. Grinning at Sunny and the others, Isabel responded tentatively, "I'm happy to be a part of your *sidanelv*...family."

"*Sidanelv*! *Sidanelv*!" Ama parroted and everyone laughed.

Colby winked at her, applauding her endeavors before he made a clicking sound, similar to the one Cary was always making, then snapped the reins commanding the mule to move along.

Isabel was glad Cary's family was seeing that she was trying to accept their culture into her way of life, even if the Tsalagi language felt foreign on her tongue and she wasn't sure about the alphabet or the letters used to even contrive the words and phrases. However, she saw herself as an educator, even if she would never be able to go away to school, so she would work hard to educate herself in the native tongue. These people were now her family, and she wanted to be a part of their world as they were a part of hers.

She and Cary watched the wagon until it drove through the trees at the end of their property. Once they were on their way, she turned to him. "Why did they leave? Did your parents change their mind about living at the house?"

Lifting a hand, he caressed along the bottom of her face as he had done once before. His touch was no less electric than it had been the first night of their introduction. When he stopped right below her bottom lip, he traced the fullness with the tip of his thumb, Isabel felt the tingling sensations left in the wake of his touch and she wanted to roll her lip in or slip her tongue out and taste him. She did neither.

He brought his gaze up from her mouth, to her eyes. "It is our wedding night, wife. They are providing us with privacy to get to know one another."

The heat in his words let her know he was not talking about the two of them sitting on the porch with coffee and talking about their favorite season or if fireflies in the summer night excited them. It was something more intimate, carnal.

"Oh." She did roll her lip in this time and worried her bottom lip with her teeth. The bit of pain she caused to herself helped her draw focus away from the current zipping from all areas of her body driving straight into her core.

"There are things we need." He placed a hand on her back and urged her toward the house.

She felt the pressure of his hand but could not feel the warmth of it through her corset. When they entered the house, the front room was stuffed with all their wedding gifts.

"I suppose we should get started on seeing what is here and getting it all put in its proper place." She picked up the closest thing to her, which was covered in brown paper, but she knew it was a painting from Sophia. Her sister had been working on something over the last two weeks but had refused to allow Isabel to see what it was.

"There is plenty of time for that later." Cary took the gift out of her hand and set it back down. He walked away, to a trunk over by the hearth. It was a black trunk with vibrant images on it. It was one of the items that had come on the train with his parents. Cary unbuckled the latches before lifting the lid. He didn't waste time in removing a bundle from inside of it.

From where she stood, close to the door, she was unsure if she should start up the stairs to their room or wait there for him. She'd come back to the house with her sister and mother days ago, to finish seeing all areas of the house, since she had not seen more than the downstairs when she was with Cary. They'd gotten distracted.

Besides the three rooms upstairs, there was a bathing room above the kitchen. Her mother and Sophia had supervised her things being moved over and placed in the larger of the three rooms upstairs. Her nightdress would be up there, something she knew she was expected to change into for her wedding night. She had bathed that morning, using her favorite rose scented bars, but after the wedding, the ride to the church then to the house, plus standing around in the heat and mingling, Isabel felt sweaty and dusty.

She watched Cary not only hold at his side what appeared to be a bundle of furs, but he then removed a rifle from the trunk as well. She was baffled by why a rifle would be required on a wedding night. Unsure what his intentions were, she headed toward the stairs. "I would like a bath if there is time."

"We will bathe." Cary closed the trunk then faced her.

His words caused her to pause. Did he mean that the two of them would wash together? Her brows pinched together. "You want to wash with me?"

The heels of his boots made a thumping sound as he crossed the wood floor to her with his items.

"Yes." He angled his head toward the stairs. "I will wait if you would like to grab a special soap."

"*Get* soap? I'm sure my soaps have already been placed in the bathing room." It was like that at her parents' house. Her mother loved baskets and had many of them in the bathing room that held soaps, Italian shampoos, various scented emollients for the skin, drying sheets, small rags, and towels.

"We will not stay here tonight, Isabel Carrie. Hurry, I wouldn't prefer to travel in the dark."

She was going to question him again, but the stern look and the arch of his brow warned her off. So, she went upstairs to get a few things. Perhaps, Cary didn't feel comfortable having their first night in a house built by someone else. She expected that maybe they also were headed to the boarding house as well. Unsure why they didn't just leave with his parents, she went into the bathing room first. It was as she expected; there were filled baskets inside on shelves around the claw foot tub. She selected one of the soaps her friend made then went into the large room. She kept her gaze away from the bed, suspecting that soon she would be in one similar to it with Cary. She went to the chest of drawers and pulled open the top one. It was filled with feminine apparel. Grateful, she removed the first ruffled items she touched. However, when she removed it and suspected it as sleeping attire, she gasped to find it was a chiffon material. It was fashioned as a sleep apparel, but it was so transparent, it would hide nothing. She tried for another, then another, but everything inside of the drawer consisted of thin, sheer, or silky items. Even the pantalets seemed more alluring than functional.

She rolled both her lips in and stifled a groan. She knew this was clearly her mother and sister's doing. Not a single one of her thick cotton night dresses was there.

"Isabel!" Cary called from the lower level. Giving up on finding anything she would deem appropriate, she decided she would just sleep in her chemise. It at least was cotton and hid more than those other gauzy things.

With nothing but the scented soap in hand, she went down.

"Let us make haste." He had added his satchel over his shoulder as he stood beside the front door.

Soundless, she followed him out as her mind wondered what other surprises she would find in the wardrobe and drawers that her mother and Sophia had filled there. She only had herself to blame for leaving them at Molly's Dress Shop without her supervising them. She'd thought they'd only been ordering her a wedding gown, but evidently those women had been up to crafty deeds, purchasing her an entire trousseau.

Cary took her hand after he closed the door. Feeling the touch of his big, strong grasp around hers, she could not help but wonder how he would respond if he'd seen her in one of those filmy creations. Would he like it, or think she was acting as one of the women who worked at The Harlot and the Hero with Mrs. Kitty? A place most decent ladies were expected to pretend didn't exist. Isabel admitted to herself, she'd often wondered what kinds of things went on behind the walls of such an establishment. Whatever the wickedness was, men must like it, because the place stayed in business.

When they continued past the newly erected barn where both Silver, his horse and the two oxen were housed and followed a path toward the thick, tree lined area, she asked, "Are we not headed to town?"

"No." He glanced down at her then up at the sky, the sun already on its descent. With spring now there, the sun did not set as early as it had in the winter months, but neither would it last as long as it would in the summer.

She followed him, not sure what the man had planned. Knowing Grover Town as she did, she only knew of one thing that was close to their property—the Kansas River. On the other side of Grover, most of the bodies of water, streams, and creeks were fed by the Mississippi River, but here, the Kansas

River that bordered the land made it prime property. The wide river ran from Kansas City to Topeka.

Animals and birds scurried around as they found their boroughs for the coming night or perched on limbs, ready to start stalking their prey.

It was that vast river that was before them once she and Cary stepped through the other side. Besides the water, nothing else was there. "Um, Cary..."

He had released her hand and stepped toward a grassy patch in the clearing before the bank. "I will lay out the furs here, then we can bathe."

Bathe. Here. She looked left then right, around the bend of the river. The water was calm here, it pooled in the deep, moving slowly, unlike in other places. "There isn't any covering here. How do you expect us..." she corrected, "...me to have privacy? I know boys and men are different when it comes to being out in the open in various states of undress, but women are different."

She knew from her youth, the boys were always allowed to remove their shirts and dive and splash in the water, while the girls had only been told they could remove just their shoes and stockings to cool themselves in the water. There was no freedom for women like men.

Cary rose beside the pile of animal skins he laid out beside the satchel and the rifle. Crossing the ground to her, he cupped her face. "You are my wife. This is our land. I will protect it and you." His rough fingers slipped around her neck and played with the strands of hair at the base of her scalp.

Even seeing the confidence in his gaze, she still hesitated. "Why can't we just go back to the house? It's what homes were built for...I'm used to a comfortable bed, not..." she waved her hands around, encompassing all of nature around them.

The big man beside her was silent as she looked at him,

still prepared to argue her point. It was then she saw the glint in his gaze. It wasn't the same desire that was always there; this time it looked more like hurt or disappointment at her prudish and snobbish words. Her heart sank as she pressed her lips together.

Giving her an abrupt nod and lowering his hands from her face, he started to step away. "I will take us back—"

Rushing toward him, she grabbed his thick forearm in her hands. "No, Cary. I-I'm sorry."

When he didn't turn and look at her, she stepped around him and stood between him and the mound. "I want to stay. I want to be here with you."

Even though she only began to say the words to soothe him, she felt the truth of them in her heart. She desired to be with Cary, to be close to him where he chose.

He stared into her eyes. "I don't want you uncomfortable."

"I won't be." She felt the tremble in her lips as she offered him a smile.

After a moment, he offered her a curt nod. "Then let us undress before the sun is gone. Let me help you."

When he turned her around, she started to turn back as she glanced. "I don't need help."

"I will undo the buttons on the back of your dress." He took her by the shoulders and turned her back all the way around.

"Oh." When he was finished and stepped away, she looked back at him. "Thank you."

Cary busied himself with gathering wood and rocks for a small fire pit.

Glad that he was distracted instead of watching her, she hurried in removing her dress, shoes, and stockings. While Cary was using his knife from his satchel, with a thick branch to hammer the big pieces of wood into smaller ones, she reached under her shift and removed her undergarment. She felt heat flood her neck and face. In all her life, she'd never been in such a state of undress before a man. Once the fire was going and she was standing only in her shift and corset, she realized she would need him again. Since she wasn't wearing one of her usual corsets that tied in the front, like she did every morning when dressing, this one was in the back and Rachel had looped and tucked the strings where she was having a hard time undoing them without causing knots.

"Do you need help?" His rich, timbred voice came from directly behind her.

Distracted, she hadn't realized that Cary was now standing behind her. She looked at him then looked away. "Yes, please. If you can simply untie... Ah!"

Unprepared for his actions, her arms had been hanging at her sides, so when he sliced open the strings in one slice of his blade, the steel and fabric material dropped heavy at her feet.

Shocked, she faced him, her hands on her hips. "Why did you do that? With a little patience, you could have untied it. Now it is ruined."

"It is of no use," he declared.

"Not now, it isn't." She swiped it up and assessed the damage. "I will have to go to Molly's and purchase another string."

"No more of those contraptions. They're not healthy for you. Summer will be here soon."

She wanted to tell him that she had worn one for years, since she'd begun to develop faster than most of the girls in the schoolhouse and boys were taking notice. However, she kept silent. She was glad that it was starting to get dark and where she stood in the shadows, she doubted Cary could see the truth of her heavy figure and why the restraining contraption had been necessary.

Laying down the item in the dry grass on her wedding dress, she picked up the soap and started toward the water's edge. It was mid-spring and the water that greeted her toes was cool, not icy as it would have been a couple months ago with winter, and not warm as it would be in a couple months once summer set in. The later the hour got, the colder the water would become, so it was best for her to wash up quickly.

When she squatted down at the water's edge, prepared to keep herself shielded from her husband's gaze, she heard him saying, "Remove your covering, wife."

Looking at him, she noticed that he'd already removed his suit coat and shirt. His chest was bare and smooth in the fire light. His upper body was wide, with broad, rounded shoulders and taut muscles on his abdomen above his buckle. It made her think of laundry day and the washboards used. At the waistband of his pants, she returned her gaze back up his chest and neck, only to see when she got to his face, he was staring at her.

Whipping her head around, she rose and moved deeper into the water, wanting to keep herself busy from gazing back at the captivating man stripping only feet away from her. She now needed the chilly water to help tone down the heat she felt rising. Besides, if he wanted her to take off her chemise, then she would use the water to maintain her modesty. She lifted her garment slowly, only moving it up her body in concert with the level of the water. When the water reached her knees, her shift met her thighs. When the river lapped at the apex of her thighs, she brought the cotton to her waist. Once her navel was wet, she was holding her last piece of covering tight around her heavy breasts with the cake of soap clenched in her fist.

"Isabel, can you swim?"

She dare not glance back at him. She could feel the

current, slow but moving, around her body. She shivered. "No."

Swimming was something boys did. She was always told that girl's clothing would cause them to drown, so they were never allowed in farther than the bank.

"Then wait. Don't go any further." There was a slouching sound behind her, and her mind teased her with elusive images of a bare Cary.

Frozen, she stood there, not having the courage to remove the rest of her clothes and tantalized by the feel of the flowing water against her nude flesh. However, Cary took that choice away from her. Under his strong grip, her shift was wiped over her head and off her flailing arms as she scrambled to grab at it.

She lost her footing on the rock and found herself beneath the surface of the dark river.

NINE

"Whoa, there." Cary flung the material toward the shore without looking then quickly grabbed hold of the sinking woman. His hands made contact with supple flesh as he dragged her toward him.

Isabel came up spitting and coughing up water as it ran in rivulets from her nose and mouth. She clutched at his neck with one hand while the other held the soap in her other, pressed against her chest as if it were some raft of safety. If she didn't look so frightened, he would have chuckled.

In the water, his body defied the coolness as it went rock hard responding to all the ample curves of his wife that were pressed against him.

"I don't want to die."

Isabel hadn't truly been in any risk of drowning. She had barely gotten a half of arm length away from him when she turned, trying to keep the article of clothing in her grasp.

"You're safe, wife," he whispered along her ear as he stroked down her back, following each vertebrae of her spine until it reached the crease of her ass.

It was that touch there that caused Isabel to still. He knew the moment she realized that her bare body was pressed tight against his nude form. He wondered if she was aware of his hard cock sandwiched between them and pressing into the soft curve of her belly.

He felt the movement of her throat muscles as she swallowed. Her feet brushed against his ankles and shin as she moved her toes below the surface. Once she contacted the flat rock on the bottom of the river that he stood on, she found her footing and pushed away.

"I'm fine now." Since the water only came to his torso and just below Isabel's breasts, she kept one arm pressed there to keep him from seeing her. Her ample bosom, no longer held down by her corset, was spilling over her small arm from above and below.

He felt the urge to peel her hand away and reveal the bounty to his lusty gaze, discovering if her nipples were rosy or soft brown. He'd allow her the moment of privacy, but before the night was over, he'd see, feel, and taste every inch of his lovely, curvaceous bride.

In the soft glow of the firelight barely reaching them, he saw her hair, wet and messy hanging awkwardly on the side of her head, some of the pins lost in her short fight for survival.

Holding his hand out, he commanded, "Hand me your soap. I will start with washing your hair."

She only hesitated a moment, before she relinquished the soap to him.

He moved in the water behind her then began to sift through her wet locks until he took out all her pins, allowing them to be lost in the water. Her hair floated in the water around the center of her back, showing him that it would fall at least to her waist, much longer than his. When he rubbed the ends over the soap, the sweet rose fragrance wafted up to meet him. Now, he knew the secret of one of her scents. He looked forward to discovering the natural scent of her essence.

Once her hair was washed, he held steady at the waist and instructed her to duck under the water to rinse it. When that was done, he began making circles over her shoulder and along her back. Isabel relaxed some under his ministration as her head rolled forward and she sighed.

He could feel the tension in her body, and he wondered how much of it had to do with the hectic nature of the day versus the awareness of what was to come that night. He didn't want her nervous to be with him. It was his plan to please her, give her repeated orgasms before he sank deep inside of her and claimed her maidenhead. His cock wasn't in agreement with the slow progression of his seduction plans, but it would have to wait. Isabel's satisfaction was his goal.

Cupping his hand, he lifted water up and over her shoulders to remove the suds. Moving closer, he pressed his chest to her back as he brought the soap around her waist.

"Cary?"

"Shh," he whispered, placing light kisses down the side of her neck to her shoulder. Licking and sipping, he drank the fresh water from her skin.

She was trembling against him, but he didn't stop his caresses.

He moved the cake up her belly toward her full breasts.

When she tensed and tightened her arms over them, he pressed his lips to her ear. "Let me care for you, wife."

"Cary." His name came out like a plea.

He waited.

They stood there for a long moment, before finally and slowly, Isabel relaxed her arms and let them lower to her side.

As he cupped one and ran the soap over the other, he didn't even attempt to stifle his groan of satisfaction. He wanted her to hear how much touching her body pleased him. They were heavy and her nipples were large, and he cursed the night sky that didn't allow him to see them. He promised himself that once he had his beautiful wife stretched out before the firelight, he would take his time looking his fill. With his hands now, he stroked and circled them, using the slickness of the lather to glide over them.

Isabel began to moan and arch her hips back toward him. When her round ass bumped along his hard shaft, he had to bite his tongue not to thrust against her and empty out his balls right then and there.

He continued to palm her breasts and hold her fast against him as he lowered his other hand under the water. She was quaking and gasping with each inch below the surface his hand went. At the juncture of her supple thighs, he rubbed the cake gently along her sex. When she started bucking against his stroking hand, he released the soap. He didn't care if it went up stream, down, or sank to the bottom of the river for all eternity, he no longer wanted anything between her skin and him.

Using his fingers of one hand, he plucked at her nipple and enjoyed her squirming and whimpering. His other hand slipped through the hair covering her sex until he was gliding between her folds. He used his fingers to part her and find the warm slickness of her pussy. Even in the water, he knew the difference of her slippery essence coating her.

Her clit was distended and needy. He stroked along the sides...once, twice, three times and felt her quiver against him. Lust pulsed through his veins as he went lower, down below her clit until he found the tight, small opening of her. With one finger, he pressed inside, just enough to feel her contract around him. Pulling away, he slipped back up to her clit. In harmony, he was circling and flicking her clit and nipple.

"Oh...ohh." Her thighs flexed closed then opened as she clutched at both his wrists in her hands. However, she wasn't using them to pull him away or stop his actions, more for purchase.

He sped up his movements, knowing where this was all leading for her. His touch became more firm, urgent, ready to feel her come apart in his arms with her first release.

"*Ayv adanvdo*...let go. Give me your pleasure," he growled in her ear. His body wanted nothing more than to bury his cock inside of her and feel her release around him, but he held back.

Finally, Isabel was screaming and rocking violently against his hand. As she came apart, finishing the mind-altering high of her orgasm, he didn't stop caressing her. He forced her to ride out every quake until she was building once more into another rise.

She was so responsive. He never would have guessed that his formal and straitlaced wife was so abandoned in her plea-sure. He doubted she knew it, either.

As her second climax ended, he swept her up in his arms and seized her mouth in a hungry kiss. He wanted to feast on her cries and the aftershocks of her passion. Blinded, he walked them out of the water as she clung to him, returning his kiss. When he no longer felt the water at his feet, he pulled away from her succulent mouth.

Making his way to his family furs, he lowered to his knees and placed her at the edge of the thick mat before the fire.

"I'll return soon." As he let her go, he saw the hunger he felt in his body reflected in her gaze that sparkled in the fire-light. It took all his willpower not to lay her down and find his existence between her thighs. He let her go then moved to his satchel and took out his soap and went back to the water. Diving in, he made quick work of his own bathing, wearing the bit of soap down to nothing before he allowed it to drift. He'd hissed and groaned as his hand circled his cock. He'd considered that it would only take him two good strokes to find completion, then he would be calm enough to titillate his wife endlessly.

Instead, he let himself go and walked out of the river. He loved the freedom of nature and had many fantasies about laying out Isabel before the stars and joining his body to hers. He wanted this first time with his wife to be just them, not the land of her inheritance or the walls of the house her father had built or even the contract that had declared her his wife, but a man and his woman.

Her eyes tracked him from the spot she sat with her knees drawn up to her chest. Now that her pleasure had receded, she was the conservative woman once again. He knew the moment there was enough firelight illuminating his body because he saw the stretch of her lids as she took in his erection.

His dick was thick, hard, and standing up proud toward his abdomen. As he closed the distance between them, she drew up tighter, shadows of fear filling her gaze. Not wanting to fixate on her apprehension, he sat beside her. Lifting a hand, he brought her mouth close to his.

"Kiss me," he commanded. He knew she enjoyed his kiss and could lose herself in it, so it was a good place to start, to get her mind off the inevitable events to come.

When she set her lips on his, he kissed her, long and slow. He didn't rush her as they had all night, regardless of what his cock wanted. Slipping his tongue into her mouth, he felt the warmth of her and tasted her sweetness. He used one hand and stroked her damp tresses from scalp to the curve of her ass where it ended, petting her, calming her.

Her sighs filled his mouth as she relaxed. Not stopping

the kisses, he lowered her down to the furs and glided their bodies up until they were stretched out, her body alongside his, their feet warmed by the fire. Her hand began to caress his chest, drawing along the taut muscles there. He pulled his mouth from hers and stared down at her.

Her body was rosy with lust and her lips swollen dark with passion. He thought about how her red lips would look around his cock, how her mouth would feel as he thrust along her tongue.

Not now, he told himself. He'd see to his wife first.

She lowered her gaze from his face to watch her hands on him.

He stared at them too. The colors different, one pale and the other dark, but they were a complement to each other.

"Do you mind?"

"Touch me all you want, wife. I know I plan to do the same to you."

There was a light tremor in her touch at his words, but she didn't stop. She never made it past his torso, but her hands became firmer in their caresses.

He started to touch her, just as he'd told her he would. Starting at her neck, he glided along skin that was warm and softer than the finest satin. He went over one shoulder then crossed her collarbone to the other. "I wish my hands weren't so rough and callused."

"I like your hands." She took hold of the one moving over her and lifted it to her mouth. She kissed the tip of each finger before settling her mouth on his palm. When she circled the center of it lightly with the tip of her tongue, he growled.

She let out a small giggle.

"Ah, you are a wicked one, wife." He leaned down and kissed her. He didn't linger but moved away to continue learning her body.

When he arrived at her breasts, he took in the lush site of them with the pale brown tips.

She quickly covered them with her hands, saying, "They are too much...too big. A distraction."

He placed his hands on top of hers, not removing hers, but using both their grips to fondle her. "Yes, wife, they are a distraction." Staring into her eyes, he confessed, "There'll never be a day that I see you, even clothed, that I'll not think of how bountiful they are. I'll remember their softness and the plumpness of your taut nipples. You, wife, will see me gaze at them and recall your own sighs as we played with them."

She was sighing now, loudly, as her body writhed against his at his words. Oh, yes, his bride was a feral cat when her lust was ignited.

He left her glorious breasts and continued down her stomach. Her waist was narrow, almost unnaturally so. He could see the scarring from the corset striping down over her ribs and stomach with horizontal markings at the rise of her full hips. She had used the material as a restraint, imprisoning the lovely full swells of her womanly form.

"No more," he growled low. When he glanced up at her, a brow arched, ensuring she understood his directive. His wife would not harm what was his ever again. She was his.

Isabel gave a single nod; her hands remained on her breasts, but still.

"You are mine, Isabel Carrie Brown." He danced his fingers over her wide hips. "Every part of you." He created patterns and circles over her fleshy, supple thighs.

When he got to the front of her knees, she giggled. As he moved his touch around the back and down her calves, she laughed louder and squirmed away from him. He enjoyed discovering she was ticklish. He played along her ankle and feet then smiled as she attempted to pull them away from him.

He brought his hand up between her warm thighs and felt the dewiness coating her skin there. She had been sensitive, but it had also aroused her to have his hands on her. Settling in beside her again, he lightly tugged at the triangular patch of hair guarding her treasure.

Gasping, she snapped her thighs around his hand. He didn't allow her to keep him out. He coaxed her to relax with a gentle caress along the seam of her nether lips. "Open to me."

She relaxed her legs slowly as she lowered them back down to the furs beneath them.

"Did you enjoy my fingers in your pussy before?"

She frowned as her lips parted, then shut, then parted again. She nodded.

Cary was sure it was the erotic word for her sex that she didn't comprehend, however by the blush he noted on her cheeks reflecting the warmth of the fire, he was sure she grasped the meaning. Rewarding her for her honesty, he slipped two fingers between the swollen, slick labia and dragged them up along the sides of her clit.

Isabel's breath hitched. When he repeated the action, her eyes rolled up and her lids closed.

"Look at me, wife." He continued the up and down motion and felt the small movements she made as she followed his strokes.

She peeled her lids open and met his gaze.

He loved staring into her beautiful green eyes and seeing the passion he ignited shining in them. "Now, I want you to offer me those pretty, big breasts of yours. I'm going to suck your nipples while I play with your wet pussy and make you feel good again."

Her eyes darkened and her red lips formed a perfect O-shape, but it only took her a beat before she cupped her breasts and lifted them slightly.

Understanding her small gesture, he smiled. Leaning down, he kissed that delectable mouth of hers then lowered his lips to one nipple. He took the beaded tip into his mouth and began to lick and suck her just as he promised.

She started moaning and squeezing her breasts tighter which only lifted them higher toward him.

Cary sucked hard on one nipple, then he moved to the other one and flicked and nipped the sensitive tip. His hand between her thighs felt the pool of cream increase around his fingers. He mimicked his oral actions with his fingers. When he sucked her nipple, he scissored her clit between his fingers. If he circled his tongue around her, then he went 'round and 'round her clit. When he licked between her breasts, burying his face in the hills of flesh, then he pushed his middle finger into her only to slip out and trace up the slit to the hood of her clit.

"Ohhh...Cary. Cary!" She was twisting and moaning his name as she fucked his hand.

He took a nipple into his mouth and inserted two fingers into her tight pussy. It took him multiple pushes in and out until he could fit both inside, but Isabel was so wet and needy, she was arching her hips to him, begging him for more as she took him deeper. He was purposely stretching her, knowing that his fingers were nothing compared to the size of his cock, but he wanted to bring her as much pleasure as possible.

When she came, she released her breasts and buried her hands in his hair, clutching him to her as she cried out.

She was still coming, her body jerking before him when he forced her hands from his hair. Situating himself beside her knees, he spoke to her, rough and commanding, to get through the haze of pleasure clouding her mind. "Bring your knees up, Isabel. Hold them wide so I can see all your pretty, wet pussy. I'm going to taste you until you come on my tongue."

Unsure and delirious, he saw her shaking her head. "No, you shouldn't—"

"Do it!" he demanded. She may not understand the act he was planning to perform, but he would still have her submission. He didn't touch her, just sat back on his haunches beside her and waited.

With tentative movements, she slowly brought her knees up. She sat with them bent but closed. Finally, her gaze met his as she wrapped her hands around her knees and drew them to her chest.

He could see the shadow of her pussy in the firelight below her heels, but he stayed right where he was until she complied fully. She finally pulled them apart until they were wide even as they trembled with both anxiety and wonder. His wife knew what pleasure was now, and her body yearned for it, even as she was unsure of what she was doing.

As her pussy was revealed to him in all its dripping, pink glory, his breath caught in his chest. His heart pounded a fierce drum beat in his chest as he looked upon the woman offering herself to him. His cock was throbbing with the same cadence. Shifting, so that he was centered between her thighs, he ran his hand down the center of her silken skin. Leaning down, he kissed her belly and felt her quiver there. He licked her skin and tasted the saltiness of her sweat. Bending lower, he moved over the short hairs and rubbed his nose over the area as he inhaled. She was a musky rose scent. It was everything that was Isabel, everything that was his.

"*Ayv adanvdo,*" he whispered softly before he dipped down into the well of cream. Her tastes exploded onto his tongue and bloomed in his mouth. She was the greatest delicacy, heady, robust, sweet, and savory. There was no other taste as refined and unique as his Isabel. She was his, all his.

Every moan she uttered was his, each arch of her back belonged to him, and shudders that racked her body as he suckled her clit were his alone.

"Cary...plea-a-se..." she implored.

He knew what she asked for...what she needed. However, he would hold her at bay, keep her right at the edge. He wanted her crying and begging for the satisfaction only he could give her. A deeper pleasure.

Slurping and licking, he drove his tongue into her. Just when she started to quiver and her orgasm started to rise, he pulled away, kissing up her thighs that she was now holding so wide, he was sure her hips would ache the next day.

She was appealing to him in every way she could conceive, using the word pussy and asking him to make her come. He enjoyed hearing how his prudish teacher was letting go of all her prim ways to be sated.

Up and down, he swirled designs along her slit and drew her clit into his mouth, painting his lips and face with her cream. When he moved beyond the small opening of her sex and pressed his tongue into the delicate rosette, she was too close to the threshold of ecstasy to shy away. Instead, she bucked and succumbed to the naughty titillation.

Finally, he couldn't take the pressure in his cock any longer; he was hard and aching, ready to split in half if he could not bury himself inside of her.

"Nooo," she whined when he moved away.

He would have chuckled at the sound, but he couldn't. He was on the verge of insanity with lust clawing at his core. His sac was drawn so tight below his cock, he could barely breathe. He positioned himself between her spread knees and set his length along her sex.

"Tell, me to fuck you, Isabel. Tell me you want my cock inside of you," he growled, his voice so raspy and deep, it was foreign to his own ears.

With a trembling hand, she reached up and placed a hand along his jaw. "Fuck me, husband. I want your cock inside me." Her voice was low, hoarse from her scream. Her green gaze was misty with unshed tears, his wife's agony echoing in his soul.

Balancing his weight on one forearm, he took hold of his shaft with his other hand then guided the head along her slippery slit. At the opening, he pressed in, just enough to breach the opening. Then he settled his chest against the pillow softness of her breasts. Cupping her face in both his hands, he whispered, "Wrap your legs around me."

When he felt her heat surrounding his waist, he pushed forward. The crown of his cock sat against the gate guarding her virginity. He began to kiss her, devouring her moans as he started to rock his hips, sliding his cock in and out, getting her used to what was to come.

Once he felt her tight walls begin to relax and her hips pick up the motion, he pulled back, almost all the way out, before he drove forward. Isabel's screams vibrated in his mouth and her body stilled. He was only halfway in, but he stopped.

He plied her lips, chin, neck, and ears with kisses as he whispered words of consolation to her, letting her know he would have taken the pain from her if he could. Moving his kisses up her face, he kissed her nose, and forehead and sipped the salty tears from her temple.

"Are you all right, wife?" He stared down at her.

"No," she sniffed.

His heart ached. "Do you want me to stop?"

"Nooo," she sighed as she arched up just a fraction and pushed him a little deeper.

"Fuck," he groaned. The feel of her hot, tight sex opening just a little as she contracted then released around him, made his head spin. Caring for her was the only thing he could think about. He pulled back then thrust forward to press further into her.

She hissed and her body was still tighter than a fist, but she made gingerly movements against him. They worked in tandem, bucking and rocking as she took more and more of his length.

"Okay, love...I'm all the way in," he informed her once he was seated at the heart of her sex, pressing at her womb. He was a big man, and it had taken both their efforts to get him there.

"Says the one of us who is not being split in two."

"True. But I'm going to ensure we both have nothin' but pleasure from here on out."

"Show me, husband," she entreated.

And he did. He pulled all the way out then drove home until the mouth of her sex was kissing him at the base of his cock. He kept his tempo slow and gentle until Isabel was clawing at him and thrusting up against him. She asked for more; she asked him to take her harder.

She came around him, her orgasm sending vibrations through her sex that quivered up along his shaft as her walls gripped him, holding him inside. The feel of her, a hot, silky, liquid paradise on Earth, shoved him into rapture's arms. He came long and hard, groaning his release as he called her name, "Isabel. Wife. *Ayv adanvdo.*"

His heart was beating so fast, he didn't think it would ever return to normal again. He lay there, his big weight comforted by her full form. This woman, whom he'd been contracted to marry, was beginning to mean everything to him.

Recovering some, he shifted his weight from her. Staring down at her, in the low light of the fire, it would be dying down soon if he didn't add more logs on it. He checked to make sure she was well. When he saw the shy smile on her lips, he exhaled, not aware he'd been holding his breath. After a light kiss, he told her, "I'll set more wood on the fire, then we will wash."

She stared at him. "Again?"

"There'll be blood."

"Okay." She nodded then curled onto her side and watched him.

His cock was already hardening again under her appraisal. Once he had the fire stoked to life again, he went back to her. Scooping her up, he headed for the river.

"I'm too heavy for you to continue to lug around."

"You are not. I like the feel of your body in my arms." He told her truth; he enjoyed the heft of it and the softness as she curled into him. "Even when you're swollen with my child, I'll carry you."

"Surely, after one time, a baby cannot be made," she declared.

"Perhaps. However, by the time we leave this place tomorrow, I will have buried my seed in you many times. Maybe one of those times will plant a babe."

She didn't respond. He wondered for a moment if she wanted a child. If she wanted his child. Just like marriage, children had not been in Isabel's plans. Children were a blessing from the Great Spirit. So if it was meant for them to conceive, then he would welcome it and pray Isabel accepted any children with joy, too.

"Ah, that's cold," she squealed and curled higher in his arms as he moved deeper into the water.

"Yes, it is, but it will also soothe any aches." The water made her body buoyant and light in his arms. He could have released her, but he kept her wrapped tight and close to him. He didn't plan for them to stay in the water long as the night was cooler away from the fire.

When Isabel looked at him with her pale green eyes and began running her long, elegant fingers over his lips, he was lost. He leaned in and kissed her lightly on the mouth. It took only seconds before that kiss became two, and then it turned heated. She was kissing him back and sliding her breasts over his chest.

Even in the cold water, his cock could not be calmed. His mind was filled with thoughts of what it felt like to be inside of her. He let go of her legs, even as he held her body pressed against him, their lower bodies entwined.

Slipping his hands down, he cupped her ass and held her to him. Now that he'd had a taste, he'd go mad for want of her.

Isabel must have felt the same way. She was arching and gyrating her hips against his length. "Is it too soon?"

He knew what she asked, what she wanted to know. He'd already been chiding his randy body to settle down, give his wife a chance to recover. However, with her eager words and the beguiling way she was grinding into him, she was not looking for a reprieve. "Hell, no. Never. Wrap your legs around me."

Once she was situated around him, open to him, he fit himself inside the hot glove of her sex again. Considerate of her tenderness, he moved slowly, simply rocking with the gentleness of the current. Their climb to pleasure's peak was a sensual one. He kissed her, caressed her, and whispered naughty things to her, all the while thrusting steady and deep into her sex.

Their orgasms weren't any less powerful because of the languid movements. When they walked out of the water, Cary stood them beside the fire with her back pressed to his chest as they stared up at the stars in the sky until they were warm and dry.

Isabel yawned.

"Come, wife, we will rest for a bit. It has been a long day." He held her hand and led her to the furs that had been in his family for generations. It was one of the only things his mother had brought with her when she married his father.

He kept two of the furs on the ground behind them for cushion and pulled the other over them. He settled Isabel along his side. She scooted closer and rested her head on his chest. One of his hands palmed her ass, enjoying the round-ness, while his other one stroked her long, thick hair.

"Tell, me how your parents met." Her voice had a dreami-ness to it, and Cary doubted she'd make it through most of the story.

"There was a trading post between the reservation in Oklahoma and Wichita, Texas. Pa said that occasionally his gramps would go there to take some of his crops to trade for items found on the road. Often when large wagon trains head west, people pack way too much and things get left along the trail. Some of those items end up at trading posts for sale or trade. A lot of times, farmers and natives alike come through to barter for goods or sell. Well, one of those trips, my ma was there with her family, looking for medical supplies. Confined to the reservations, her people could not go in search of the herbs for medicines needed for the sick. Pa saw her and she smiled shyly at him."

Cary felt the soft caress of Isabel's fingers, letting him

know she hadn't fallen to sleep yet, so he continued, "As you can imagine, my grandpa did not have any trust for white men. Pa said he knew the only way he could plead for Ma's hand was to offer my grandpa what he could not resist. So, Pa spent a year saving every cent and working not only his family farm, but doing other odd jobs. When the year was over, he'd saved enough to buy two horses and a trunk load of medicines. Pa rode all the way to the reservation, not even knowing if Ma had been married off by then. At first her pa refused him, even with all the items. However, it was my ma who convinced him that she wanted to marry the white man. It brought shame to the family, and my grandpa forbid Pa from living among their people."

"Did your grandfather ever accept your pa?" She slid her leg along his.

"No. Even going back every year. My pa was a simple farmer who didn't even own the land he worked. My grandpa died without ever giving their marriage his blessing."

"Remembering what you said about your pa's family, it is sad to know that your parents were caught between two worlds that never recognized the beautiful love they have."

He pulled her tighter to him. "I have learned that you cannot change ignorance."

"No, you can't..." Her words drifted away, and her hand stilled as her body rested heavily along his, a clear indication that she was asleep.

The animals of the night rustled in the brush and hooted from the trees as Isabel lay in his arms and Cary was completely at peace.

ISABEL AWOKE with her body feeling achy and sore as she was caught in a salacious dream as she'd never had before, with Cary kissing and touching her all over her body. There were erotic images of his shaft, thick and heavy, buried deep in her body, bringing her to one release after another. The fantasy was so real, vivid, that she could feel his strength around her and smell the earthy sandalwood that always accompanied him.

"Wife, if you do not stop grinding your pussy on my cock, I will fuck you, whether you are awake or not."

"Uh...what?" The words and masculine voice didn't seem to make sense. It was pre-dawn and her bed was warm, comfortable. Where the rumbling, husky voice was coming from had her at a loss. It was the feel of big, callused hands squeezing her backside and one thick digit stroking along the seam of her cheeks, the touch was intimate and very real. Startled awake, she found herself face to face with said man. The sun hadn't risen, but the strong features staring back up at her in the gray dawn were unmistakably Cary's. Her husband.

Everything from the day and night before flooded her mind and sent heated coils of lust through her body.

"Mornin'." His hands were working their way between her thighs and down along her sex. She could feel her wetness coating his fingers, his touch made possible by her sprawled position on his chest.

Blushing, she hid her face on the side of his neck and mumbled, "Hello."

"Did you sleep well?" he whispered then nipped at her lobe.

"Too well, it would seem. I forgot myself." She was trying to remain still, but his fingers rubbing up and down her folds had her rocking and pressing her little nub of pleasure between her legs against his length. It felt wonderous as her body started the delicious climb towards climax.

"Yes, but your body remembered."

Oh, gracious life, it did.

"I don't know if I want to fuck you or taste you first, Isabel." Two of his fingers entered her, gliding in and out.

She groaned and wanted to tell him she didn't care which he did if he brought her to that glorious satisfaction that only he could provide. She was mindless as she pushed back into his hand then pressed forward onto his shaft.

"That's right, *ayv adanvdo*...take what you need," he encouraged.

Gripping his shoulders, she sank her teeth into the corded, taut muscle of his neck as she worked herself on his hand. She couldn't stop; her body seemed to have one aim, one goal, to reach the pinnacle of pleasure. Then she was coming, his weight beneath her, the furs caressing her legs and back as Cary's grip squeezed tight and his fingers drove her to madness. She was bucking and trembling, and she couldn't stop as one orgasm became two.

"Shit. Come here." Cary's fingers slipped from her, creating a void.

Before she could question where he wanted her to go, he had her by the waist and hauled her up his chest. She was confused, but the confusion didn't last long when she found herself straddling her husband's shoulders and his face between her thighs.

"Cary, what-t-t..." Her words broke off as his tongue swirled around her clit. It was the word he had used for the tight little bundle of nerves at the top of her sex, the bit of flesh that caused her great delight. He was licking and sucking up along her wet sex. His tongue was either buried inside of her or flicking the needy, stiff peak. She would have thought after two orgasms, she would have been sated, but she wasn't. It was as if the man beneath her had unleashed some beast within her that could not be satisfied.

He had one hand on her hip, holding her fast to him, while his other hand reached up to her bountiful bosom and palmed one. His fingers were tweaking the nipples, causing more sparks of desire to ignite in her body. Just like she had done to his hand moments ago, she was driving herself to another climax against his mouth. She didn't even know who she was anymore. The only thing she was sure about was everything Cary did to her body felt so good and made her hunger for more.

His firm lips latched onto her clit; he was drawing her out as he flicked it rapidly. The sound of someone screaming as she quaked above him was unknown to her. She'd never heard such a sound come from her mouth before. It was a combination of pleas, whimpers, and demands, filled with 'yeses' and 'don't stops'.

She was still coiled inside and pummeled by a storm of ecstasy when she found herself bowed forward, her knees on the cushion of the furs, her hands sinking deep into the dirt as Cary drove into her from behind. His thick cock was stretching her, making her accept every inch of his length. The gentle man of the night before was gone, and in the grayness of pre-dawn, he was taking her rough, hard. His knees were inside of hers, pressing her open and wide as he held her hips tilted high for his thrusts.

There was pain with his taking, an unbridled, animalistic bent to his passion. She reveled in it. She didn't want the kidgloves; she wanted his lust. Within the fiber of her being, she needed to know that she could drive a man to wicked, fierce levels of passion.

"Harder. Harder. Fuck me, husband." She didn't know

how such words tumbled from her mouth, but she couldn't recall them. Didn't want to recall them.

He growled. He didn't even spout a single audible word as he gripped her hips tighter, spreading her cheeks wider, allowing him to go deeper. He pummeled her sex like a hailstorm in the summer, unrelenting.

Something began to press between her cheeks. Wide and thick, it fit itself inside the puckered opening. By the width and size, she surmised it was Cary's thumb. She wanted to tell him to remove it, tell him the touch was wrong and that nothing should enter her there. However, when he began to move it in and out in time with his cock, the wicked touch caused a frisson of heat, like a flame that licked from her back entrance up to the back of her neck and set the nerve ending ablaze. She shouldn't want it, such a naughty, nefarious penetration, but she did.

Cary was playing her like a fine-tuned fiddle, taking her outside of herself. It was as if she were staring down at the impish woman on all fours before him and instead of being shocked or appalled, she was lusting at everything she was getting and craving it even more.

This time when she came, he slammed home, holding himself at the hilt, her sex speared and spread wide at his base. He emptied into her as she contracted around him. When she'd dropped on the far side of pleasure, Cary slipped from her aching sex, still hard. He stretched out onto the furs and pulled her on top of him.

He brushed her wild locks out of his way and kissed her. His kiss was gentle but thorough as he slowly slid into her once again.

She whimpered, feeling thoroughly used, in a good way. "I'm not sure how much energy I have left in me," she admitted.

"Take it slow. I just want to be inside you, wife." His steel gray eyes held hers.

She nodded and allowed him to hold her by the waist and settle her into a seated position. Straddling him, she felt him deeper as she rocked and rolled her hips and stared into his eyes. The sun brightened the sky in oranges, yellows, and reds as the rays warmed her from the outside. Cary's loving and attention as he softly caressed her thighs, fondled her breasts, and whispered words of her beauty heated her from the inside out.

Their final climax by the river didn't have either of them yelling or clawing at each other but was more powerful as they found completion holding each other's gaze. Isabel felt as if her heart was laid bare in those moments.

TEN

Isabel awakened for the second time Monday morning, with the sound of the bedroom door closing. It had just been a couple hours ago that she had woken with her husband sliding deep inside of her from behind. With her on her side, and her leg over his forearm, Cary had taken her to her first of four climaxes even as she was opening her eyes. Following that release, he had rolled her onto her back and plied her sex with his roguish tongue. She dragged a pillow over her face to tamp down her screams of pleasure. Even though the children were in a room on the other side of the bathing room and her in-laws were in the room off the kitchen, the farthest point away from Cary and her bedroom, she still didn't wish to wake the house. Her husband's stamina was blue ribbon worthy. Once he covered her body with his and drove deep into her, he'd pulled two more orgasms from her before he had his release.

She'd fallen back into a dreamless and exhausted sleep. Now, she needed to get up, wash and dress if she planned to make it to town before Miss Beadle rang the bell for the students. Their house was farther from the schoolhouse, on the opposite end of town than her parents' home. Before, she could walk, but now, she'd have to take the wagon. After she'd bathed at the washstand in the room and donned a fresh chemise, she stood at the wardrobe, frustrated. Yesterday, she had discovered that all her high collared dresses, as well as her corsets, which Cary had told her not to wear, but it didn't much matter since her things were gone. Her sister and mother had taken it upon themselves to replace all her clothing with the fashionable shirtwaist dresses that other ladies in town wore.

It was a far cry from what Miss Beadle dressed in, but they would have to do until she could order herself some of her old style. She knew that Cary liked the new look, because every time he'd been around her yesterday, she saw the heat in his gaze. The way he stared at her breasts, sitting high and distinct in a corset-less top made her feel as if she were once again bare and riding his thick length in the morning sunlight. Even now, she fanned herself from the memory. Thank goodness, he and his father were already out in the field for the second day, because she would be hard pressed to get out the door without him pulling her into a closet or back up to their room to kiss her senseless. Yesterday, following the noon meal after the family had returned, he'd made up some excuse about him needing her to help him find something, only to get into the room and have him unbutton her top and ruck up her skirts so that he could suck her nipples as he fingered her to a climax.

She'd collapsed on the side of the bed in a daze, while he had washed his hands, winked at her, then went out the door whistling and back into the fields. The man was insatiable.

Dressed in a peach skirt and white blouse, she was mixing the batter for flapjacks when Sunny exited the door of the room off the kitchen. Isabel knew that her mother and sister had the room built for a cook if she ever decided to get one, but Isabel liked to cook and could not see using it for anything other than guests. Sunny and Colby had selected it, liking the privacy it offered until their house was built.

"Morning, Mrs. Brown." Isabel offered a smile to the woman whose silver and black hair was parted down the middle and hung in two braids over the front of her shoulders. "Breakfast should be done shortly. Hope you don't mind flapjacks and sausages."

"Not at all. You are up and about early."

"I've always been an 'up with the sun' kind of person. I get it from my papa. Mama and Sophia could sleep until noon meal." Isabel added lard to the cast iron flat griddle on the burner.

"May I assist with something?" Sunny asked.

"No. I'm well on my way. I've already got the batter made and I'll get the meat sliced and in the oven. However, I do have water heating if you would like a cup of tea."

"That would be wonderful. I like to have a sit in the morning. It gives me a chance to thank *Unetlanvhi* for the day. The Great Spirit."

Isabel ladled the first four cakes out then poured tea to steep in a porcelain mug she knew had been her grandmother's dishes.

Sunny took the teacup from her but declined sugar or cream. "I don't like many sweet things."

"Ah, so you are where your son gets that from." Isabel smiled as she turned and flipped the food.

"It is true. Garmin was like Colby. They both could never get enough sweets."

Nodding, Isabel went to the pantry and removing one of the smoked links hanging there. Taking it to the counter, she grabbed a knife and set it beside it. She took a moment to set four more flapjacks to cooking after she placed the first set on a platter. She'd need to make plenty; the men would be hungry by the time they came in from the field for breakfast.

"Well, if you have all of this under control, I will go enjoy a little solitude."

Isabel was about to wish her well with her morning meditation, when she remembered something she was curious about. "Mrs. Brown?"

The older woman turned back to her and smiled. "Now that could be you or me. If you would like, you can call me Ma Sunny."

Isabel nodded. "Thank you. Um...can you tell me what..." She paused for a moment, trying to recall the word Cary used. He only said it in passion, and she was a little embarrassed to ask. The way he said it, it didn't seem like a naughty word. Her cheeks felt hot as she asked. "...*Ayv a-dan-v-do* means."

Sunny tipped her head to the side and looked at her. The older woman's wise brown gaze, different from her son's, held hers. "Where did you hear the word?"

Turning, she tended to the food then patted her cheeks, hoping that Sunny would think she was just heated from the stove. "Cary. He's said it...says it."

The older woman paused for so long, Isabel actually thought that she wasn't going to say. Then she spoke, "Are you sure this is what he is saying?"

Thinking long and hard, she closed her eyes and replayed the words he'd even whispered to her a few hours ago. "Yes."

"It is probably something that Cary should tell you. But *ayv adanvdo* translates into my heart."

The word sounded smoother and poetic coming from the native woman, compared to how Isabel had stumbled over her broken interpretation. Hearing the meaning robbed Isabel of her breath. Her heart pounded as she tried to keep the words in perspective. Cary had never said the words to her in

English, so it was a strong possibility that he was using it like he did when he called her lovely or wife.

"It seems as if you and my son are getting on well." Sunny held her cup sandwiched between her palms.

"We are finding our way." It had only been a few days since they married, even though they were going on three weeks of knowing each other. She was trying to keep everything in perspective.

"Good to hear." With a nod, Sunny continued on her path out of the kitchen.

Over the next twenty minutes, Isabel completed the breakfast. She placed a towel over the high stack of flapjacks. A bowl of scrambled eggs sat on the stove, with the tin of sausages on top to keep them both warm. It would be at least another hour before Cary and his father came in for their morning meal. She wrapped two sausages in cakes for herself and folded them into a linen napkin. She would eat them on the way to town. At the front door, she grabbed her bonnet from the hook. She fit it on the tight coil of hair at the top of her head then tied it beneath her chin. When that was done, she picked up her satchel with her books and journal that she'd brought down from beside her wardrobe.

She stepped out onto the porch to find Sunny sitting there with her eyes closed. Isabel wasn't sure if she was sleeping or praying. She waited semi-patiently for a sign the older woman knew she was there.

Finally, when she considered calling her name, Sunny opened her eyes and looked over at her.

"Oh, good. I didn't want to disturb you, but I must get going."

Sunny looked from her bonnet to her satchel. "Where is it that you are off to before the western meadowlark flies?"

Isabel smiled. "The schoolhouse. I assist Miss Beadle with the students."

Cary's mother sat silent for a moment then asked, "What about the children? Yours and Cary's children?"

"Well, of course, they are too young to attend now. Once they are older, I will surely take them in with me." She glanced back into the house at the stairs. "I would have liked to see them this morning before I left, but they are still abed, and I need to get on my way. Do you mind terribly caring for them today?"

"They're my grand little ones. I never mind their care."

There was something in the weight of the older woman's words, but Isabel didn't have time to unpack it all. She wondered if Sunny was concerned that she would have to keep minding the children even after she and Colby moved to a house out back. To alleviate Sunny's concern, she offered her a smile. "I plan to hire someone to watch them while I am at the schoolhouse for a few hours a day. I can either take them in town to someone or the person can come here." She huffed, needing to skedaddle. "Nothing has to be decided today."

"Maybe some things."

"I am saddened I won't get to see the children when they awaken. But I will be home after the school day in time to make supper. Maybe Ama would enjoy helping me."

"Children always enjoy spending time and learning at their parents' side."

Isabel didn't know what that meant, but she was already moving down the stairs. With a wave, she was crossing the yard to the barn. Glancing over the field, she could barely make out the two big men on the other side of the field with the oxen. The area closest to the house had already been overturned and she could see the rich, dark Kansas mollisols with all its plant roots and sediment revealed from the deep tilling Cary and Colby had done. Both her pa and Cary spoke about the richness of the earth in Kansas and how it would yield some of the finest crops if someone farmed the right plot of land. This was one of the best in Grover, her husband confirmed when they lay in bed at night before sleep. Cary had big hopes for the crops they would harvest come fall.

Once she arrived at the barn, she was happy to see the wagon parked on the side and the mule inside. Silver was there too, and when she walked by his stall, she ran a hand over his muzzle. She continued to the mule who was in one of the two stalls across from the horse then grabbed the bridle on the hook beside it. Having seen Mr. Peter ready horses and wagons for her, most of her life, she had no problems getting the mule hitched to the wagon in fifteen minutes. Settled on the seat, she snapped the reins to signal to him she was ready to go. As she came past the house, she saw the children were now on the porch with Sunny. Atohi was standing at the railing and Ama was seated in her grandmother's lap.

She waved and smiled at them as she rode on. Isabel wished she'd still had a few minutes to stop and give them both hugs. The two children had had their life turned upside down in a matter of months. Not only did they lose both their parents, but they had been sent away from the only world and family they knew. Now, they were in a different state, with a different surrogate papa and mama. There was a tightness in her chest as she thought of the pain the two little ones would be feeling. However, being at the schoolhouse for so many years, she knew that children were resilient and they bounced back better than most adults.

As she rode, her mind ticked away at ideas that could help the children acclimate in Grover Town. She decided while she was in town, she'd post a letter to Greta Spencer, Holly

Morgan, Eileen Taylor, Bell Green, and Daisy Mae Dilbert. All of them had small children who weren't in the schoolhouse yet. Perhaps they all could meet once a week and let their children play together. Whomever she hired for the weekdays could shuttle Atohi and Ama to the little group. She smiled and even whistled a little to herself as she bumped along in the wagon and removed one of the flapjacks from her satchel and nibbled as she went along.

Forty-five minutes later, she was walking across the field to the schoolhouse as the bell rang, the mule and wagon at the livery until she needed them later.

The children were all laughing and waving as they rushed past her like a stampede of cattle into the school, dust kicking up behind them. When she climbed the stairs, Miss Beadle stopped pulling on the cord that rang the big copper bell on the roof about the door.

"Good morning, Miss Beadle, it is a fine day today." Isabel smiled at the older lady with silvery threads at the temples of her red hair. The woman was in her early forties and had been in Grover Town for over twenty years, teaching.

"Why, Mrs. Brown," she stared at her, her expression wide, "I'm shocked to see you here today."

"Oh, I know. Please forgive my absences the last two weeks. I hope you got my letter. My father, as you know, can be quite difficult."

"Yes. Lots of fathers don't see this as a life for their daughters. Times have not changed in the years I've taught and mentored."

Miss Beadle's words weren't anything new. Isabel had cried many times after the school day had ended, pouring out various frustrations her papa had caused in attempts at blocking her dreams of teaching.

"Very true. However, now that I'm married, Papa doesn't have a say any longer in what I do."

Freedom. Sophia had called marriage freedom, and to Isabel, the words couldn't be more appropriate as she thought about the relaxed ride in from the farm.

"And your husband? Mr. Brown is all right with it?"

Such a curious question, Isabel thought. *Why would Cary mind? He has his farm work; we will rarely see each other in the day anyway.* "He knows I like teaching."

"Well, if you're sure." The schoolmarm placed a hand on Isabel's shoulder. "I'm always eager for another set of hands and eyes to help."

"We best be getting in. I'm sure the children are wondering what is keeping us."

Miss Beadle crossed the threshold inside, and Isabel followed.

By the end of the day, she was both exhausted and energized by the time she gathered her satchel and headed for the door, the students already up and moving out the door, where Miss Beadle bid them good day. During the lunch and recess break for the children, Isabel had helped the teacher with a stack of grading papers then managed to get to the post and pen the letters to the other mothers in Grover. She also checked the employment request list there, to gather a list of names of women in need of positions. After supper, she would ask Cary to ride out with her to the different women's homes to interview their situation and if they would be best to assist with the Brown children. Before making it back to the schoolhouse, she'd stopped in at the mercantile and picked up a few candy cherry sticks to take to the children when she got back home.

"Well, I'll see you in the morning." Isabel stepped onto the small landing at the door.

"Perhaps," the teacher mumbled absently. Miss Beadle had been looking off in the distance, then she glanced at her, concern in her gaze. "I think you have someone waiting for you."

"Me?" Curious, Isabel shifted her gaze in the direction of the lone man and horse about sixty feet away from the stairs. She smiled when she recognized it was her husband.

"Thank you for your help today," she heard the woman say, but Isabel was too consumed by the big man standing next to the white stallion. Even from the distance, with his brown hat pulled low, she could feel the intensity of his stare. Her heart began to flutter, and her body heated in response. She wondered if the sight of him would always cause such a reaction in her. She prayed it would. She was truly looking forward to spending a life with such an all-consuming man.

As she drew closer, she noticed he was still dressed in his dark work pants and a blue shirt. Both were covered in dust, dirt and sweat. He hadn't taken any time to wash up and change, as if he'd left the ranch in a hurry. Since there was still so much daylight, she wondered why he was here.

When she closed the distance, she saw the austere set of his features. "Is something wrong? Are the children all right?"

"I assume you are speaking of Atohi and Ama...they are fine, wife." Cary's tone was flat, controlled, giving nothing away.

"Oh. Is it Sunny or Colby...my parents?" They weren't touching, but standing so close to him, where she normally could feel his heat, now it felt as if there was a wall between them. It concerned her. She admitted to herself she was just getting to know her husband and grow accustomed to all his moods, but something seemed out of sorts with him.

"Everyone at our home is fine. I've heard nothin' to cause

alarm concernin' the Reynolds' household." He was still staring at her, not touching her, not smiling.

Her heart started to sink. She swallowed and licked her bottom lip, her mouth feeling suddenly dry. "What is it?"

"We'll discuss the matter at home." He took a step back, to the side of Silver.

She glanced over at the magnificent horse and noticed even Silver's head was turned away from her, as if he knew something serious was going on. Wracking her brain, she could not come up with a single issue.

"Um, all right." She started around him. "I'll just go get the wagon from the livery and meet—"

He caught her wrist, halting her steps. "Pa already took it back to the farm. You'll ride with me."

Cary took her satchel from her shoulder then secured it to the saddle. In a flash, his large strong hands were at her waist. then he was lifting her onto the big horse. "Straddle it," he commanded.

Once she'd followed his orders, he swung up behind her in the long saddle. He took up the reins with one hand, holding it loose as he wrapped the forearm of his other hand around her waist, holding her tightly to him. Without the benefit of her corset, she could feel everywhere they touched and the heat of his hand on her lower belly and his chest along her back. It was comforting, even with the strange tension she felt between them.

He spoke to Silver with a Tsalagi word that sent the horse on its way.

"Oh. Did you need the wagon today? I suppose I should've made sure you all didn't need it." She was babbling, not even sure if Cary could understand her words at the speed they galloped.

Her husband remained silent.

She was sure that instead of it taking the normal forty-five minutes or so to get from town to the house, they had made it in half the time. With the pressure of his leg on the side of Silver, Cary directed the horse around the back of the house, skirting their property. She could see the sticks that had been hammered in the ground, marking the area for the foundation of the small house planned for Colby and Sunny. They kept going, not stopping at the barn, but Cary drove them into the forest before he slowed Silver to a trot.

Having the dense trees around them and surmising their destination, her heart kicked up in beat. She recalled the last time Cary had brought her there. It was days ago, their wedding night. They'd made passionate love under the stars and with the heat of the sun on them. For a moment, when he ordered Silver to a stop, in the clearing before the river, she hoped all the intensity and rush was due to her husband needing her physically.

However, once he was down and reaching up to her, she could clearly see the tension around his mouth and hard steel of his gray eyes. Whatever was going to happen here, her husband had not brought her for a passionate rendezvous.

Cary smacked Silver's flank and the horse took off back through the trees in the direction of the barn and front of the house. Her husband walked over to the bank and stood staring out at the river.

"Cary, talk to me." She came up alongside him.

He took in a deep breath and let it out slowly before he turned to face her. "*Unitsi* isn't here to be our nursemaid."

His words would not have shocked her more if he'd yelled at her instead of speaking in the calm, controlled voice he used.

"Of course, your ma is not here to care for the children. I only needed her to watch them for a few days, until I can hire someone permanent. I have names." She made a gesture toward her satchel that was still strapped to the horse. Isabel didn't see Sunny as malicious, but perhaps she had not told Cary the whole story.

"Someone permanent?" He arched a brow. "That is what *we* are."

"Yes. But during the day while you are tending to the farm and I am at the schoolhouse, we will need someone to be with them."

"You and the schoolhouse, Isabel. It seems the only thing you can see. The only thing you care about."

"That's not true." She closed the gap between them and placed a hand on the side of his face. "I care about you and Atohi and Ama."

"There's no proof of that in your actions." He stepped back from her touch.

Now, she was angry. This felt like the old argument with her father. "Because I want to teach? What is so wrong with that?"

"Because you *chose* to leave the children to work with others with not a moment of consideration about your actions."

"I told you I did consider. I thought about hiring help for them all the way into town. I even took time during my lunch to collect names. I thought we," she made a gesture between them, "would ride out to a couple of them after supper. If none were to our liking, I would draft an announcement for the position and post it in town."

He growled. Literally, growled. "Will you do the same for our children? The ones you birth? Hire someone to be their mother? Nurse them."

She gasped. "No!" She tossed her hands up at her sides. "The thought is ridiculous. I'll be everything for our children."

There was a heaviness in her lower belly, and she wondered if even now she was carrying a babe.

Folding his arms over his chest, he stood there, staring at her. Finally, he spoke, his voice low. "Then why wouldn't you do the same for my nephew and niece? Two children who have lost everything, who have no need of formal school, but of something greater. Love. Our love. They're our children."

And it struck her. She lowered her gaze to the ground before her feet as her guilty conscience rained down onto her shoulders. She could understand everything now. Her mistake. Ama and Atohi were her children, and she'd left them. Not in the care of someone ill equipped to tend to them, no...but she was now their mother, and she'd rushed away to get to the schoolhouse because it was what she wanted. Her eyes began to burn as she remembered how liberated she had felt riding away from the farm. Her life had changed in many ways over the last few days, but she had not. Even her own mother had tried for years to warn her about her stubborn determination.

"I'm sorry," she whispered, squeezing her fist an attempt to keep control of her emotions that were welling up.

When Cary didn't respond, she lifted her head. He was still standing before her, his hands now on his hips, his thumbs shoved into his pockets. "Why didn't you talk to me, Isabel?"

The real truth was that she didn't think she had to. However, she was afraid those words would hurt him, so instead she offered another. "Maybe a part of me thought you'd forbid it. That you would see my love of teaching as trivial."

He shook his head. "A person's dreams are never silly. Sometimes, you just have to consider another way of doin' it."

She felt shaky inside, as she realized that today had been her last day in the schoolhouse.

It wasn't until she felt Cary's touch on her face that she realized a tear had escaped from her eye and was rolling along her cheek. He used his thumb and brushed it away gently.

Reaching up, she cupped his hand at her face. "I won't teach anymore. I promise."

Pulling her in his arms, he held her. "Not in the day, especially if the children cannot be there yet. But there's an announcement in town; you still can help adults learn to read and write."

She sniffed. "Yes. One night a week before supper."

"How safe is it for you doing that?" He caressed her along her back.

"Rachel used to ride with me, just in case it was dark when I was leaving. Deputy Nelson is there also, to ensure there are no issues."

Leaning away from her, he stared into her eyes. "How about I meet you in town and ride back home with you. We can talk to Ma and Pa about tendin' to the children that one night."

Her heart lifted. "Do you mean it, Cary?"

He drew her in and kissed her softly on the lips. "Yes. I know you want to find somethin' that's yours, use your talents and all; somethin' will come about that fits you."

Giving his lips another quick kiss, she smiled, glad the disagreement was over.

"Let's go. I need to get supper started." Turning, she started toward the path to go back to the house.

"Not so fast, wife." Still holding onto her hand, Cary tugged on it.

She stopped and looked back at him. "Yes."

"There's the issue of your behavior this mornin'."

"We just settled that. I said I was sorry. I'll send a message to Miss Beadle that I won't be there any longer. I'm sure she'll not be surprised. She'd said as much when I arrived today." Isabel realized that should have been a hint.

"True. We came to an understandin' now. That doesn't remove the consequences of your actions."

"Consequences?" Her voice squeaked out of the tightness of her throat.

"Yes, love. I told you before I believed in a disciplined household."

She recalled his words the time he'd brought her to see the house. Her hands started to shake, and she rushed out the first excuse that came to mind, "B-but...we were discussing me trying to leave on the train."

"No. That had been what you'd done to raise your pa's ire. I clearly explained I had a way of dealin'."

He never said what that way was. She looked around at all the trees then back at him. "Is this when you send me to pick a switch?"

"No." Turning, he walked down the bank, pulling her along with him, until he arrived at a boulder. Cary sat down on it.

When she made a move to sit beside him, he grabbed her hips and kept her before him.

"Lift up those skirts, then place yourself across my lap. If you have on drawers, drop'em. I want that ass bare."

"Here? Now?" She stepped back from him and stared at the big man as he sat in his makeshift chair.

"If you delay, then it will be a longer event for you." He lifted an eyebrow, barely visible beneath the brim of his hat.

"How long will I have to be there?" She took another step back, wondering if she started running if she could make it to the house, even the barn, and hide.

"Until you've received your licks." He leaned forward and rested his elbows on his knees, looking too calm. "I wouldn't suggest you run. Or you'll earn yourself more."

"There will be how many now?" she asked, still not giving up on the idea of running.

"You'll get ten for every hour you were at the schoolhouse instead of being home with our little ones."

"Wait...school is from nine until two. That's fifty!"

"I see why you like teachin'; you're real good at arithmetic." He winked at her. "The amount will ensure you remember to put our family first."

"I'll remember, I promise." The flesh on her backside was throbbing and she hadn't even gotten one strike yet. She couldn't do it. She couldn't just lie over him and take the punishment. So, even though he warned her not to try to run, she grabbed two fistfuls of her skirts and hightailed it toward the house. The fancy kid boots her mama and Sophia had purchased for her were not made for running, even with the low heel. It didn't stop her from putting them to the test.

In four steps, the test failed. Not because the shoes had let her down, but because she forgot she was trying to match herself against a big man with long strides. He'd caught her before she even made it into the tree line.

"Let me go." She kicked as he held her fast to his chest. "I promise I'll do better. I won't be selfish ever again."

He ignored her rants and pleas as he carried her with ease back to the large rock. "Oh, wife. I am going to enjoy tannin' that purdy hide of yours."

"No!" she screamed when he sat then flipped her deftly over his thighs.

Her skirts were tossed up over her head in a flash as he used one of his arms to press the center of her back, to keep her layers in place.

"You may want to still your flailing before you wind up face first in the Kansas River." He chuckled.

Stopping, she stared before her. Her face was three inches or so from the ground. When she lifted a hand to move the layers of her skirts out of the way, she saw that she dangled two feet away from the water. Unlike down the embankment where they had been the other night, where there was a gradual slope into the water, here was just the giant boulder hovering on the edge. "This isn't safe, Cary."

"Not if you don't keep still." His other leg came over hers. She figured it was to keep her from pitching to her death. She felt a tug then a ripping sound. Sunshine kissed her backside.

She realized she'd just lost her drawers. Her husband took hold of her hands and fastened them together at the small of her back; she assumed with strips of her ruined undergarment.

"You are a beautiful sight, all pale, plump, and round." Cary was running his callused hand up and over her bare skin that was revealed to him.

"I really don't want this."

"That's not going to stop you gettin' it." He squeezed the supple flesh of one cheek then the other.

Hanging upside down, she was already feeling light-headed, but she didn't complain because she figured that would be the least of her problems soon.

"You ready, wife?"

"No."

It didn't matter what she said, because the first smack landed. It smarted like the dickens.

Smack. They rained down fast and hard. She tried to keep count in her head, wanted to know when it was going to be over, but the pain and heat radiating from her backside over-whelmed and confused her. She couldn't keep track; she couldn't count. If someone had asked her name at that moment, she would not have been able to tell them.

"Ah! Oohhh," she whimpered and whined as tears poured from her eyes and ran over her forehead to saturate her hair and the ground below her.

Whack. Whack. Whack. The slapping of her husband's big strong hand on her butt cheeks and the back of her thighs had her delirious. Her ears were ringing with the sound, and nothing else got past it. She didn't know if birds took flight at her screams or if coyotes were howling. The only high quavering cry she knew for sure was happening was coming out of her throat.

"It hurts! Cary...husband...Ow!" She kicked her legs, but they only pounded into the dirt; with them locked beneath his big thigh, she could not do more. One of his hands was holding hers, interlocked, and she dug her nails in it and squeezed hard, trying to cause him some amount of pain as he was inflicting on her. However, nothing stopped him.

She felt branded by him. She didn't doubt that for the rest of her life, her backside would carry his handprint, marking her ass his.

When the strikes finally ended, she became aware of the changes in her body. Even as she whimpered from the throbbing of her rear end, she also noticed that there was an ache just south of her backside. Her clit was pressed along the inside seam of Cary's breeches and the friction caused wetness to pool between her thighs. She could feel the slickness. Her unbound breasts had been swinging freely under the soft cotton of her mutton shirt, sending sparks into her nipples, now drawn tight.

Recognizing her body's response, she sniffled as fresh tears ran out her eyes. She was embarrassed. It was evident to her that her desire for Cary knew no bounds, even in this.

"Shh... *Ayv adanvdo*. It's over now." He smoothed a hand lightly over her hot, pulsing skin. He lifted her up gingerly and settled her against his chest, her knees on the sides of his hips.

She pressed her face into his neck as he caressed down her spine and back up. He had called her his heart. Even after her actions, he still thought of her in such a special way.

"I'm sorry," she whispered. She leaned into him and inhaled the sandalwood, earth, and sweat of him. Her hard-working, sexy, big husband. She thought about the places he was big and how he fit around her, inside of her. Her sex remembered his cock and how it filled her, stretching her in such a deliciously painful way.

His hands paused in stroking her hair, hanging wild and loose around her and her back. "Isabel?" he groaned.

"Yes," she sighed.

He lowered his hands to her hips and squeezed.

She hissed. The spark of pain reminded her of the pulsing flesh of her backside. It also made her aware what she had been doing. She hadn't realized that while her mind was seducing her with images of her husband's loving, she'd been grinding her sex over the closure of his breeches, where an extremely hard length was flexing under her sex.

"What's going on?"

Shielding her eyes, she lowered her lids and turned away from him. She didn't want him to see the lust she was certain would be there. "I can't."

"Tell me," he commanded as he maneuvered a hand beneath her skirts and pinched her tender skin of her backside.

"Oww." It hurt, but it didn't stop her from thrusting her hips forward. Then a second time, to feel him right where she needed him. "I'm aching," she confessed, still not looking at him.

"It's a spanking; it is supposed to ache." His hand stilled below her skirt, cupping her curves.

"No." She shook her head. "Not just there." Her voice sounded small to her own ears.

Taking her face in his hand, he used his thumb to force her gaze up. Steel gray met her pale green. He wasn't allowing her to hide from him. When his hand moved down between her thighs and slipped along her parted sex, his eyes darkened to a charcoal gray.

"Shit. Fuck. Your pussy is soaked." His eyes lit with understanding. "Do you need my cock inside you, Isabel?"

"No. We shouldn't. Not after such a punishment. It's wrong." *I am wrong*, she wanted to say as she shook her head.

"Says who?" His fingers entered her, three of them pushing deep, wide, in and out. "We're husband and wife. We say what's good and bad between us." He withdrew them then pressed his fingers on her clit.

She arched toward him and cried out as she set her forehead against his. She needed release.

"Tell me to fuck you," he ordered.

"Cary..." She stared at him, his eyes a gray blur. She was so close, but she could see the intensity there, hear the command in his words.

"Come on, love. I want to hear you beg me to put my big cock in your tight pussy until you're comin' around me, milkin' my length."

His erotic words had her core quivering with need. When he began circling her clit, she couldn't deny herself any longer. The words tumbled out of her mouth as she pleaded with him to take her.

When he began to release her hands, she shook her head. "No. Don't."

Cary's eyes darkened more at her words, almost appearing black. He worked fast, tucking her skirts below her waistband so that they both could see him unfasten his pants. Then his big, thick shaft sprang forth, and she could not hold back her whimper of need. He took her by the waist and lifted her high, so that he could stroke his crown through her wetness.

When he was there, at the heart of her womanhood, she wiggled down, not wasting any time to take him in. Her sex burned with the stretching, her knees stung from the rough surface of the boulder, but she continued, uncaring.

Once he was all the way in, his hard cock throbbing in her tight sex, she looked at him, the man she loved, who cared for her. "Kiss me."

He glanced down at her full lips then back up. He reached up and took off his hat and flung it toward the clearing somewhere; neither of them watched where it landed. His lips met hers and they brushed hers once, and then a second time, before his rough command vibrated between them, "Fuck me."

Cary cupped the back of her head and kissed her hard, taking control of her mouth. In turn, she controlled their pleasure. Too new to this, she wasn't sure what to do, but she was too much in need to argue with him. She moved on instinct, did what felt good to her, and hoped it satisfied him as well. She rode her husband, slamming down on him and rotating her hips to grind her aching clit against him.

He unbuttoned her shirt to avail himself of her breasts. His strong hands fondled them and pinched the nipples.

She cried into his mouth as the spark of heat went from her tips to her clit. It didn't take her long before she was quaking, moaning out her orgasm. However, she didn't stop. She rode it out, wanting Cary to come along with her. Squeezing and releasing her walls around his length, she pumped him.

Soon, he tightened his arms around her, holding her as he shouted his release. They sat there, on the bank of the river with their bodies humming the last bars of orgasms as dusk began to settle around them.

"We need to wash up and get back to the house." He kissed her cheek, ears, neck as he blindly worked the knots from the strips holding her hands. "I need to feed you."

"Do you think they waited on us for supper?" she asked as Cary rubbed the red markings on her wrists. She knew they were most likely caused by her pulling against him as she rode him than actual tightness of the restraints.

"Not if they know what's good for them, they didn't. Pa would have seen Silver come back and known where we were."

Her face felt hot as she blushed. "Do you think they heard us?"

Cary chuckled as he lifted her to her feet. "Love, I think the whole town heard you."

She shook her head. She didn't feel shame about enjoying the satisfaction her husband brought her, but she'd have to learn to temper her cries when others were close by.

"I wouldn't have your passion in any other way," he responded as if he could read her thoughts. Reaching up, he removed the remainder of her pins that had not been lost between the spanking and the loving.

Her hair tumbled around her shoulders to her back. "It's too much." She shoved it back over her shoulders. "It will look wild in minutes."

"I like it down. When you are home, let it stay loose." He held her gaze. It was the way he looked at her, as if she was the most beautiful woman in the world.

"Okay." Isabel was beginning to understand that in their marriage, there would be nothing of herself she would deny her husband.

Cary picked up the shreds of her bloomers before he walked them to the sloping bank at the water's edge. He used the material as a clothe to clean them both. Once their clothes were righted and they looked as presentable as two passionate lovers could, he folded his hand around hers and they headed into the trees toward the house after stopping to swoop up his hat.

"What does *u-wo-ha-li* mean. I hear your ma call you it often."

"Eagle. When I was younger, she would tell me that like the eagle, I would fly away from home. That I would fly high enough to talk to God, and he would direct me to my home. A place that was mine." He lifted her hand and kissed the back of her hand.

Her breath got caught in her chest at his words. She understood that he was saying she was his home. She fought away tears at the awe that filled her heart. After only a few days, he was becoming her home...her world.

That night after they had filled their bellies, Cary taught Atohi how to play checkers. After two games, they all sat in the living room. Atohi sat beside her, while Ama curled up in Cary's lap in the chair. She smiled at the painting over the cold hearth of their house, with Silver grazing before it. Sophia had done a marvelous job on it; she loved the wedding gift.

"Tell us a story," Atohi bid.

"Me?" Cary clarified as he nodded toward his mother knitting on the couch beside Colby, who was reading a copy of the Farmer's Almanac. "*Enisi* tells a better fable."

Sunny looked at him but remained silent as she went back to her work.

"*Edutsi* tell story." Ama banged on Cary's chest then rested her ear against it.

Isabel could see in Cary's eyes what she understood; Ama missed her papa and she liked to listen to the rumble of Cary's voice, most likely to remind her of Garmin.

"Okay. I will tell you all of *A New Bow for Tani*." Cary wrapped his arms tighter around his niece as Ama closed her eyes and settled in against him.

Isabel's heart ached for the little one, even as it swelled with thoughts of Cary one day holding their child in his arms and telling them stories that had been passed down through his people.

Her husband began, "Tani was a small Cherokee lad who lived during the great Hundred Year War..."

ELEVEN

Cary loved this time of morning, an hour before dawn when the world was silent. He lay on his back with one hand behind his head as he felt the final threads of the night's coolness settle around him before the heat of the day stole it away. Nothing made this time of day better than his wife's pretty, full, red lips wrapped around his cock. Her ardent mouth was hot and wet as she glided him deeper and sucked him harder. Over their last two months of marriage, she'd become skilled in providing him oral pleasure, as she'd flourished in many ways of taking pleasure.

He dug his fingers deeper into her thick auburn hair, tugging it just the way she liked. She rewarded him with a moan that vibrated along his shaft and into his balls, drawing them tighter. At this rate, he wasn't going to last much longer. He loved it. She'd continued to keep her hair down when they were home and only pinned it up when they rode into town. On their land, his proper wife had become free in expressing herself. She'd loved on the children, taught them; Atohi was already starting to read under her tutelage and Ama was blossoming, smiling, and laughing more, and loving being in the kitchen alongside Isabel.

His lovely wife took time daily with his mother to learn the language and history of their people. She took notes, jotted it down and allowed them to review it for accuracy. Seeing her talent and instinct when it came to telling other people's stories gave him an idea. One he'd already put into motion. Today, they had a few surprise appointments in town.

"Shit," he groaned as the head of the sensitive crown of his cock brushed over her soft palate and bumped the back of her throat. When she made a swallowing motion and clenched around the head, his cock hardened more, swelling, ready to explode.

"*U-dal-ii*," he was panting as he arched his hips up, pushing a little further before retreating.

She let his cock pop out of her mouth as she gazed up at him, her pale eyes barely seen in the shadows of the morning.

"Yes, *u-ye-hi*. Do you want me to stop, my husband?" Her wicked tongue flicked over the tip right along the responsive opening. It jerked in her hand, dancing away from her teasing mouth.

"Fuck, don't stop." He wasn't sure how his mind had even formulated a response, let alone gotten his mouth to function beyond the growls that came clawing up from his throat.

She giggled before she claimed his cock again with her mouth. This time she hollowed out her cheeks and sucked him hard, with vigor.

He couldn't take it, both of his hands were on her now, cupping her face. Not to stop her, but to feel every movement of her mouth as she pushed him into his second climax that had him bucking and seeing stars in the morning. She licked and drank in every drop of his thick release.

As his body still quaked through the remaining threads of

release, he pulled her up to his chest. Her plush breasts and curvy body lay bare and soft on his. He ran his thumb over her mouth, now blood red from her exertion.

"Morning," she sighed, as if she'd gained as much pleasure from her deed as he had.

He kissed her and tasted the mixture of him on her tongue that blended with her essence on his. They stayed that way for the moment, kissing and caressing in the dark. He wanted to roll her to her back, slide inside of her or taste her again until she was coming for the third time on his tongue.

Finally, it was that moment in his day where he had to set his beautiful wife away from him and start his day.

"I always feel guilty that you have to get up so early while I get to laze around for another hour or so in bed."

"Don't." He kissed along her neck, over her breasts with their large nipples, where he paused to draw one into his mouth. He loved the way her breath caught in her throat and she palmed the back of his head. She had always been sensitive here, but over the last few weeks, they had become even greater. Releasing her full mounds, he continued down to her navel. He had to stop there, for if he went any further, he would wind up late meeting his father, fucking his wife for the second time that morning. Her body smelled deliciously of roses, sandalwood, and sex. He loved it. He loved her.

He slid his body to the edge of the bed before rising and staring down at her. "I like thinking of you in this bed like a bare goddess. It makes me imagine I can turn around at any moment and join you, slip between your thighs and bury myself inside of you."

She moaned and writhed on the sheets as her gaze traveled over his body.

His dick started to swell again. He groaned and stepped back twice from the bed. His wife was too tempting. Across the room, he filled the bowl on the washstand with water from the pitcher. He scrubbed his face, then used the tooth powder before utilizing the rest of the water to wash up.

When he turned around, his wife was asleep once again. That was happening more often over the last month. He found her asleep in the oddest of places; even his mother had commented about it. Isabel had said it was all the energy she used keeping up with the children. However, his mother advised him to take her to the clinic soon.

It was one of the things he planned to do that day. After he dressed, he pulled a piece of vellum from her satchel and a pencil and wrote her a note about taking her to an early supper at Drummonds' in town before she had her tutorial session that day. He'd go out and check the field, water the germination stage of the crop, and then work some with his father on the small house before taking his wife into town.

After placing the note on the small stand beside the bed, he took a moment to brush her lustrous hair from her face then left.

"YOU AND MR. BROWN are newly married. The changes of a new life can be exhausting at times." Doc Clarkston squatted down beside the table where Isabel sat in one of his clinic rooms, dressed only in her chemise, as he checked her toes. He moved his examination up to her ankles and calves, asking her if she noticed any pain or swelling.

"No. Nothing."

Cary watched the doctor rise and move around Isabel, checking her in various places, shoulders, spine, arms, and hands. The man then used a light instrument to check her eyes and mouth before listening to her heart with a stethoscope. Cary had been glad the physician was in when they got into town. When he told his wife on the way in that they would stop in and see the doctor after supper, she balked, telling him that she was all right. She said she'd just worn herself out spending time with the kids and farm life, that she would adjust soon.

He would have believed her words if not for his mother. Sunny was convinced that his wife was breeding. Since he didn't have any experience with pregnant women, he would take his mother at her word. However, he figured his wife would need to hear it from a doctor to be persuaded, the reason they were there.

"What other things are you experiencing?"

"I'm hungry all the time."

"Mm-hm." Doc Clarkston instructed her to lie back. The man then walked his hands over her stomach and asked about any tenderness.

"No," she responded as he went.

It fascinated Cary to think about all the things doctors would know about a person's body simply by touching them.

When the doctor got to Isabel's lower abdomen, he rolled over the area slow, pausing at times and pressing. "How are your menses?"

Isabel blushed, redness moving from her neck and flooding her face, competing with the color of her full lips. She glanced away. "Um...fine and regular since I was ten and two."

"When was your last flow?" Doc Clarkston still palpated along her abdomen.

"A few weeks...last month..."

When his wife's words broke away, and she glanced back at the doctor, Cary realized what had not dawned on him, even though his mother had told him weeks ago that Isabel was pregnant. His wife had not had her woman's flow in the nine weeks they had been married. Enjoying loving his wife night and day, it had not crossed his mind that something was askew. To himself, he chalked it up to not knowing a single thing about it. In his adult life, as a single man, he'd visited places that cater to pleasure activities of the flesh. There was always another whore if a certain one wasn't available, or young widows in towns could discreetly decide not to entertain men during those times.

"When do you recall your last flowing?" the doctor questioned when Isabel fell silent. Doc Clarkston held a hand toward her and assisted her in sitting up.

Isabel's brow creased as she considered. "The week before Cary and I married."

Doc nodded then glanced at him. "Describe your wife's breasts, Mr. Brown. Specifically, if there have been any changes to them."

His wife gasped.

Cary stepped from the wall and rose to his full height, eyeing the man directly. The doctor was almost as big and tall as he was, but Cary had a couple inches over him. He wasn't sure why the doctor was asking such a personal question; however, he was willing to give the medical man the benefit of the doubt...for a moment anyway. "They seemed to be a bit bigger and tender...you know, around the tips."

"Just as I expected." Doc Clarkston glanced at Isabel, who was even more red faced. "What's going on with you, Mrs. Brown, is that I'm fairly positive your pregnant."

"What?" Isabel wasn't looking at the doctor but at him. His wife's eyes were stretched wide and they began to fill with water as she whispered, "A baby?"

Crossing the small area, Cary stepped to the other side of

her as the doctor picked up a board with some paper attached and began jotting things down.

With his arms around his wife's shoulders, he smiled. "Guess Ma was right."

She smiled up at him, her pale green gaze filled with wonder. "*Unitsi* suspected this? She said nothing to me."

"Are you happy, *udalii*? I know we already have Atohi and Ama. Will this be too much for you?" He caressed the wisps of hair at the back of her neck that always refused the restrictions of her simple coiffure.

"I love our children, just as I will love all the others who come along." She set a hand on her stomach.

"Mrs. Brown, I'll need you back in a few weeks. I should be able to get a better impression of how far along you are." The doctor eyed them both for a moment, his expression serious before he headed toward the closed door.

"Is there somethin' you're not saying, Doc?" Cary kept an arm around his wife but faced off with the man.

The doctor shook his head. "I'm not one to judge anyone's relationships. Or how they conduct themselves before marriage."

Cary frowned. He stepped away from Isabel, shielding her. "I'm not sure I like what you're gettin' at, Doc."

Seeming unfazed, the doctor held his gaze. "Mr. Brown, you and your wife have been married barely over two months. From her report of her last cycle, she could at the most, by calculations, be six weeks along. However, the impression of her uterus could already be felt from the outside. That usually doesn't happen until weeks later, around ten, maybe twelve, weeks. I'm goin' to say this plain, with no offense or censor intended. You all had to be together before the wedding and perhaps Mrs. Brown has her menses time mixed up. She feels further along. I'll do a more internal check in a few weeks, when there's less risk."

Cary felt the growl as it caused his words to come out broken, fierce. "My wife was a virgin when we married, and it wasn't until our weddin' night that we were together physically. I don't take too kindly when someone puts shadows on her reputation."

The doctor remained calm. "If that's true, then there's a medical anomaly happening inside your wife. You're a big man, Mr. Brown, but a single babe at seven weeks can't be that large."

"What about two?"

Isabel's soft voice came between them and calmed his agitation where the man's words had gotten him riled.

They both looked back at her, but it was Doc Clarkston who spoke first. "That would be a sure cause. Why would you suspect that possibility?"

His wife looked at him and grinned.

Seeing her smile, eased a lot of the tension in his shoulders. Cary smiled at his wife even though there was still sadness in his heart. "I'm a twin. My brother was the father of the two children my wife and I now raise."

"Ah. Yes. My wife told me about the mother and young children's circle your wife has created," Doc Clarkston declared on an exhale. "Multiple birth would cause the rapid growth and elevated signs in the mother. So, we will keep a close eye on you, Mrs. Brown. I'll leave you a moment for privacy to dress."

When the doctor left the room, Cary pulled his wife into his arms, holding her firmly to his chest. "Twins. Damn. You all right, love?"

"Yes." She held him tight around his torso and buried her face in his chest. She inhaled deeply and he could feel the tightness leave the muscles of her back where he touched. "I'm apprehensive, but if your ma could do it and she is half my size, then I should be fine. Right?"

Leaning back, he touched her chin and tilted her face up to his. He stared down into her luminous green gaze. "Yes. You're goin' to be fine. You're my heart, Isabel. *G-v-ge-yu.*"

Her breath caught in her throat, and those eyes that had been cloudy with concern at the doctor's news now glistened with fresh tears. "*Gvgeyu.* I love you, too."

He lowered his mouth to hers and kissed her deeply but pulled away in moments before his body got other ideas. This wasn't the time or place. She was clutching his shirt at the sides, and feeling her need made it hard for him to put a halt to their desire. "Come on, so we can get you dressed and give the doc his room back."

A few minutes later, they exited the room to find the Doc standing behind his own wife and whispering something in her ear that made her giggle. She was adding Isabel's name to a large slate mounted to the wall of the clinic.

"What's with the board?" Cary asked.

The doc and his wife turned toward them. The missus appearing flushed and extremely swollen in the middle.

"It's where I place the visits my husband needs to handle. Isabel's name is up here, but I won't officially put her on rotation until Doc says it's not safe for her to ride into town."

"With two babes, your wife is high risk and will need to stick close to home earlier than most pregnant women. So, I'll make my rounds then," the doctor clarified.

Cary nodded.

"Twins. Such exciting news. A double blessing." Elizabeth Clarkston's eastern accent laced her words as she waddled across the area to Isabel with a wide smile on her face.

"Very much a blessing." Isabel accepted the woman's

embrace, a little awkward around Elizabeth's protruding stomach.

"Do you have time for tea? Now that I'm confined to the house, I don't get to see many people besides Eileen, my sister-in-law. But she just gave birth a few months back and she's had her hands full since returning back to her shop. I'm lonely."

"Well..." Isabel glanced over at him.

"I've got an errand to run in town. You can hang out here. I should be back shortly."

His wife's sexy red lips pulled back in a smile, and for a moment he was transfixed and couldn't help but recall those lips on him that morning.

"Great. If you need a little more time, just meet me at the schoolhouse."

"You sure?" he asked. Now that they had confirmation of her pregnancy, he wanted to keep her close.

"Yes. The deputy will be there. So, take your time."

He leaned down and kissed his wife's cheek. "Doc, you mind walkin' me out?"

"Not at all." The physician set down a journal that he'd been scribbling notes in.

Cary assumed it had to do with Isabel, which was perfect, because he had a lot of questions for the man that he didn't want to ask around Isabel. He didn't want to worry her.

The two women headed through a door that led into the Clarkston home, while he and the doctor went out the clinic door.

TWELVE

"Gracious. I need to get going." Isabel set the teacup and saucer onto the table as she rose from the chair in the Clarkston's front room. "Do you need help cleaning things up?"

"No, no. I'll take care of it. I need things to do in this house." Elizabeth pushed herself up from the couch in a graceless, wobbly manner, so out of character for the proper and fashionable woman who ran the town's etiquette school.

Isabel smiled. Soon the babies would be here. With the two children she and Cary already had, it would give her plenty to occupy her time.

This woman was a business owner and a wife, soon to be a mother. Elizabeth had found a way to balance her independence with her family life.

For that, Isabel enjoyed the hour she'd spent talking with her. Isabel had confessed to her that now that she'd discovered she was pregnant, she would soon have to let go the last cord of her autonomy. Teaching had been hers, something she was good at and it saddened her that it would end soon. Cary had been supportive, after they'd had a bottom warming conversation, but she knew there were babies coming, and there would be no way for her to continue...not right now. Possibly not ever. She knew Miss Beadle would pick up the one night a week once Isabel had to let it go.

"Thank you again for all the advice." She moved to Elizabeth and embraced her before her mind stared down a road that would make her emotional again.

"Please come anytime." Elizabeth escorted her to the door.

With her satchel on her shoulder, Isabel headed toward the schoolhouse. She thought about the babies growing inside of her and the new life that she'd had over the weeks with Cary, and it made her heart sing. She loved the man, and he was always kind to her. He listened to her and talked to her about the farm. Things were going well.

When she arrived at the building, she was almost at the stairs before she noticed that Deputy Nelson wasn't waiting for her on the steps as his usual habit. He now only stayed with her until Cary arrived, then Nelson would head in to the sheriff's office. His horse wasn't hitched out front, either. There was only one horse out there. She didn't recognize who the horse belonged to. She wasn't early but running a minute or so late. She glanced behind her to see if Robert was coming up, but beyond the road headed back to this end of town was barren. Adding to that fact was the schoolhouse sat some distance back from the main throughway, to give the children space to run and play at recess without worrying about someone rushing by with a wagon or horse would make them unsafe. With the train station and so many busier establishments down on the other end of town, it was quiet. She never realized how desolate it seemed when others were not around.

Figuring that the deputy would be here soon, and Cary after that, as her husband's mysterious errand should be complete by now, she continued up the stairs. If someone had come to learn, she'd teach them.

When she got inside, she saw a familiar figure taking up the space at the last desk. She smiled to herself, seeing that the grumpy man had returned. It happened often that a man would find that their pride and embarrassment were keeping them from the thing they wanted most, freedom from their ignorance. She continued up the side aisle; the entrance was on the other side, away from him, so she went to the desk and laid her things on the chair then faced hm.

"Welcome back. I hadn't seen you in some time, and I was starting to think you weren't going to give the tutoring another try." She smiled as she walked down the center aisle, trying to put the man at ease.

He shrugged. Once again, he kept his hat on and it obscured his features. "Where's all ya men?"

Her smile waivered a little, not liking that he referred to the other hands that came to learn as *her* men. "Well, I'm sure they will be along soon. Or perhaps, something has kept them tonight." She shrugged this time but forced her lips into a bigger grin. "However, once most have learned enough to continue on their own, they don't have to keep coming."

She hoped hearing this would encourage the man.

"Guess it's just us this evenin'."

"I didn't get your name last time."

He was silent for a long moment, during which time she could feel his gaze on her. It moved from her face down to her shoes, almost inappropriate in the way he stared. He was at her breasts so long, she wished for her corset. His stare made her stomach fill with uncomfortable emotions from her past. She was back in the schoolhouse and too young to be budding and getting glances that made her ashamed. A feeling Cary had never incited when he looked at her with tenderness or even passion.

"Um. Mister..."

"Luther." His dark eyes were bright when lifted to her face again.

She wasn't sure if it was his first or last name, but she'd treat it properly as she did the other men.

"Well, Mr. Luther, since it may be just us tonight. I wondered if you wouldn't mind doing a little reading for me, so I can hear where we need to start to help you best." She took the opportunity to go back to the desk, to place some distance between them for a moment. Taking longer than needed, she pulled out the things from her satchel then chose one of her beginner books. She took a deep breath and refused to allow herself to be intimidated. The man was just rough around the edges, nothing new. He'd come back, so he wanted to learn.

When she started back to turn, she caught a piece of paper folded on the desk. It wasn't completely closed, as if it had been open and then haphazardly closed again. She reached for it, expecting it to be from one of the other men, explaining their absence. Instead, she saw the signature on the bottom of the short note was from the deputy.

MRS. BROWN,

Emergency outside of town. Had to assist the sheriff. Cancel the class. I'll meet you next week.

Deputy R. Nelson

HER HEART SANK, and her skin felt tight with apprehension. Robert wasn't coming to offer his presence. Even though she'd only had one rowdy student a year ago, who had gotten into a fight with another man that had to do with a woman they both were seeing and not her lesson, still, having the deputy there always brought a calm. Now, she could feel the uneasiness building inside of her.

Cary, please come soon.

She knew that her husband would think Deputy Nelson was here and there was no urgency to arrive before the end of her session, but she silently prayed that he would come earlier rather than later. With the book in hand, she turned and discovered Luther was standing a few feet away from her instead of at the back desk. So caught up in her own thoughts, she hadn't heard him move.

"Oh. Mr. Luther. There was no need for you to come to the desk. I was going to bring the book back to you." Her grip tightened on the book, hoping to still the tremors.

"Guess it's just us tonight." He repeated his earlier words, but having his burly presence so close to her now brought an eeriness to the room. It was at that moment, seeing his full height and his style of dress, with the leather vest and worn chaps over his dark clothes, she realized his had been the stranger at the wedding.

"Yes. Seems so. Others may still come. So, if you'll take your seat again, we can get started and not keep either of us here long." She gestured toward the seats, mentally prodding him to go.

"Heard there was a body found out on vacant land by the Spencer Ranch. Reckon his workers is out helpin' the lawmen." He offered her information on the whereabouts of the deputy and the regulars who came to her tutoring.

Even more dread filled her heart, sending icicles through her blood. Her fingers felt numb. She wondered if he had something to do with the person's death but shoved it away. "Well, the sheriff is smart. He's kept us all safe for many years; he and his men will figure it out."

He chuckled, hoarse, rough.

An odd response to someone's life ending, she thought. "Let's get to the lesson." She waved her arm again toward the seat.

"First time I come here, I noticed you was a purty gal, Miss Reynolds."

"It's Brown. Mrs. Brown." She raised her chin, looking him square in his dark eyes. She would not be intimidated.

His guffaw came out rough and taunting. "Ya got a body and comely mouth made for thangs. Thangs a man can't help dreamin' 'bout."

She stepped back. "Evidently, you're not here to learn, sir. So, let's not waste either of our time." She used the same stern tone as if she were speaking to a disobedient or bully pupil.

When he took a step, she side-stepped, not wanting to get trapped with the desk at her back.

"Cain't believe you'd let that redskin, a savage, under your skirts."

Gasping, she shot him a hard look. Cary had explained about the derogatory things people and kids, even his pa's family, had said about his ma and him and his brother, but hearing it cut deep, a painfilled cut in her core. "This conversation is not appropriate. That man is my husband. I think it's time you leave, Mr. Luther."

He turned his head and spat on the floor.

Bile rose in the back of her throat and she had to swallow twice to choke it back down.

He stepped closer, closing in and surrounding her with a vile cloud of tobacco, sweat, male must, and dirt. Not the rich earth sent of soil that her Cary always came home from working in the fields smelling like, blended with the leftover traces of sandalwood. No, this man smelled like the grime of dirt was caked in his very soul—a malicious decay.

Grabbing her satchel, she quickly shoved the books back

in. "Better yet. I will leave." She made a move to pass him and head toward the side aisle.

She'd almost made it to the end of the second row of chairs before he grabbed her arm. He gripped her arm in a tight hold and snatched her back into stumbling steps. She could feel the heat of his body along her side, as he stared down into her face.

"Ah! No! Get your hands off me." She raised her voice as she leaned back from him and struggled to pull her arm away.

His clutch held, tightened to a painful level as his meaty fingers dug into her flesh.

"Ya ain't too good to let some injun fuck you like a squaw, but ya stop a decent man getting' 'tween your thick, purty thighs," he hissed, then growled.

"Get off me!" She shoved at him, tried to pull away as she started to realize just how dangerous this man was. She thought about the two babes she carried in her stomach and struggled with more determination to get far from him.

As she fought him, he chuckled, a sick, low sound. He grabbed at her skirts and began yanking fistfuls of it up. "I saw ya liked it rough. Hard. On land your pa should have given to a white man. That's al'ight, Luther goin' show ya he can give it better than some redskin."

"Get your filthy hands off me!" She wasn't having it; her free palm connecting against the side of the man's face resounded in the room. Her strike was so hard, her palm stung, and it snapped Luther's head to the side and knocked his hat off, revealing dark, oily hair.

He didn't let her go. Instead, he responded by slamming her against the wall.

The impact knocked the air from her lungs when her back struck the wood.

"Oh, yeah. We goin' play real rough. I ain't got no rope to

tie ya like you like, but we'll make do." He grabbed one of her breasts and squeezed. Excruciating pain shot through her chest.

Isabel gritted her teeth and tried to stifle the cry that came up. She realized that this man had been around their property. He'd seen her loving her husband months ago, on the rock in the afternoon sun. She wondered how long he'd been stalking them, following her. It made her sick to hear his words, not because she'd freely loved her husband in the open, but because this despicable man tried to soil what they had.

She wasn't going to let him taint the goodness and passion she found in her husband's arms, his heart. When Luther kicked one of her feet out, she didn't waste a second. She brought her other leg up quick and high, kneeing him between the legs as she aimed for his balls. She tried to unman him.

"F'uuuck! Shee-it!" he groaned and cupped his crotch.

His hand slackened just enough on her arm for her to shove away and make a run for it. Her boots clacked and smacked loud on the worn wood floor as she made her escape. She burst through the front door, hell bent on seizing her freedom and hauling it to town. The man was so hefty, she figured if she lifted her skirts and ran, she could outrun him.

She never made it to the first step before she was yanked by a fist in her hair. Pins dug into her scalp as his fierce grasp burrowed them deep.

"You bitch! I'll teach ya some manners," he taunted.

"Luther, let go of me!" she screamed at the top of her lungs as she swung and kicked at him.

"Woo...wo! Woo...wo! Woooooo..."

If she was ever asked to describe a Cherokee war cry, it would be the sound she heard coming from her husband as he ran full speed across the lot toward them. A fierce, soul-roaring shout that shook the air like rolling thunder and sent animals and humans scurrying.

RED. Cary saw red as bright as the blood he wanted to watch streaming from the man who dared touch his wife. His heart. His legs pumped as his feet pounded; long strides ate up the land between them as he rushed toward the schoolhouse.

He'd been delayed longer than he had anticipated as he'd met with Mayor Sneads, who'd been in a longer meeting with the judge, in town from Topeka to handle a few cases. By the time the two men had walked out of the mayor's office, with the judge saying he'd stay in town a few days longer to see if they discovered the person connected to a man found dead that day on Mr. Reynolds' vacant field. Cary recalled that place would have been where he'd have settled if he had turned down the offer to marry Isabel. A foolish decision, he now knew, if he'd have taken it.

He knew his time was limited, because he'd need to get to his wife at the schoolhouse before her session ended so that Deputy Nelson could get to work. Over the last several weeks, the three of them had fallen into a routine around Isabel's sessions. She'd drive herself there, where she'd meet the deputy who'd be there while she taught people, mostly cowboys and field hands, and he'd ride Silver after his workday to meet her and escort her home. He and Isabel would need to talk, because now that they had confirmed the pregnancy and discovered she was most likely carrying two, it wasn't safe for her to travel alone to town. She wouldn't like it, but soon she'd have to stop the tutoring sessions. It was why he'd spoken with the mayor; it was time for his wife to see she had other talents that would give her the self-sufficiency and independence she craved.

The mayor had wholeheartedly agreed to give Isabel the position of Grover Town Historian. Mayor Sneads stated that since Grover had grown exponentially in the last seven years, and explosively with the trains arrival, it had been on his mind to advertise for someone to get down stories and the history of the diverse townsfolk for posterity's sake. Sneads would even allow her to use an office in town. Next year, after the babies were born, he would order a printing press for her to record the information in a more permanent fashion and hire a few staff.

Cary had left the meeting feeling good, excited to share the news with his wife on the way home. Perhaps they'd celebrate after they tucked the children into bed by him placing kisses all over her luscious, curvy body until she came on his tongue.

Now his mind went blank as he turned the corner and saw Isabel screaming and fighting on the stairs. The only thing he could think or see were the two figures before him. He felt the presence of all his ancestors who preceded him fill his blood and *Unetlanvhi* give him speed of flight. He saw himself as *Uwohali,* the eagle his mother had always seen marked within him from birth, sure flight in his attack to rescue his mate and devour his enemy.

The man Isabel had screamed at, tagging him as Luther, released his hold on her hair at Cary's war cry. However, the piece of shit made the mistake of stepping before Isabel as if he would keep Cary from his wife.

"I've wanted this chance, redskin—"

Cary's fist connected with the man's face and he felt the crunch of bone under his knuckles.

"Aww... Fuck!" Luther grabbed his nose but squared off

against him. He stepped forward and beckoned him with bloody fingers of one hand, dirt caked around the other. "Come on!"

Silent, crouching low, Cary circled him and waited. He knew he was going to kill this man. He'd violated what was his with his filthy hands. Luther wasn't any different than the bullies in the play yard of his youth, but unlike them, he wouldn't show this man any mercy.

People hearing the commotion came from various places, starting to gather around them.

He and the desperado were equally matched in size, except Luther's brawn was just as wide across his middle, a clear indication the man was strong but lazy. Luther shifted and side-stepped, trying to keep Cary in his sights. It was the wrong move, because the shuffle took him away from Isabel, still on the stairs with both her hands covering her lower belly, where their children lay.

Cary launched at the man with fists of fury.

Luther swung, fighting back, but his blows grazed off Cary's shoulders or chin. Cary was coming at him too fast, too hard, and striking at the man's eyes and mouth. Spit and teeth flew, but Cary didn't stop.

When Luther's foot swept out and kicked Cary in the calf, he stumbled back and landed on one knee.

Luther blinked away blood and sweat then lunged his big body toward him. Acting fast, Cary shifted his weight to his knee and placed a supporting hand on the ground and kicked out. The heel of his boot caught the other man right in his gut. When Luther folded over, Cary rose and went for the man, encircling his meaty neck with his hands. His steps and the struggling man attempting to move back from his grip as he clawed at Cary's wrists and hands, propelled them toward the side of the schoolhouse.

People were scrambling and kicking up dust around them as Cary continued to hold.

"Come now, son, turn the man loose." Mr. Reynolds, his father-in-law, who must have been called from his property management office in town and notified of what was going on, gave Cary's arm a tug as he spoke.

Even as much as he cared about the man's opinion of him, it wasn't more than Cary cared for the man's daughter.

"Cary, please." Isabel's voice met his ears. She was the only one he cared about, but it was the assault on her that fueled his fury and would not allow him to release the man.

It was his job to protect her, keep her safe, and today he had failed. He had made the mistake of trusting someone else, even a deputy, with her care, and it had backfired on him, allowing this man to put his hands on her. His mind flooded with thoughts of what could have happened to her, to his two unborn children. Even as he continued to keep a firm grip on the man's throat, Cary could feel the quakes in his core as the fear of those thoughts rested there.

"Hell, CB, if I'd known you were giving me an open invitation to join a fight, not farmin', maybe I'da been here sooner." The brown face of his friend came into view a foot away from Luther's purple one.

He'd sent Rufus a wire a month ago, lettin' him know the job on his farm was open-ended whenever he wanted to stop working the rail line and come.

Rufus didn't attempt to stop him from choking the man; instead, he pulled one of his forever matchsticks out of his shirt pocket and put it in his mouth.

Cary kept both hands around the man's throat, wanting to feel Luther's life slip from his body. It was only in Hell that putrid scum as the likes of this asshole would get what they deserved.

"Cary, don't." Isabel's whimpers reached him, even through all the crowd that was gathered now at the schoolhouse. However, this degenerate had made the mistake of touching her. He had put his hands on what belonged to Cary, and for that, he wanted to rip Luther's head off his shoulders.

Pink spittle was coming out of Luther's mouth, combined with the copious river of blood flowing out of one nostril from his busted nose.

"I'm sure you've got sound reason for killin' this here man." Rufus spoke again, staring off into the crowd.

"Rufus. Can't you shut the fuck up for one damn second?"

"I just want you to answer one little question." His friend shifted his gaze to him. "What you 'pose should be done with your purty lady? I'm s'pect that's her standin' behind you wringing her hands with worry."

"What?" Rufus bringing up Isabel worried, jolted him. Cary glanced at the ex-slave briefly before turning back to Luther whose eyes were turning glassy and starting to roll up.

"You know. Even if you's justified in murder, law don't take too kindly to us colored folks, red or black, killin' white men. So, when you hangin' from the judge's noose what's ya last Will and Testament. Just so I got it all straight. You know, make sho ya missus cared for and your chilin'."

"Fuck!" Cary moved his hands abruptly.

Luther, semi-conscious, dropped like a cast iron pot to the ground. The impact knocked his head hard, but the man let out a strangled gasp. He scratched and clawed at his neck, breaking skin as his burly body flopped, skidded, and shoved over the dirt terrain like the wounded snake that he was as he tried to fill his lungs with needed air.

Sheriff Silverman came galloping back into town, both his deputies on either side. Hell bent for leather, the lawman was rushing directly toward the large crowd that had gathered around Cary and the vermin.

Cary disregarded everyone as he moved to his wife and took her by the shoulders. He stared down in her face and saw the tear stains and apprehension shadowing her eyes. Seeing her hair hanging askew, some pins poking out in odd directions and one sleeve of her blouse torn, made Cary want to get his rifle out of the wagon and blast a hole through the man. "Are you all right?"

She nodded, a fresh round of tears streaming from her eyes. "I thought you were going to kill him. And I'd lose you." Her voice was hoarse, most likely from all the screaming she had been doing.

Dragging her into his arms, he crushed her to him. "I'm sorry, *ayv adanvdo*. Forgive me for scaring you."

"I'm just happy you're all right," she mumbled, her face buried in the curve of his neck. He heard her inhaling, as if she was drawing in his scent, as the tension released some from her.

He took in her sweet rose scent; it was his balm, his solace.

"Mr. Brown." It was Sheriff Silverman who spoke to him.

Cary took a beat before he stepped back from Isabel but kept an arm around her. His heart swelled as she tucked herself in at his side. He figured the man wanted to take him down to the office and read him his rights. He'd damn near killed a man with his bare hands. Cary eyed the sheriff. "Before you drag me off to your station, let me get my wife settled with her pa, so I know she's home safe."

"No. I won't leave you." Isabel clutched at his shirt. "That man was trying to...to..." Isabel glanced at the people still gathered, looking on curiously then at him. "...hurt me, and Cary arrived and stopped him."

"Isabel, don't justify my actions." He cupped her face, seeing the fear darkening her green gaze.

She shook her head. "But—"

"Hate to break up a family discussion, but I don't need you at the station. Well, not right now. Tomorrow will do jus' fine, to get your statement."

"My statement?" Cary frowned at the lawman.

Deputy Nelson and Deputy Dilbert now had Luther cuffed and hauled to his feet, one on each side of the big man. The two young deputies were slim and smaller than the desperado.

"If you try us, I'll put a bullet in your ass before you take two steps." Deputy Nelson settled a hand on his gun and eyed Luther.

"He's one of the best shots in town; I wouldn't even think on it," Deputy Dilbert confirmed as they pulled the reluctant man along.

Luther squawked on about an Indian getting more respect in this town than a decent white man. The two deputies ignored his rants and insults.

Silverman chuckled.

"What were you sayin' about tomorrow?" Cary asked the lawman.

"I've got eyes. They may be old, but they're still in there. I can tell by Mrs. Brown's hair and clothing that something untoward went down." He took off his hat and dragged a hand through his own hair. "Anytime I come upon a scene as such and a wife's husband is attemptin' to rip a man's head from his shoulders, I can put the pieces together. That one jus' better hope he ain't got nothin' to do with that body." The sheriff gave them a sharp nod. "Good evenin', folks."

"Since my son-in-law will see about Isabel, you can fill me in on the man on my land." Mr. Reynolds offered him an intense, collaborative look, communicating that if Cary hadn't gone after the man, James Reynolds would have, after a firm nod before he walked off with the sheriff.

Now that all the excitement was over, the people began to disperse. Some of the men clapped him on the back, sayin' they'd have done the same, while the women stepped to Isabel and told her to send word if she needed anything.

"Some town you settled on. Don't remember it bein' so excitin' the last time we came through with the line." Rufus stepped over to them now, carrying a big bag over his shoulder. He brushed the dirt off the hat in his hand then passed it to Cary.

"That it is." Cary thanked him for the hat and settled it back on his head, not even sure at what point he had lost it. "You know, most folks do the polite thing and answer back a wire and tell a friend when to expect them."

"Ain't no one ever mistook me for polite...that's too close to a gentleman." Rufus winked. "We must be cut from the same cloth, cuz it's taken ya awful long to make introductions." Rufus was smiling over at Isabel.

"Isabel, this is Rufus Abraham Lincoln, the friend from the railway I told you about." Cary laughed, feel more of the stress of the evening ease away. "He's come to help us on the farm."

"Am I correct, Mr. Lincoln, in thinking we have met before?"

Rufus stretched his lips wide into a smile that showed even white teeth. "Yes'm, you are. You let me sit in on a few of ya classes a couple years back when the line came through here."

"Well, now, Mr. Lincoln. It is nice to see you again. And thank you." She tilted her head in the direction of the wall

Cary had hemmed Luther up against. She moved from his side and hugged his friend.

"Shucks. He'd do the same for me. And it's just Rufus to my friends and family." Rufus gave Isabel a quick embrace then stepped away.

"Well then, I'm Isabel. You're welcome to stay at the house, Rufus. We have plenty of room," Isabel offered.

"Ah, naw, ma'am. I just need a good pile of hay to lay my head on at night. Dat be more comfortable than the cots I've stretched on for the last few years."

Cary took a moment to remove the pins from his wife's hair, letting all the waves of her auburn tresses hang free like she kept it at home. She was his world. He leaned in and kissed her softly on the cheek and whispered, "*Gvgeyu.*"

"*Gvgeyu,*" she repeated.

Rufus whistled.

"Watch it," Cary teased.

Isabel blushed.

"Yea, you take a stall instead of the loft in the barn." Cary slipped his wife's hand around the crook of his arm and started the trio toward the livery for the wagon.

"Don't faze me none." Rufus chuckled as he moved in step.

"Sunny and I will make sure the loft is good and comfortable for you, Rufus. And I won't take no for an answer when it comes to meals at the table."

"I ain't never turned down a good meal when offered."

"My wife is a good cook, so I'll ensure I work you twice as hard to work it off."

Rufus chuckled. "Sure you will, boss."

Cary kept his wife close, enjoying the feel of her thin, long fingers squeezing his muscle, her security. He glanced over at her and watched her smile kindly and converse with his friend, not caring he was a man of color. Once they were home and he had her luscious breasts deep in a bath, he'd take his time washing away the horrors of her day and replacing each memory of another's cruel touch with kisses, sucks, and licks until his lovely wife was screaming through more completions than she could count, then he'd tell her about the historian position.

"I guess my teaching days are over." There were shadows in her gaze, more of nostalgia than true sadness, and that eased his heart some.

"To everything there is a season under Heaven. There's something new just around the bend. I promise."

"Even if there isn't, I have everything I want with you, *ayv adanvdo*." She was staring into his eyes as she stroked along her belly.

Cary's heart swelled and thumped hard in his chest then settled in place. He'd found his home.

AUTHOR'S NOTE

I hope you are enjoying the Grover Town Discipline series, and I especially hope you felt the worth of love in Cary and Isabel's story. This was a fictional story, crafted from my great-grandparents' lives. A lot of times, the simple history and stories of people's lives don't get told and seem to vanish with each generation. Talking to my grandmother years ago about my great-grandparents, of whom I only had the amazing opportunity to meet my great-grandmother. She passed when I was fifteen. She was amazing and truly the rock of our family. Asking questions about my great-grands and hearing just the little bit that my grandmother recalled, because stories of families don't get passed on, made me want to begin writing stories in late 19th century America and drove me to bring their story to life, even if fictionally. Their lives weren't extraordinary in any way, but it's just theirs. Here's a little of their tale.

Cary Brown, Native American—Cherokee—'hopped the train' to Spring Hope, a little town in North Carolina. No one knows where he was coming from when he met and married Carrie Reynolds, a fourteen-year-old girl who was born to

James 'Jim' Reynolds and Lillian Reynolds. At the time of their marriage, Cary Brown had already been previously married to an Indian woman who had passed and left him with five children. Carrie became an instant mother and additionally bore eight children with her husband, giving them a total of thirteen in all, only losing two who didn't live beyond the age of seven. They lived on and worked their own farm, where they grew tobacco, corn, green beans, and other vegetables. My great-grandmother had not been schooled and could not read or write, and it was my grandmother who taught her how to sign her own name. My great-grandmother, even though she could not read, had managed to memorize the Bible. At some point, my grandparents separated but never divorced, and Carrie moved to southeastern Virginia with the five youngest children, to live with her single and childless sister Josie. Cary, my great-grandfather, closed the farm after the harvest, with the older children, who then went on their way, while he relocated to Philadelphia to work on skyscrapers. Monthly, he still made his way to Norfolk, Virginia to visit his wife and children until he tragically fell from one of the skyscrapers while working, severed his arm on the way down, and died of shock.

It was an honor for me to craft my great-grandmother, who my family lovingly called Gramps, into a schoolteacher and someone who was interested in the history of other families' lives. Family and God were the most important things to her. I enjoyed giving my great-grandfather a life on the railway line and showing his desire for having his own land and his love of family and farming.

DICTIONARY OF CHEROKEE WORDS

Cherokee word list:

Tsalagi (Cherokee language)

E-du-tsi (uncle)

Uwohali (eagle)

U-ni-tsi (mom)

E-ni-si (grandmother)

E-du-da (grandfather)

Ayv a-dan-v-do (my heart)

T-sa-wo-du-hi (You are beautiful)

G-v-ge-yu (I love you)

U-ye hi (husband)

U-dal-ii (wife)

Unetlanvhi (the Great Spirit)

Salali (squirrel)

Sequoyah (sparrow)

YASMINE HYDE

USA Today Bestselling Author, Yasmine Hyde loves romance and writing it is one of her greatest pleasures in life outside of her daughter. Her belief in happily ever after began when she was sixteen and started reading romance books. Now as an erotic romance author, she tries to show that every woman, no matter color, age, shape or size, deserves a high level of passion in her life. She resides in North Carolina with her family and is a RomVet.

Visit her website here:
https://yvettehines.com/yasmine-hyde-erotica/

Don't miss these exciting titles by Yasmine Hyde and Blushing Books!

Grover Town Discipline
Guiding Gretchen
Handling Holly
Servicing Serenity
Educating Elizabeth
Instructing Isabel

BLUSHING BOOKS

Blushing Books is one of the oldest eBook publishers on the web. We've been running websites that publish spanking and BDSM related romance and erotica since 1999, and we have been selling eBooks since 2003. We hope you'll check out our hundreds of offerings at http://www.blushingbooks.com.

BLUSHING BOOKS NEWSLETTER

Please join the Blushing Books newsletter
to receive updates & special promotional offers.
You can also join by using your mobile phone:
Just text BLUSHING to 22828.